A life of crime—or a lifetime of love?

Mary Billing knows her solitary mountain life is over when a handsome stranger blows on to her land in an unmarked chopper. Terry McCoy is not only dangerous to the pretty widow's shattered senses, he's a hardened criminal no woman in her right mind would fall for. Yet there's something tender about Terry—something that makes her surrender to his searing touch. Now Mary is in deep—deep enough to be taken hostage by a villain whose true target is Terry...

The son of a notorious crime boss, Terry is about to take over his murdered father's multi-million dollar empire. But first there's the little matter of avenging his father's death—and rescuing the one woman he knows could turn his hard-bitten life around. Terry never wanted a life of crime, but suddenly he's ready to do just about anything to bring Mary back...

I0677524

Books by Shady Grace

McCoy's Boys
Beautiful Criminal
Never Give You Up

Published by Kensington Publishing Corporation

Never Give You Up

McCoy's Boys

Shady Grace

LYRICAL PRESS
Kensington Publishing Corp.
www.kensingtonbooks.com

Lyrical Press books are published by
Kensington Publishing Corp. 119 West 40th Street New York, NY 10018

All Kensington titles, imprints, and distributed lines are available at special quantity discounts for bulk purchases for sales promotion, premiums, fund-raising, and educational or institutional use.

Special book excerpts or customized printings can also be created to fit specific needs. For details, write or phone the office of the Kensington Special Sales Manager:
Kensington Publishing Corp.
119 West 40th Street
New York, NY 10018
Attn. Special Sales Department. Phone: 1-800-221-2647.

Kensington and the K logo Reg. U.S. Pat. & TM Off.
Lyrical Press and the L logo are trademarks of Kensington Publishing Corp.

First Electronic Edition: June 2016
eISBN-13: 1-60183-725-9
eISBN-10: 978-1-60183-725-7

First Print Edition: June 2016
ISBN-13: 978-1-60183-727-1
ISBN-10: 1-60183-727-5

Printed in the United States of America

Chapter 1

The 1969 Charger RT weaved through traffic two cars behind.

Terry McCoy adjusted his rearview mirror and eyed the shiny black beast. The car had been following him for thirty minutes since he'd left the estate near Saanich Inlet, and the driver wasn't even trying to be discreet.

So, you want to play games, eh? He glanced into the rearview mirror again, and grinned at the driver's side of the windshield as the car darted around traffic behind him. A good game of cat and mouse always got his blood pumping.

With the engine revving high, he took a left and whizzed past a minivan packed with unruly children. He winked at the frazzled-looking mother and punched his Camaro into fifth, blowing ahead of her as if she were pulling those brats by hand.

Like an angel of death, the Charger was right on his ass.

He jerked to the right then the left, veering around other vehicles as he neared the main drag along the wharf, but still he couldn't shake him. The Charger nudged his bumper, making Terry grip the wheel tighter.

"Fucker."

He sped up and slowed down, making the driver behind him veer around another car to his right, barely avoiding a crash. Terry laughed and accelerated again, only a few hundred yards from his destination.

As he neared the hotel parking lot he jerked hard to the right and stepped on the gas, skidding to the side then punched it harder into the parking lot, missing the hotel sign by mere inches. The Charger blew straight ahead toward the downtown core, its engine screaming, and disappeared from view.

Terry chuckled and eased the Camaro into the rear parking lot at his family's Sea Scape Hotel. He shut off the engine and took a deep breath. The hotel was the last place he wanted to be right now, but he had to tend to his own personal business.

He glanced up and stared at the man reflected in the rearview mirror.

Tired eyes. Gaunt cheeks. Pale skin. Pathetic life.

He looked like ten pounds of shit in a five-pound bag.

Still staring into the mirror, he released a pent-up breath and tried to clear his mind, before pulling out his cell phone.

As he dialed the number he pictured her lovely face on the other end of the line. He really needed to hear her voice. Maybe it would make him feel better. Maybe it would make his negative thoughts go away. He didn't know why, but her sweet, seductive voice made him feel as if the world could be a good place sometimes. Right now he needed a good place.

To his bitter disappointment the answering machine kicked in.

"Hi. You've reached the Billings. We're probably outside right now so please leave a detailed message and we'll get back to you as soon as we can. Thank you!"

He couldn't think of what to say and hung up. Low, that's how he felt. Low and lost, and for some stupid reason he thought she would make him feel better. He punched the dash and shouted, "Fuck!" before he lowered his head against the steering wheel and closed his eyes. Now what was he supposed to do with himself? He let out a self-loathing groan and shook his head.

She still hadn't changed the message on her machine. Obviously Mary Billings couldn't let go of her dead husband. A dead husband who did nothing but hurt her. He deserved to be in the cold ground. He deserved to no longer be on that goddamned answering machine. It physically pained Terry to hear her speak as if everything was perfect in her world. He knew better. She should be back to her maiden name by now. Shouldn't she? Over four months had passed since Tom's death. How could a woman cling to a name that made her miserable? He'd never understand females. Most of all, he'd never understand Mary. Maybe that's why he couldn't get the woman out of his head.

A rap on the driver-side window jerked him back to the present. He looked up and into the eyes of the doorman. Terry rolled the window down. "What?"

"You're late, that's what. Gabriel's already here."

Terry blinked. "What? But I saw him go downtown." He glanced to his right and was stunned to see the Charger parked beside him. How did he not notice him pull up? He shook his head, grabbed his briefcase, and exited the mustang, disgusted with himself and his recent inability to concentrate.

"Everything okay, Boss?" The doorman walked with Terry to the side entrance, conveniently hidden by tall flowering shrubs. "You seem out of it lately."

"I'll be fine, Ezra. Just keep an eye on the door, will you?"

"Sure thing, Boss."

Terry strolled into the hotel with all the energy of a man on Valium. He couldn't focus on much these days and the headaches were debilitating. He tried his best to make light of his life, to find humor in everything, but fuck all seemed to work when we was sick and tired of the same old routine. What he really needed was a vacation.

Maybe he needed a new life. Something that didn't involve walking on eggshells every day.

Massive plants covered the vast waiting room where leather chairs and antique tables covered the black-and-white tiled floor. Several well-dressed men were gathered in one section, talking business and smoking fine cigars. Classical music resounded from the doors leading into the Tail Wind Lounge, one of the finest restaurants in the city.

The Sea Scape Hotel was well known for its old-world atmosphere, and after sixty years in business, nobody knew that today it was a fancy front for the biggest dealer this side of the border.

Hell, shipments were boated right to the hotel dock at night and brought through the back to be distributed amongst certain wealthy guests. Business didn't get much easier than that, although the shipping runs by plane and boat held many risks, especially when Terry or one of the others had to skip countries. At least at the hotel, and on their own domain, business ran smoothly.

Even the cops had a cut, and often spent their evenings wining and dining in the Tail Wind. They had the pick of the finest rooms and the best women—as long as everybody played by the rules and respected each other.

It was a rare occasion when a room was vacant at the Sea Scape, but if a man with a briefcase and a promise walked in, they always had something available. And if his promises turned to lies then he'd never be seen again.

Terry's apartment spanned the top floor, a place where he was the top man, for Colton McCoy preferred his estate near Saanich Inlet, a short jaunt out of the city. Despite being the boss's son, and second in line, the hotel was Terry's domain. Even his father didn't question him here.

His Oxford's clicked on the tiled floor as he made his way to the group of men waiting in a private seating area, hidden by several large palm plants. "Gentlemen." He set the briefcase on the side table next to an elderly man. "You'll find it's quite potent this time around. Enjoy."

He accepted a different briefcase and headed for the front desk, smiling as he approached the dayshift receptionist. "Good afternoon, Sal. Any messages for me?" He handed her the second briefcase and she discreetly deposited the leather case into the safe beneath the desk.

Sal looked sassy as ever today, her red locks pinned up in a loose bun with a pencil poking through. Her trademark black-rimmed glasses gave her the look of a naughty librarian.

Everybody loved Sal. Terry trusted her with his life. She was a good woman, and even though he'd nearly started something with her a few years back, he decided to be smart and not touch her. Bad shit happens when you mix work and pleasure.

Sal smiled, her cheeks rosy, lips bright red to match her hair. "No messages today, Sir, but I'm done at six." Long black lashes—he guessed must be fake—fluttered as she winked.

Terry chuckled. "Good to know." Sal must be the biggest flirt he'd ever met, but their relationship would never go beyond that. He paid her no further mind and disappeared into the private elevator hidden in a small alcove behind the front desk.

He couldn't help imagining little Mary with her caramel hair all in disarray and wearing a pair of those same spectacles—every teenage boy's dream to unfold the pages of the mysterious librarian.

Terry punched the keypad and the elevator descended into the basement, only accessible by certain staff members. When the door opened, his gaze moved directly to the man secured to the metal chair centered in the room. Terry adjusted his shirtsleeves and squared his shoulders before stepping inside.

"Adolfo Montesano. It's been a long time, old friend."

Adolfo lifted his face. Blood oozed from his busted nose. Dried blood covered his face and hair, and the wide slit from upper lip to ear looked painfully gruesome. Terry cringed at the view, glad he wasn't in Adolfo's shoes.

The traitor's head bobbed and he groaned beneath the duct tape covering his mouth as he tried focusing bloodshot eyes on Terry.

Duct tape perfected crime. With Adolfo's wrists taped to the chair arms, he'd never free himself. It didn't matter how strong a person was.

Wrapped three times around wrists and ankles, even the biggest man couldn't wriggle free as he could with rope.

It took three months to locate Montesano's son after the disaster Ben caused in the mountains. Now the traitor was about to meet his maker as well. He promised Ben the world if he took out Terry and Gabe, and stole the stash of Peruvian flake. Adolfo was the bones behind Benjamin Cain. They'd almost lost it all, including Terry and Gabe's life.

Terry's shoulder still ached from the bullet Ben slammed him with. Now it was time to take out the trash and get the business back on the straightaway.

On the other side of the room the eerie sound of steel on stone invaded the silence as Gabriel Miller sharpened his hatchet. Terry studied his partner in crime with a mixture of emotions.

How could he be so calm at a time like this? He should be enjoying retirement with a good woman like Mima and leaving this crazy bullshit behind. If Terry had even a scrap of the life Gabe accidentally found in those mountains, he'd never set foot back here again. As much as he loved his hotel, he didn't want it to be a place of crime. He wanted his guests to feel happy and secure. To know that when they set foot in here, they had a decorative, safe room to stay in, a classy restaurant to dine in, and staff to wait on them hand and foot for all the *right* reasons.

But a wrong reason sat in front of him right now while Gabe sharpened his hatchet.

Having a Montesano tied up and bleeding in the basement was testament to business taking a new turn. Terry didn't want to be in this position, it was beyond dangerous, but when Colton McCoy gave an order, everybody listened.

He focused his attention back to Gabe and released a deep breath. They may be the best of friends, but Terry and Gabe were the complete opposite of each other. Gabe, always cool and in control; Terry stressed about every little thing. Perhaps their differences made them such a good team.

"I didn't even see you pull in."

Gabe kept his back to him, still sharpening the hatchet. "Probably too busy yanking it in the parking lot. Thought I'd give him a few rounds on the house until you were done."

He couldn't help his rumble of laughter. "Smartass. I haven't yanked it in months." It was a total lie, but no way in hell would he ever admit to Gabe that when Mary's face haunted him at night his hand automatically drifted down.

Adolfo groaned again. Terry shifted his gaze to the captive and actually felt a little sorry for him. As he stared at the man's bruised and bloodied body he wondered why everyone had to suffer all the time. Why not shoot him in the forehead and get it over with? He knew well that nobody would dare betray the McCoy's and get away with it, but why did everything have to lead to all this blood and chaos?

Adolfo was just another rung on a steep ladder, which could start an even bigger threat. They'd never really know until it was too late, because no matter how hard they tortured him, Adolfo would never talk.

Nobody worth their salt talked in this business, and Terry knew how far up the food chain Adolfo Montesano really was. Cocaine royalty bled on his chair right at that moment.

Terry focused back on Gabe. "You're supposed to be enjoying retired life between your old lady's thighs, or is making a man bleed more of a turn on for you?"

Gabe chuckled, not at all put off by Terry's sick humor. "I wanted to be here because of what happened in the mountains. Besides, Sam's on an errand for the old man so he can't do it."

Terry moved toward Gabe, slipped off his suit jacket and tossed it over the long metal table spanning the entire side wall, before rolling up his sleeves. "You're gonna miss this, aren't you?"

Gabe glanced over his shoulder and winked. "Nope."

He was bullshitting and Terry knew it. Knew it like he knew a shot of vodka would be perfect right about now. Not once did Terry ever take pleasure in killing or torturing a man, it was just a job that had to be done. Maybe that's why he'd taken to the bottle lately. He couldn't be happy without being drunk most of the time.

Gabe on the other hand thrived in this lifestyle. He was born for this. Terry often wished he could switch places with Gabe, but he knew his old friend would never accept.

"Was Mima pissed about you leaving?"

"Yes and no. She knew I had some things to finish up before I was done for good. But I think she believes I'll never return every time I have to leave."

Terry chuckled. "Can't blame her, I guess. She doesn't understand what we do."

"Speaking of women, how's Mary?"

Terry shrugged, unsure how to answer him. But inside he cringed at the mention of her name. He wanted to see her again, face-to-face, but he was afraid she'd reject him because of who he was. She didn't need a man like him in her life, and for that he felt ashamed.

Business always got in the way of personal life, and it was different for him than it was for Gabe. Terry was the boss's son. Any relationship with a woman made him and the business vulnerable. He didn't dare get in too deep with a broad or risk everything. He couldn't handle another repeat of what happened to his mother. He couldn't allow an innocent woman like Mary to suffer as his mother did.

And Mary still hadn't changed her message on the damn answering machine.

He stared down at the leather satchel rolled out to expose Gabe's toys, wanting to forget his twisted thoughts and the sexy caramel eyes that tormented him.

The ice pick was fast and efficient, easy to hide. The handsaw made dismemberment a breeze. Several other gadgets Terry knew nothing about looked grossly sophisticated, but the one that shocked him the most was the oversized eyelash curler used to slowly and painfully sever a man's nut sack.

His balls shriveled at the thought.

"Mary's too good for me. I haven't spoken to her in a while." His answer would have to be good enough.

Gabe grunted. "Mima's too good for me too, but that didn't stop me from moving in. Quit being a fucking dumbass and go take her out to dinner or something."

Terry smacked Gabe's shoulder, all in good fun of course. He knew Gabe could take him in a second. "Shut up about me. Soon enough you'll have Mima knocked-up, buddy. Then you can worry about telling your kid what to do." He cleared his throat, unable to stop himself from staring at Gabe's profile. His long-time friend had the look of a happy man. He appeared more at ease these days. His smile was quick and sure, his eyes held a spark of something Terry didn't recognize in his own. Terry looked tired and fed up, whereas Gabe had the happy face of a man who just got laid.

Terry was suddenly overcome with a pang of jealousy. "Do you have any regrets?"

Gabe turned with the razor sharp weapon in hand and studied him for a few breaths. "The only thing I regret is the lack of power and running water out there. First two things on my list as the man of the house. Oh, and adding a driveway. I'm tired of parking the truck a kilometer down the road. I'm getting too old for that much exercise."

"What about Diana? Are you going to bring her there or have her parked here?"

Adolfo struggled but the restraints held him fast.

Gabe spun around and glared at him. "Do you mind? We're having a conversation here. Just be thankful you're not going to the pigs."

Adolfo's eyes widened and his body stilled.

Gabe turned to Terry with an annoyed look on his face. "I'll keep Diana here for now until we have a proper driveway. Mima refuses to move to town even when I offered to buy the biggest house in Silver Creek. And she'll never move here. I already let go of my apartment. But I know she loves her land. Maybe one day I'll build her dream house right there... with a pool and a helipad and the whole shebang. My princess would need a new suspension if I brought her up there."

Terry chuckled. He couldn't picture Mima agreeing to a pool and a helipad, but he respected what Gabe wanted in life. He was like his big brother, and even though Ben had managed to trick them a few months back, Terry trusted Gabe with his life. His buddy deserved everything good, and that included Mima Etu.

Terry's thoughts drifted to the incident when Gabe crashed his plane in her backyard. Even though his dad questioned Gabe's motives, Terry never gave up on him. He wanted to be there with Ben, and he was right not to trust him. In his heart, Terry knew Gabe never would've taken off with all that blow. Besides, Colton promised Gabe a tidy retirement package for all his hard work over the years. Gabe didn't need to steal to walk away big from the family business.

Fate had taken over and made Gabe a different man when he crashed his plane and Mima found him.

"Are you really happy with her? I have a hard time imagining you gutting a deer instead of a man."

Gabe's big shoulders lifted as he took a deep breath. "I've never felt more at peace out there. It's so quiet in the mountains I can actually hear myself think."

The weird smile on his face almost made Gabe look childish.

"Which must be boring as hell," Terry added with a grin.

"Not really. I thought it would be at first, but all this—" Gabe waved the hatchet around and Adolfo shrieked beneath the duct tape, "makes me happy to live quietly for a change. You know what I mean? No more looking over my shoulder. No more doing what everyone else wants. Nice walks along the property. Outdoor sex. You should try it sometime instead of making your dick raw with your hand."

"Fuck off."

Terry knew right then Gabe was exactly where he needed to be. "God you're pussy-whipped already, aren't you?" He didn't dare admit he was jealous. Before Gabe could respond he continued quickly, "I thought Dad wanted him to go to the pigs?"

After giving Terry a deadly glare about being pussy-whipped, Gabe walked over to Adolfo with all the calm in the world and ripped the duct tape from his mouth. Adolfo squinted hard as part of his thick black mustache tore off with the tape.

Terry cringed. *God, that must've hurt.*

"Wanda put a stop to that after Ben. The pigs are on a diet."

Adolfo's eyes widened but he made no other sound, only pursed his lips shut and glared at them.

"Any last words, amigo?"

Terry's heart hammered as a sly smile curved Adolfo's bruised and bloodied mouth. His black eyes held no remorse. He wasn't afraid to die. "Yeah. This is only the beginning . . . *amigo.* You boys are stupid if you think killing me is going to be the end of this."

"What the hell are you talking about?" Gabe blurted.

Adolfo smiled as he eyed Terry, completely ignoring Gabe hovering over him. "You kill me, everything you love will burn."

Fear gripped Terry by the enemy's stark threat. He rushed him, grabbed his blood-soaked hair, and violently yanked his head back. "What the fuck is that supposed to mean? Answer me!"

Adolfo's evil laugh sounded hollow off the three-foot thick cement walls. He had nothing left to say and they weren't going to waste any more time.

Gabe separated Adolfo's baby finger from the rest. With a perverse calm he wielded the hatchet with brute force. The weapon slammed down with a distinct *thwack* on the chair's metal arm. The finger fell to the floor, blood spurted from Adolfo's fleshy knuckle.

His whimper of pain and pure terror made Terry's blood pound in his ears. And just as quickly as his face contorted in horror as he looked down at his hand, Adolfo pursed his lips, lifted his chin high, and glared at Gabe then Terry. He was tough. He could probably lose his whole hand and still keep his shit together.

Disgusted, Terry turned away. Watching a man suffer didn't give him any satisfaction, whether the guy deserved it or not. He didn't want to kill him. He didn't want any of this, but he couldn't stand back and do nothing if everything he loved would burn.

"Colton wants his finger with the gold ring, then he's going for a dip." Gabe leaned down and smiled at Adolfo's hazy eyes. Tears streamed down his high cheekbones. "You hear that, *amigo*? I hear the ocean is nice this time of year." Gabe stood back and held up the bloody finger. "When your father gets this, he'll be sure to play by the rules. No more jumping over the fence."

Having seen enough, Terry withdrew his favorite Beretta Neos and took aim at Adolfo's forehead. He didn't want to do it, but he had no choice—not when he felt threatened. As he exhaled and pulled the trigger, nothing in the world eased his turmoil more than the blood spurting from Adolfo's mangled forehead, and his desolate eyes, frozen in sudden death as his blood sprayed the wall behind him.

Terry didn't want to think about Adolfo's family getting his finger.

With a heavy heart and more weight on his tired shoulders, he put his piece away and set the finger inside the tiny velvet box, before retreating into the elevator. "I need a fucking drink before I deliver this to Dad. How about you?"

Gabe wiped the spatter of blood from his arm and released an annoyed growl when he realized the blood trail ran all the way up the side of his shirt. "It's not even noon yet." He gave Terry a *"what the fuck is wrong with you"* look.

The elevator doors silently inched closer together. Terry put his hand out to stop them and said, "So? It's close enough to lunch time for me." He removed his hand and the doors closed before Gabe could argue with him.

As the elevator smoothly ascended, Terry wondered if they made a huge mistake.

Chapter 2

Brown, soggy leaves. No vase of fresh or artificial flowers. No colorful cradle to crest the headstone. Nothing but a dismal carpet of dead leaves to grace her husband's grave.

Mary Billings, widow of little more than four months, absently toed some of the leaves around with the tip of her boot.

Nestled near a tattered and lifeless tamarack, the headstone rested in the furthest northern section of Silver Creek Cemetery. In bold letters, his name, along with birth and death dates, engraved the existence of his life. Now he was just a lone monument, tucked away from all the others in this depressing place.

That's what you deserve.

Maybe she was a cruel person for not missing him. Did her lack of hysteria mean she was as nasty as he had been when he was alive? Now she questioned everything in life because nothing made sense anymore. She had been devastated when the RCMP first arrived with the news of his death, but with the continuing silence came acceptance. Tom had hurt her both physically and emotionally for years. Now that he was gone, Mary had a strange sense of peace.

Sometimes she wondered how drowning would feel. Did it hurt? Did you simply feel cold and fall asleep? Maybe that wasn't harsh enough for Tom. Maybe he should've suffered more, as she suffered through their marriage.

Look where your stupidity got you, Tom. Look where it got me.

His sudden death had set her free. Sad to say, but she was too afraid to leave him when he was alive, and today would be her final visit to his grave. She couldn't do it anymore. Couldn't pay her respects to a man who did nothing but hurt her since the beginning of their toxic marriage.

She may have loved him from the start, when she was younger and he'd put a spell on her, but it quickly turned poisonous shortly after the wedding. His control over her was as strong and unyielding as granite.

"Goodbye, Tom." Despite her will to be strong, her voice sounded weak, distant, as if it came from somewhere else with the wind.

She had to be tough now. Soft people never survived out here.

With a heavy heart, but an odd sense of relief, Mary returned to the north gate of the cemetery on the outskirts of her small town. She untied the reins attached to her big bay stallion, lifted up onto the saddle and urged Blue onto the road leading home. She needed the crisp air to fill her lungs and feel the connection of woman and horse today, rather than a lifeless drive in a lonely vehicle, listening to the same old boring voice on the radio. At least the noise of the wilderness sounded different every day.

She patted Blue's neck. "Time to go home, boy. I'll give you an apple."

Blue had been her saving grace many nights when Tom was still alive and she needed an escape from his violence. At least Blue could take her places no vehicle could traverse. He was sturdy and strong, never afraid of an unfamiliar or rough trail, and he never argued. Blue gave her a sense of security, and belonging. Right in this moment he was her only friend.

Spring filled the air in her little mountain town, but the cheery, fresh air and new growth did nothing to set her mind at ease. She felt like that dead tamarack in the cemetery.

She was alone—alone in a small town with nobody to share her time. Her best friend was busy being in love with her new man, and everyone else stared at Mary as if she was a husband killer.

Rumors traveled fast in small towns. Some of the story was true, some of it stretched beyond belief. It first started at the café shortly after Tom's funeral service. She heard the whispers, noticed the glares. A helicopter and a group of thugs were mentioned, and apparently they had been Mary's friends, or maybe her father's. Probably sent to help her kill Tom so she could keep the trapline and the house.

Maybe she was just like her father they had whispered. Crazy and alone in the middle of nowhere. But they knew nothing about her, not really. She was a quiet woman who kept to herself and plodded through life as best she could.

She didn't have a group of female friends. She didn't get mixed up in other people's affairs. Maybe that was her problem. She'd never taken the time to really get to know anybody. Not in a true sense. Her only real friend was Mima.

Look at her. She pushed our beloved Tom into that freezing river. How dare she show her face here?

Sometimes she wished she did push him. After all, he thought nothing of hitting her whenever he felt the need, or whenever she didn't do anything good enough. Did the town not know what kind of animal their precious Tom really was? Just because he was a tall figure in town and supported local businesses and charities—didn't make him a great husband. No. People did bad things behind closed doors all the time.

She resented being treated like an outsider simply because she wasn't well-known like Tom. And because of their shallow minds and ignorance, Mary became sour. She wanted nothing to do with most of them. Only a few treated her with respect and kindness, and they were few and far between.

Ambling along at an easy pace, she guided Blue along the side of the dirt road leading home, trying to forget the townsfolk and their notions, not at all happy to return to a house with nothing but seven dogs and a hut full of furs to be skinned and tanned, waiting for her.

The road toward home curved around huge boulders, thick wilderness, and beautiful rolling hills, all beneath towering mountains. The scenery never failed to impress her.

An hour later she unsaddled Blue and urged him into his stall in the little barn beside the house. Once he was tucked away and content with an apple treat, hay, and water, she made her way across the yard.

It was well past dinnertime, but she didn't feel like cooking. Instead, she grabbed a bottle of rum, put on her favorite jazz CD, and settled onto the chair beside the living room window.

With the beautiful view of the wilderness around her home, Mary sipped her drink and stared outside, until the jagged tips of the surrounding mountains no longer felt like her prison guards.

* * * *

A cool blast of air whipped her hair about. Evergreen and poplar branches swayed in the wind. A mountain fresh scent filled the swirling air.

She glanced up at the pale blue sky, wondering if Tom was staring down at her with his ever-present scowl. What would he think of her now, surviving without him?

One of the dogs wined, followed by a long, low howl from the others. To anyone else it may have sounded like a pack of wolves lingering nearby. To Mary the sound was eerie and beautiful.

She paused along her trek by the river. The hairs on the back of her neck tingled.

A familiar hum resounded through the mountain range.

Her eyes widened as that all-too-familiar black chopper crested the nearest mountain peak.

Oh God. Not him.

She made a mad dash for the house, hoping to have a few minutes to do something reasonable with herself. Maybe put half a face on, or powder her puff. Thank God she had power and running water out here on this side of the mountain.

Time to play.

She tossed her hat and coat somewhere near the hallway table and ran into the bathroom. Quickly, she washed her hands and set out to fix herself up, excited yet angry that her unexpected guest could be a tall blond man with dangerous blue eyes. If it was him she'd slap the crooked grin right off his sexy face. Since Tom's death, the handsome criminal couldn't seem to leave her alone.

The dogs barked with excitement. Mary's hands shook as she removed her clips, whipped her shoulder-length hair about and clouded her head with hairspray. She applied some concealer and powder, pinched her cheeks, and rushed to the back door just in time as the unmarked chopper set down in the clearing on the other side of her driveway.

Frozen in the back door, Mary watched, transfixed, as the passenger door to the chopper opened. He stepped down, tall and lithe, dressed in a black leather bomber and blue jeans. He hunched low to avoid the blades whirling above his head, his golden hair whipping around as he came toward her with intent, with dark purpose, eyes flashing deep sexual desires. She should step back and lock the door. She should grab her rifle.

But she couldn't.

There was something about him that made her stand there like a nervous fool, unable to tell him to leave her alone.

Since his last visit, her dreams had been plagued with hot, sweaty nights, naked in his arms. She'd awaken with her fingers between her legs, shrieking in delightful orgasm or on the very edge, it tormented her all day. Her cheeks heated as he slowed his pace and took the first step at the back door.

"Hello, Mary."

His voice. His voice did things to her insides that should be punishable by law. Maybe he had a handful of women waiting to please him back in the city. Maybe he had all the wrong intentions.

Today she didn't care.

She'd been through too much to care about anything but feeling something good. Something tangible.

Without a word, she grabbed the lapels of his jacket and yanked him into the doorway. If he was surprised by her actions he didn't say anything, didn't pull away. His lips felt like wicked perfection against hers, as she forced him to give her what she wanted.

Her heart lurched as his strong arms went around her, crowding her against the doorframe. The sturdy wood pressed against her back painfully, but she didn't care. Not when his hot mouth made her tremble and burn under his searing touch.

Fast and frenzied, they backed into the house. The screen door banged against the frame. Terry trapped her between the hallway wall and his hard body, and when Mary felt his erection press against her abdomen, she boldly reached down and stroked him over his jeans.

"Mmmm," he moaned, and rocked into her hand.

"Yes," she moaned, excited and surprised by how large he felt in her hot grip. "Give it to me."

Without finesse, Mary unzipped his jeans and pulled his cock out, eagerly dropping to her knees and took his bulbous head into her mouth—

A loud knock rapped on the back door.

Mary jerked up in bed and blinked from the bright beam of light shining through the bedroom window, and looked around in stunned delirium.

Panting, she ripped her fingers away from between drenched lips, painfully close to orgasm, and sucked in a shuddering breath.

Jesus Christ.

Another loud knock pounded the door, followed by a few more. She rubbed her head and groaned, the knocking right on her fragile skull.

How did I get to bed? The last thing she remembered was crying at the window after polishing off half a bottle of rum.

In her dazed and flustered state, she whipped her legs over the side of the bed and shouted, "Who is it?"

"It's Gabe. Are you awake?"

I am now you son of a—"Yes! Just a minute."

With an unladylike curse, Mary plodded across the chilly wooden floor and grabbed her housecoat from the hook by the door. Still in an aroused yet angry state, she made her way to the back door and yanked it open.

"What do you want?" She tried to control her heaving chest.

Gabe raised a teasing brow. "What, no hello?"

She folded her arms over her bust and glared at him. "Hello. Now what do you want?"

With a casual shrug and a disarming grin, Gabe brushed past her, into the hallway toward the kitchen, as if he had a share in the property. "I thought I'd swing by and check up on you. Good thing I did. You smell like a pub. Everything okay with you?"

Mary made a face behind his back and shut the door. She tightened the sash of her robe and followed him into the kitchen, annoyed by his horrible timing, yet grateful when he saved her the trouble of having to make coffee.

"I'm lovely. Where's Mima?"

"At home," he said over his shoulder.

Curious to the strange visit, Mary took a seat at the kitchen table and watched in tired silence as he patiently waited for the brew then fixed each of them a steamy cup. Apparently his untimely visit needed coffee before more words were exchanged. She was okay with it, for now.

Mary eyed him up as he puttered around. Gabe may have swept her best friend off her tough feet, but Mary still felt awkward around him, even when he came by with Mima to help with some of the more difficult tasks Tom used to handle. Gabe may be somewhat of a decent man and wouldn't harm her, there was still something about him she couldn't trust, and it had nothing to do with who he was, but what he did.

Her life had drastically changed when he crashed his plane into their woods. Sometimes she wondered if Gabriel Miller pushed her husband into the freezing Athabasca River. It made no sense that a strong man like Tom, who lived in the woods for thirty years, would drown so easily.

She eyed him with mixed emotions as he spooned cream and sugar into his mug and lifted it close to his lips. "How've you been lately? I haven't had the chance to swing by in a while." His expression turned more serious. "Mima had to put one of the dogs down. She's not in the best of moods."

He sipped his coffee and absently glanced around the room.

Mary's heart ached for her friend, knowing those dogs were like children to Mima, as Mary's were to her. "Poor girl. Which one had to be put down?"

Gabe shrugged. "No idea. I can't keep track of them all."

She glared at the heartless man across from her. "There's only five of them." Of course he wouldn't remember the name of the dog, but he'd never forget his *Lady Diana* specially kept in the city. After all, he

NEVER GIVE YOU UP   21

constantly talked about how fast and smooth she was. Men like Gabe had their cars, while she and Mima had their dogs.

She took another deep pull of her coffee, watching his demeanor. He appeared calm but the puffed out vein in his forehead didn't go unnoticed. "Come out with it. I know you didn't come here to check up on me."

Gabe rumbled with laughter. "You got me all figured out." He rubbed the back of his neck and let out a deep breath. Once he set his cup back down, he eyed her more seriously. "Actually, I have a business proposition for you."

The mere mention of that word made her tense up. "What does your business have to do with me?"

"I have a friend who needs a place to unwind. Nothing gets more private than this."

She tried not to react physically to those words, but her heart pounded and every nerve jumped to life when she knew who he was talking about. "No." There was only one man who'd want to come here, and he made everything in her body come to life without her consent.

Gabe's comical look grated her nerves. "What if I told you it was Terry?"

A strike of fear and unwanted excitement ripped through her, but she tried her best to appear passive. Why did he have to say his name and confirm her wicked suspicion? "Terry?" She shrugged, but her stomach fluttered with anxiety and it became harder to sit still on the damned chair.

"Got your attention now, don't I?"

Despite the chaos they'd created in her life, she couldn't help thinking about the man with eyes like a glacier that made her stomach flip, and a sexy smile that made her want to let him do things with his hot mouth. The same man she lost her control with and kissed on a lonely night after one too many beers, one month after Tom's death.

Her cheeks burned at the thought, not only from the shame of kissing a man this soon after her husband's death, but also from the heated memory of that night. Despite her inhibitions from drinking, she remembered how his sensual, exploring kiss made her feel bold, brash. If he hadn't pulled away, she would have given him much more.

And the dreams . . . .

She squared her shoulders, forcing herself to think smart. By all means, a group of gangsters could come charging in and flip her world over just when she was getting back on her feet again. Having Terry here would end in disaster and possible death, and the kind of heartbreak a woman couldn't get over. She already had enough heartbreak to last a lifetime.

Gabe at her kitchen table was bad enough. As much as she appreciated his help, having a criminal swinging by to visit didn't seem natural. She couldn't imagine regular folks hanging out with drug smugglers and murderers over coffee and deer sausage.

Gabe's sharp gaze settled on hers and it cut right through her. "Seriously. Terry needs a vacation. He looks like shit."

She eyeballed him right back. "So?"

He lifted his steaming mug and took another sip before answering. He was taking too long to explain himself. "You don't want him to come here?"

She rubbed her sweaty palms over the robe covering her thighs. "Not really. And since when does Terry McCoy need a vacation? Did something happen and he needs to hide out with a convenient little widow like me who lives in the middle of nowhere?"

"Of course not."

"Bullshit." Mary glared at him, regretting opening the door this morning when she could've enjoyed an earth-shattering dream.

Gabe shrugged. "Look, all I know is, he wants a break and he wants it to be here with you."

Her back stiffened. She looked around the room, anywhere but directly at Gabe. He seemed pushy about this apparent vacation, and it scared her. When she had the nerve to finally look back at him, something strange lingered in his calculating eyes that made her think this visit was a cover-up to something else. She had her dumb moments like everyone else, but she wasn't an idiot. The McCoy's probably owned several vacation homes across the world. It made no sense to Mary he'd want to come here to her quaint little cabin in the woods, where nothing but hard work was the highlight of the day.

"Why didn't he just call me if he wanted to see me?" She didn't bother to mention she'd left messages on Terry's voicemail, and his lack of a response hurt her feelings. Now she was frustrated and angry.

Right now all men were the same in Mary's eyes. They couldn't be relied upon or trusted.

Gabe's smile faded slightly. Perhaps he sensed she wasn't comfortable with the conversation. "He's been busy, Mary, and to be honest, he's been out of sorts lately."

"When you two flew into my life my husband wound up dead." She took another long drink from the mug, needing a rush of caffeine. Maybe something stronger would be more appropriate during this strange conversation.

Gabe cleared his throat and looked down at his cup. "I'm sorry for your loss." He tapped his hand against the cup, the silver ring on his baby finger ticking the seconds away.

She blew out a shaky breath. "Don't mention it. The asshole treated me like garbage anyway. Now I finally get to do what I want." She hoped to God he couldn't tell how hard it was for her to say that. How much it hurt to be alone, even when the pain didn't physically hurt anymore. She didn't want him thinking she was still the same terrified woman he'd first met a few months back. All this back talk and toughness was only a front. Deep down, she was a lot like her father.

Gabe's brow arched but he made no further comment.

"Why doesn't Terry stay with you and Mima?" Mary picked up her coffee cup, pushed her chair back and strolled over to the kitchen window, which faced a thick stand of pines. Maybe Gabe wouldn't notice how upset this conversation made her.

All alone with Terry. The criminal who kissed me then left me hanging.

Even when he'd come to say hello and checked up on her, he always had some kind of bodyguard with him, which in itself made her uneasy. Even if she agreed, there'd be men with guns behind the trees. She didn't want to live in fear again, even if it was for a short while.

"Mima's cabin has one bedroom. We'd be packed like sardines."

She glanced over her shoulder. "I'm sure he has other friends in your *business* that could show him a good time."

"I wouldn't say he's looking for a good time. More like a good rest, with someone he trusts."

Mary sighed. It seemed as if everything she said was going in one ear and out the other. "I'm sure there are many other private locations, resorts, small towns, *hookers*, to keep him busy."

"No."

"Why not?"

"He wants to be here with you. It's really that simple."

Nothing is simple these days. She closed her eyes tight, wishing she could be somewhere else, and rubbed the sudden ache in her forehead. "We barely know each other." A part of her wanted to run and hide, but the other wanted to hear more.

She opened her eyes and stared out the window, feeling hopeless and alone, picturing that night. He'd told his man to wait in the chopper. Then he closed the back door before he pressed her against the hallway wall and made her mind blank with lust. It happened so quickly after a few drinks that, like a common floozy, she'd held him tight and taken everything he'd given. Those criminal lips still held an imprint on her soul.

To say that she felt ashamed of her actions was an understatement.

Pushing aside her wayward thoughts, Mary sought out the picture of her and Tom standing in front of the house a few years back. She knew damn well the smile on her face was fake, his grip on her arm too tight. Everything was a lie. Everything was forced. Terry would probably hurt her, too.

"Did Tom really drown? Be honest with me."

Gabe's expression remained the same. Calm, cool, and completely unreadable. "Yes. He drowned. It's a common way to die."

She shook her head in disbelief and turned back to the window, trying to fight the tears rushing to the surface. Her whole body trembled. Why did she have to be leery of everything? She wished she was strong enough to throw caution to the wind and be like everybody else who didn't give a shit about action versus consequences. She cared too much about every little thing it physically pained her.

A hand touched her shoulder and she jerked around in horror. "Jesus, you scared me," she panted. "You guys are always sneaking up on me." She backed away. "Don't do that anymore."

"I'm sorry." Gabe stepped back and looked down at her with what appeared to be sympathy in his eyes. "I would never hurt you, and Terry wouldn't either. He's not an evil man."

Mary swallowed the lump in her throat. What was the true meaning of evil anyway? A man who hit his wife or a man who took another man's life?

Gabe frowned. "I'm confused. I thought you two were really hitting it off? He hasn't shut up about you since the doc took that bullet out of his shoulder."

Mary couldn't look him in the eye. "I don't know what to tell you." She blew out a deep breath and stared out the window again, her gaze lost in the endless sway of green. Knowing Terry talked about her lifted her spirits, but there were still many questions left unanswered. "He made me feel like I was beautiful." She bit her lip, realizing she'd said that out loud, and turned back to Gabe with her shoulders square. "But now I know better than to believe anything a player says."

Gabe appeared to be taken back by her words but didn't say anything else in Terry's defense. "Would fifty-grand make it easier on you?"

She'd just taken another sip of coffee and nearly choked on it. "What?"

"I'll pay you to babysit him. Think of yourself as an innkeeper, or bed and breakfast hostess . . . whatever."

Mary threw her hands up in frustration, cursed out loud, and opened the cupboard door. "I'd have to cook for him too?" She grabbed a bottle of liquor and added three fingers to her coffee. The bottle rattled against the cup. She sorely needed hair of the dog.

Fifty-thousand dollars. Holy shit.

Gabe stood there completely silent as she took a shaky drink. "And if I say no, then what? People come banging down my door anyway, like I have no say in the matter?" *Why am I shaking so much?* "I don't think I've ever seen fifty-thousand dollars before."

She set her coffee cup down, unable to keep a steady hand. It would take her several years of hard work to earn that much money.

Gabe shrugged as if he was talking about beer money. "Put it this way, if after his little vacay is over and you still want him gone, then I understand. Take the money and run if you want. Nobody is telling you what to do. I'm just asking for your help."

She breathed a little better knowing she wouldn't be forced into anything, yet this whole situation was so crazy she didn't even know what to say. Gabe's proximity, and the fact that he was such a huge guy didn't help either, even though he let her have her own space.

A long, awkward silence fell over them until Gabe cleared his throat. "Ben has been dealt with."

Mary swallowed. The mention of that psycho's name made her skin crawl. "Why are you telling me this?"

"Because I want you to trust me, and Terry couldn't tell you himself. He can't call you and report our actions." He lifted a teasing brow and Mary wanted to hit him. "I'm sure he'll make it up to you somehow. So, what do you say?"

She took a shaky breath. *Why am I even having this conversation with him? Fifty-thousand dollars.* Maybe she could skip town and go on a vacation or something. Let Terry stay here on his own and fend for himself.

"I don't know, Gabe. This is insane."

"Not really." He chuckled. "It's not like he's a complete stranger to you. Think of all the fun you could have." He waggled his eyebrows then winked, showing that strange humor she was still trying to get used to.

"I . . . ." She turned and moved a safe distance away, her cheeks burning knowing he was right. "I have a hard time trusting people, especially after what happened."

"You can trust me, you know."

She whirled around. "Why? Why does Mima trust you after everything that happened? We had a simple life until you guys showed up." Tears filled her eyes from the harsh memory of Ben cutting her breast. Almost of its own will, her hand lifted to the scar, a small ridge about an inch in length above her right breast. Physical proof of how crazy some men really are. It didn't seem to matter who set foot into her life, if he was a man, he was bound to eventually hurt her both physically and emotionally.

Gabe glanced around the room, perhaps trying to find the right words. "Terry and I both feel horrible about what happened. I certainly didn't plan to crash my plane, and we didn't know what Ben was up to."

She blew out an impatient breath. Her hand settled back to her side, but the scar would never be forgotten. "I know, but still. Our lives aren't the same anymore. *I'm* not the same anymore."

"None of us are the same anymore. Look, all I can say is Mima's my world. I truly believe fate brought us together, and I'm about to give her this." He reached into his pocket and when he opened his enormous hand a gorgeous diamond ring twinkled in his palm. "I'm going to ask her tonight, but I thought I should tell you first." He shrugged, but Mary saw the color of embarrassment in his cheeks. "Kind of like asking your permission, I guess, since you're her only family."

Her throat felt tight. Her heart felt empty. What did Mima see in this man? She eyed him critically. He was built like a brute and had the face of a man weathered by a harsh life. He may be handsome in his own way, but nothing to die for. In her eyes Gabe wasn't a sex symbol, he was a symbol of take it to the death by any means necessary kind of man. But Mima fell in love with him. She was attracted to him, and Mary would probably never understand why. Maybe they were perfect for each other. Big versus small. Harsh versus soft.

A slow smile touched her lips. "You don't need my permission. I know she loves you. I have no idea *why*, but I know she does."

Gabe nodded, his grin almost childish. "Not all men are assholes, Mary. You'll find out soon enough."

She cleared her throat and wiped her eyes. "My answer is no, Gabe." *Fifty-grand you idiot!* But Mary walked him to the door before she changed her mind. "Please tell Terry I'm sorry, but I can't do it. Good luck with your proposal tonight. I know what her answer will be."

Gabe nodded and let the screen door smack behind him. "Take care, Mary. We'll see you soon." He started his old Ford pickup and backed out of the driveway.

Mary returned to the kitchen with a heavy heart. How lucky Mima was to have such a big and powerful man love her so much. She was envious, even knowing Gabriel wasn't exactly a model citizen. Not everybody is perfect, and not everybody gets what they want. Mary was well aware of the brutality of people and life in general.

When she heard the truck pull away she returned to the kitchen and polished off the rest of her Irish coffee.

A vision of Terry filled her mind. He was the opposite of Gabe. Terry had a long and lithe body, and his face could grace any popular magazine. He was tough but he had class. He could be deadly, but he could kiss her into liquid, too.

She closed her eyes and allowed herself to imagine how pleasurable it could be in his arms. It was just a fantasy. A dream. Nothing good could ever come from a tryst with Terry McCoy, son of a notorious crime boss. But she was allowed to fantasize in her own home, on her own kitchen chair.

She pictured his soft, kissable lips on a face with a hint of stubble to scratch and excite. She imagined his smooth, low voice whispering sensual words against the soft spot below her ear, before he trailed those hot lips down her body.

Naturally, she parted her robe and slid her middle finger between wet lips and softly stroked her sensitive clit, wishing a bad boy was giving the attention.

God she was pathetic.

Her finger moved faster, more forcefully.

She wanted more. Wanted it all. Needed to be touched and loved and spoiled.

What she really needed was to let go.

With a heavy sigh, she let her head fall back as she slid her bum closer to the edge of the seat, while her finger brought her closer to the edge of release.

What have you done to me, Terry McCoy?

Chapter 3

Terry pulled onto the teardrop driveway at the family estate near Saanich Inlet. He bounded up the massive stone steps, velvet box in hand, and walked right in. The house was silent as he entered the parlor and made his way into the great room, where his father liked to read the paper by the windows.

"Dad? Wanda?"

He strolled over to the round table. The paper lay untouched, his reading glasses sitting atop. No Colton. Terry stared out the big picture window as a sailboat drifted along the waterway. With his mind in chaos, he stared out over the water, wishing he could disappear in those clear blue depths.

Too many windows. Too exposed.

The McCoy estate, designed by a wealthy old coal baron, had sweeping ocean views from every waiting room, and all seven bedrooms. Even two of the four bathrooms had a lovely view of a natural waterfall with its immaculate surrounding gardens. The property even had a creek and a small beach to add to its list of perfections.

The imperfections consisted of the people inside.

To Terry this place held no more meaning than a pretty decoy, like the hotel in Victoria. A convenient lie covering the nasty bones of this business his father worked hard to build. A business that would be his one day—whether he liked it or not.

This is only the beginning.

Adolfo had him all worked up wondering what the hell those words were supposed to mean. Should he be scouring the house for a bomb? Was there a hit man on the property ready to put a bullet through the window right where he stood? *Fuck, I hate living like this.*

He scowled at the happy couple on the sailboat, drifting at a languid pace only a few hundred yards from the house on the shore. They embraced each other by the wheel. No worries. No end in sight. Champagne and strawberries. Maybe they weren't even married. Maybe she was his mistress or perhaps an expensive escort. Hell, she could be his best friend's daughter.

They may not be able to see him through the window, but he saw everything.

He saw too much and knew too much. Felt too much. Emotions always got the best of Terry, and Colton was quick to remind him: *"If you're going to survive in this business you have to shut yourself off."*

Not Terry.

He honestly believed he'd never be able to flip off the switch and continue to live like a puppet. This life his father had thrown him into was seriously getting to him. It all came down to being accepted. Would he ever be good enough? It seemed like his life revolved around pleasing his father no matter the cost.

He'd almost got Gabe killed—the one man he'd promised to protect all those years ago when they were kids, after Gabe's dad died in a plane crash up north.

The guilt bore a massive hole in his soul.

The sailboat disappeared. Just like the innocence of his youth.

He stared at the wake from the boat. A long time ago he was a boy living the life of a regular kid at this estate. He didn't know then what he knew now, that when his father told him to go outside and play, somebody was getting their throat slit in the library.

Even his mother didn't know the real man to whom she'd given her heart. She saw only the best in her husband. When men came to visit, Eliza believed they were business associates, married with children, living in their perfect glass houses. Everyone else knew better.

Eliza loved Colton McCoy beyond the moon and believed the man who swept her off her feet was simply born of a family with old money—not a man who earned his wealth from drug smuggling.

How naïve and beautiful she was. He was her spitting image—reminded of her every time he looked in the mirror. He missed her every day. Missed her long golden hair, blue eyes, and warm, genuine smile. She was a child born of nature, loving her gardens and every bird perched high in this dark place. A place bloodied by death.

Life wasn't fair, and an innocent woman lost her life because of what she saw that day. The day Terry's life had changed.

Doc said the heart attack killed her instantly. If only that was true.

He hung his head, accepting the great weight upon his shoulders. A weight his father held even more than him, for Colton worshipped the ground Eliza had walked on. Even though Terry knew he couldn't be to blame for his mother's tragic death, in some small way he wished he'd been old enough to know better. To have had the opportunity to take her away from this place before the business sunk its claws into him.

But she never would've left her husband. If her heart would've held fast, Terry knew, deep down, she would've stuck by Colton's side no matter what.

There was too much pain and heartache in his life. All the jokes and jabs were a mask to cover the lonely beast he'd become.

A beast who deserved to be alone. Just like Gabe had been, before Mima pulled him out of his mangled plane.

He pressed his palm to the glass. A dark vision filled his eyes of that night he'd reached out and grabbed Gabriel's hand through the bars of the cell a Columbian cartel had trapped him in. They'd ripped away his clothes and his pride. Stabbed him. Thrown the wreck of the man he already was into a watery pit to be slowly eaten alive by the bugs. Terry and his team arrived in the nick of time. One more day and Gabe would've been dead.

Terry was the one who'd pulled him out, but Gabe always had Terry's back. He was so full of regret it made his stomach turn. Even the memory of Ben hurting Mary haunted his dreams at night.

What could he possibly do with a good woman like Mary? How did Gabe win the heart of Mima? How did anyone fall in love and stay there?

Maybe I should try calling her again, or will she tell me to fuck off?

Everything was his fault, and his alone.

Mary deserved better than him, but he couldn't stop thinking about her.

He pulled his cell phone out of his pocket and listened to her last voicemail for the hundredth time. *"If I don't hear from you in a couple days I'll assume I'll never see you again. It's okay, you know. I'm a big girl."*

God her voice sounded so sad; so beautiful. But how could he see her without his father sending a tail? How could he possibly be alone with her to explain himself?

Everything tortured him. He was sick and tired of this life. If he really had his way this business wouldn't exist. He'd gladly run a proper hotel and leave all this torture behind. If only he could step up to the plate, be a man and walk away, without guilt making him turn around and run right back.

"Are you all right, sweetheart? You look ill."

He blinked, realizing how pathetic he must look standing there touching the window like a blubbering fool. Maybe there were tears in his eyes—he couldn't be sure. He turned to face Wanda, his father's second wife, and forced a smile for her benefit. After all, if it wasn't for her his father probably would've killed himself in his grief.

He stepped away from the window and slipped the velvet box into his jacket pocket.

"I want to see it," she said, and lifted her hand.

Terry cleared his throat and stared at her in disbelief. "What? Why?"

"Because I want to see. Don't argue with me." Palm up, she fluttered her fingers impatiently.

Against his better judgment he reluctantly handed her the velvet box.

He watched her in confused silence as she held the box in delicate fingers and opened the lid. She didn't cry, didn't bat a lash, didn't even make a sound, but to Terry it seemed as if seeing Adolfo's finger hurt her soul. He didn't want her to suffer as his mother did. The dirty bowels of this business should never be seen by innocent eyes.

He may be a monster, but he'd never intentionally break another's innocence.

Wanda sighed deeply. "Some people never learn." She closed the lid and handed him the box, her smile tight. "Nobody messes with my family."

"I know." He led her toward the plush sectional couch—a white and grossly modern monstrosity—in the middle of the parlor, before making his way to the liquor cabinet. "Drink?" He held up a crystal tumbler.

Everything in his family home was original, right down to the floral wallpaper and fainting couches. But Wanda insisted on "pops of modern and contemporary furnishings," as she'd told Colton. Terry thought the mixture to be highly unusual and in very bad taste. But he'd never tell her the bitter truth.

Wanda shook her head and frowned. "Terry, darling, what is going on with you? You have me worried with your drinking lately."

Ignoring her pleading eyes, he focused on pouring a healthy measure of vodka, clean. "I'm an adult and I'm fine."

With her thin eyebrows arched high, the wrinkles in Wanda's forehead deepened. "What would your father say if he knew you drank a forty a day?"

He blinked. "How do you know how much I drink?" He shook his head. "Never mind." She probably knew everything. She was a smart cookie and kept tabs on them all.

"Where's Dad?"

She sighed again, her expression full of worry. "He hasn't been feeling well lately. I don't think he'll be joining us for lunch. You'll have to entertain our business guests, sweetheart."

Wanda clasped her hands together as she always did when deep in thought. Terry stared at the beautiful woman who devoted her life to his father. She was a raven-haired beauty with mocha skin and dark eyes that whispered scandal. Tall and thin, she was a rare gem who commanded attention and made many women jealous. No wonder Colton fell for her quickly. She epitomized grace and charm and brass balls.

"I wish you would open up to me, my boy. I only want you to be happy. Don't be like your father, Terry."

More guilt weighed on his shoulders. "I know. You're the total opposite of the wicked stepmother in every other book."

She slowly eyed him up. "Is there a woman in your life? Someone to make you happy?"

He swept his hand out in a gesture of indifference. "There's many of them. They're only good for one thing."

"Terry!" Wanda's eyes widened in surprise, then she chuckled softly. "One day you will learn the power of a woman. One woman. And if you're lucky you might survive what she does to your heart."

The power of a woman.

Terry grinned as an idea sprung to mind. "What do you think of the mountains?"

Wanda appeared confused. "What about them?"

"I read an article recently about mountain women who trap animals and rely on dogs to get around in the winter. Totally self-sufficient. Impressive, don't you think?"

Wanda shook her head, eyes wide in disbelief. Her massive diamond earrings twinkled in the light. They probably cost his father no small fortune. "Why would you read a silly article like that?"

Coming from the finest, wine infused circles in Los Angeles, she wouldn't understand Mary if her life depended on it.

Terry shrugged. "I was just curious."

"Who could possibly tolerate a bunch of filthy mutts in the wilderness anyway?" Wanda leaned forward, staring hard. "Do these . . . females . . . go to town to bathe?"

Terry's head filled with a gorgeous vision of Mary rubbing a bar of soap along her soft flesh in the middle of a river, in the middle of nowhere, with nothing but the wilderness in the background.

I hope not.

One of the housekeepers entered the room. "Lunch is served."

Thank God. "See? It's officially noon." Terry lifted his drink in a salute to his stepmother, took it back in three swallows, welcoming the burn down his throat. He was thankful to have such a large stash of Finlandia Vodka nobody else seemed to like.

After lunch and a brief meeting with new and old business associates, Terry headed back to the Sea Scape and tried to forget what Adolfo Montesano said before he shot him in the forehead.

* * * *

Sometime in the wee hours of the morning, Terry whipped his legs over the bed and grabbed his robe off the floor. With his heartbeat in his throat he stumbled to the en suite. Every step became forced, as if his feet held the weight of the hotel. Sweat trickled from his forehead into his eyes. A disgusting bile filled his mouth. He could hardly swallow and his vision blurred.

He stared at his pale skin in the mirror, his entire body trembling with weakness, before splashing cold water onto his face. His pupils were so dilated he could hardly see the blue, while red veins spanned across most of the white. This wasn't the flu or some nasty hangover, there was something seriously wrong with him.

Maybe it was only a nightmare. Maybe a drink would settle him. No. It was more than that. He tightened the sash on his robe and made his way to the study. A wave of nausea hit him like the force of Gabe's hatchet. He stumbled against the hallway wall and tried to keep his head straight. The door at the end of the hall expanded and shrunk like in a cartoon. He leaned against the hallway wall. Bile scorched his throat more forcefully. He shook his head and fought the rush of dizziness, his hazy vision trained on the study door.

Determined to make it there before losing it in the hallway, he pushed forward, gripped the doorknob and shoved the door open. He groaned and wiped the sweat beading into his eyes. Somebody had moved the furniture. He shook his head, trying to navigate the unfamiliar floor. The objects in the study molded together, danced in a sea of blurring white. His knee hit something and he crumbled to a state of submission as a streak of lightning spread across his stomach. He whimpered as pain unlike anything he'd ever felt before gripped him hard.

Somehow he managed to pull himself off the floor and stumble to the desk, where he picked up the phone. With a shaky hand he pressed the button for the front desk.

"Help me," he groaned, his strength completely sapped.

He heard the click on the other end before the receiver fell from his shaky hand and banged onto the desk. His knees buckled, the lights went out, and he hit the floor.

Sometime later he blinked and rolled to his side, just in time to hurl into a mop bucket. How it got there was a mystery, but he was glad for it. He wouldn't want to ruin his favorite Navajo rug. He puked so hard he thought his eyes would pop out and fall into the bucket.

After long, agonizing minutes, he finally lifted his head and breathed as if he'd completed the longest marathon in existence. Two blurry bodies filled his vision.

"What happened?" He spit into the bucket, not daring to look up too fast and feel that hot sickness again. He already knew who occupied the room with him, and only one of them had a key.

"You're drinking too much, dickhead," Gabe blurted.

"No. He was most likely poisoned, shitstick," said the other man.

"What?" Of all the ways to try and kill him in this day and age, being poisoned would be his last guess. And he didn't drink *that* much.

He lifted his heavy head to find Gabe and Sammy Hayes sitting opposite him. If not for Sam—who knew pretty much every way to kill a person—Terry might not be alive right now. Barely alive, but still breathing at least.

"Hey, Sam," he mumbled, completely baffled and ill to the bone. He wanted to die and get it over with. "What are you doing here?" Every word he uttered sounded like drunken gibberish.

Sam chuckled. "What, no thank you?"

"Thanks," Terry muttered. "How did this happen? How did you know?" Saying the words took great difficulty.

"Well, you were disoriented, mumbling shit that didn't make sense. You were burning up, and drooling and twitching. Top signs for poisoning, and most likely arsenic."

"Why the hell—"

"You just lie there and be quiet, boy."

Terry tensed at the sound of his father's voice through the speakerphone. Of all the people he wanted to chat with, Colton would be the last. He sighed and shook his head, prepared to have his ass handed to him, even though this wasn't his fault. "Hello, Father. Nice of you to check in."

"Shut up and do as you're told. You're not invincible, you know. Time to watch your ass and quit fucking around. Now, what are we looking at here?"

Gabe sat forward in his chair and spoke loud enough to be clear to Colton. "Good thing Sam knows his stuff, sir." He directed his attention to Terry. "Once you finish puking you'll need to eat something and drink lots of water. You'll be sitting on the toilet more than puking. I truly feel sorry for you." Yet his grin totally belied that, the snarky bastard.

Ugh. Eating was seriously the last thing on Terry's mind. *I just want some fucking vodka.*

"Well, it's obvious this person didn't know what they were doing. This is not the work of a professional."

Terry watched in silence as Gabe closed his eyes and took a deep breath. "Hard to say, Boss. Could be this person was interrupted and had to compromise, or poison isn't their usual method. There's no easy answer. Terry took your place at the meeting today. There were several new faces in the mix. They should all be questioned."

"Well, it's clear to me my son needs a little vacation and we'll figure this out, quietly, without him. God knows he needs to sober up anyway. You know what to do."

Terry glared at the phone as Colton hung up.

At least it was the three of them now, and he could speak his mind. Terry, Gabe, and Sam were like brothers, although Sam wasn't always around. His missions usually consisted of eliminating unsavory characters in all corners of the world. Right now Sammy was on the home front, and nobody knew why.

Either way, he was a smartass like Gabe. Terry had the pleasure of constant mockery at his hip.

"Colton's right. We can't risk your health when he's already under the weather. You're all he has left." Gabe leaned forward, his expression hard. "And you're my only brother. Don't fuck this up."

Terry wasn't afraid to die; to take a number and wait for it. Death was the one sure thing in life. But he understood his father and Gabe didn't want to lose him. But why did his father have to speak as if Terry was at fault? All he ever did was try to be the best he could be, yet it wasn't good enough. He knew his father loved him, but sometimes it felt as if his father had no choice. He didn't *want* to love him, he *had to* because Terry was his son.

Sam on the other hand seemed bored by the heartfelt exchange.

"He talks to me like I'm a fucking kid and all I do is disappoint him." Sam chuckled. "Awww. Chin up, bud."

Terry glared at Sam and flipped him the bird. He loved Sam like a brother but he could be a jackass at times. Maybe living his life through the eye of a scope made him God or something, like doctors and their "live or let die" mentality.

"Not long ago you were shot by Ben and now this," Gabe tossed in.

Adolfo's last words repeated in Terry's hazy mind. When he felt strong enough not to puke, he pushed up to a sitting position and stared at the two men. His guts turned and the need for food became stronger by the second.

"Do you think Ben's wife hired someone to poison me?"

Sam shrugged. "It's possible, but I doubt it. She had the hots for Gabe and was only with Ben out of necessity. I doubt her heart is broken. I could probably unzip my pants right now and she'd fall to her knees."

"Then Adolfo's family or his contacts must be behind this. Someone must have poisoned my food either at the hotel or at the house today. I haven't been anywhere else."

Sam glanced at Gabe, who nodded in agreement.

"Well, you need to go somewhere and you'll need to be watched at all times."

Terry settled back against the couch and took a deep breath. "I don't want to hide out like some rat." The queasiness in his stomach died down a bit but the hunger was like a living thing raging within. Either that or Gabe was right about the toilet. He forced his mind away from the ugly thought. "A vacay would be nice. How long is this going to take?"

Gabe shrugged. "Hard to say. Maybe a couple of weeks, or longer. Don't worry, someone will watch the old man, too. What about spending some time with the trapper?"

The power of a woman.

Terry closed his eyes and sighed. "We haven't talked in a while. She'll probably tell me to fuck off, or shoot me right there on her doorstep. I have to admit I would deserve it."

Gabe chuckled. "I think you might be surprised what she does to you."

Terry frowned but his nerves jumped to life. "What do you mean?"

His best friend shifted in his seat and cleared his throat. "I paid her a visit the other day and sort of mentioned you needed a vacation."

Terry sat up straighter. If he had the strength he'd fly through the air and take Gabe down right through the fucking couch. "Why the fuck would you ask her without even asking me first?" His chest tightened and his stomach turned to knots. He couldn't believe Gabe took it upon himself to talk to Mary. Yet his curiosity screamed to know the answer. "What did she say?"

"First of all, you're a stubborn idiot, that's why I didn't ask you first. If anybody needs time off around here, it's you. And after this disaster, I guess I did the right thing."

Terry glared at him. "Or you poisoned me as some sick joke, and you're trying to play matchmaker."

"Shut up for a second," Sam said, and sat forward, suddenly interested in the conversation. His crooked smile was wide enough to show a hint of a gold tooth. "Who's this *trapper woman*?"

"Just some broad," Terry answered, avoiding Gabe's intent stare.

"Bullshit," Sam interjected, and folded his arms over his chest. "*Some broad* is a bimbo you find on a dance floor with fake tits and a fake onion bum. This woman sounds like a lot more to me."

"Anyway, she said yes," Gabe finished, his smile teasing.

"What?" Terry's heart pounded. His upset stomach turned to a twisting ball of barely suppressed excitement. *She actually wants me there?*

"On another note, I asked Mima to marry me, and she accepted," Gabe added nonchalantly. "It'll be a fall wedding, I guess."

Terry and Sam gaped at him and then each other.

"God you're pathetic. Marriage. Already?" Terry blurted. "You've only known her for like five months. And Dad thinks *I'm* a reject."

"You are," Gabe and Sam voiced at the same time.

"Well isn't this perfect? Maybe you'll get married at this trapper shack and throw bacon bits for confetti," Sam said and hollered with laughter.

Gabe glared at him. "Fuck off."

Terry slouched back against the couch, his sickness completely forgotten. "Mary actually said yes to me going there?"

"Yep."

"That's a good thing, right?" Sam asked, clueless to what exactly was going on. He was away on a mission in Australia during the mountain escapade.

"Yeah." The room fell silent as Terry eyed Gabe, who stared intently back at him.

Terry looked out the window, remembering a darker day in the distant past. "As long as she doesn't find out the truth."

Chapter 4

The cool, crisp air hitched her lungs this morning.

Mary lifted her old skinning knife and studied her handiwork. The carcass exposed pink flesh from the bottom lip to the tail of her latest catch: a forty-pound beaver with a lush pelt.

"Well, buddy. You'll probably fetch me a tidy thirty-five, maybe even forty bucks."

A warm blast of air loosened a few strands of unruly hair from her bun. With a frustrated grunt she swiped them away with the back of her hand.

Next she set out exposing the castors and separating the fur from the front and back legs, before skinning the pelt away from the sides and back. Once she completed the tedious task of removing the pelt from the head, she fetched her fleshing tool and began scraping away any remaining flesh and fat, before grabbing a tin of nails and the stretching board.

She folded the pelt in half across the marked rings on the board, allowing the pelt to shrink back to its natural size. After nailing the nose, tail and each flank on the appropriate ring, she then added another nail every inch around until the pelt expanded to its maximum size.

Once the task was complete, she set the hide to tan in the smoke hut and returned to the house. She fed a few logs into the wood-burning furnace before she readied to head into town for supplies.

The dogs yipped and barked on top of their little houses. She wandered over and gave each of them a motherly pat on the head before getting into her old Bronco and driving away.

The scenery on the way to town never failed to take her breath away. In the daylight hours the glistening white-tipped mountains jutted high above the treetops. The gravel road wound around thick brush over foothills and down through valleys. At every turn there was always something beautiful to see. Even the old cutovers from loggers breathed new life with saplings and moss and an endless painting of green.

Few people lived this far from town, although like herself and Mima, some still chose a more rugged lifestyle. Though Mima lived completely off grid without power and running water, or even a driveway all the way to her home, she still managed to make due. Mary, however, lived twenty-minutes from town on this side of the mountain. She had her own septic system, a phone line, running water, and power. Convenient, yet still far enough to be in the middle of nowhere. She could walk around her property for hours and never see a single person.

Winter lasted too long in these majestic woods and mountains. Now that the buds were sprouting, the sky bright and cheery, her winter melancholy should subside. But nothing made her feel good these days. Work, care for the dogs, and sleep. That was the gist of her life. Boring yet consistent.

Nobody prepared her to be a widow. Nobody ever expects to be left behind. Despite feeling alone, Mary felt oddly relieved. With Tom gone she had choices in life now, yet sometimes she didn't know what to do with herself. He'd controlled everything for many years, and now he was gone. No warning that she'd be fending for herself. No signal that one day she'd be woman and man of the house.

Sometimes she'd wake up in the morning, alone, wondering what she should do with herself. Nobody yelled at her that she slept too late or that the house wasn't clean enough, or supper didn't taste good enough.

Nothing was ever good enough for Tom Billings, which included Mary.

Now she could do as she chose, but she still found herself doing those things he wanted without a second thought. It was as if she still lived as his little puppet on a string. But as each day passed she found herself growing more independent, and emotionally stronger. She had to, because if she didn't force herself to lift her chin and square her shoulders, then she might as well throw herself into the river as well.

She was alone now. Alone with seven dogs and a million trees, and one friend a mountain away.

Mima had a future to look forward to with Gabe. Mary didn't know what tomorrow would bring.

What did she ever do to deserve this meaningless existence? Tom had swept her away, and with rose-tinted glasses, Mary didn't notice the change in him until it was too late. Gone was his ready smile and gentle touch, replaced by constant bickering and a hurtful hand. She did everything she was told, always kept the house clean, did her wifely duties, and for what?

Not a shred of happiness, that's what.

Her love life consisted of a few quick flings when she was a teenager before she got married at nineteen. Not once did she ever feel loved.

Mary drove the old Bronco up the steep hill into Silver Creek—another place where she didn't want to be. As she approached the first stop sign she took a deep breath. Since Tom's death most people looked at her with suspicious eyes. As if she was the one who pushed him into the river.

They were wrong. But maybe she was wrong too for every choice she'd made in life.

Tom was a seasoned bushman and survivalist. How could he fall into the river he'd trapped on for years, and drown so easily? Nobody had any real answers, not even the authorities, and she didn't want to search anymore. Sometimes she wondered if he gave up and committed suicide to get away from her.

Maybe I should sell the house and move away. Start fresh. Pretend to be somebody else.

She pulled up to the only available parking spot in front of Byron's Hardware and shut off the engine. The town boomed with tourists this Saturday afternoon as they rushed in to set up their tents, park their trailers or motorhomes for the summer. Silver Creek was well-known for its numerous campgrounds and resorts on the outskirts of town. June was beautiful around here. Everything came to life in a short span of time.

Despite being treated like a traitor, Mary did love the old world feel of her tiny mountain town. Several shops proudly hung Canadian flags. Flowering baskets adorned street lamps. Every shop was painted a different color. The sidewalks were always kept clean, and at every turn one had a sweeping view of the mountains.

She exited the Bronco and shut the door, forcing a winner of a smile for the tourists. At least they knew nothing about her. They held no grudges, no suspicions, not a single reason to be rude to a young woman who did nothing to nobody. In their eyes she wasn't a husband killer.

The doorbell to the shop chimed as she entered. A couple of women stood by the counter, chatting with Byron. They turned and stared at her like she had some horrible disease, but old Byron had a quick smile for Mary, even if it was fake.

"Ah, Mary Billings. How are you doing, my dear?"

"That's her," one of the women whispered.

Her muscles tightened and she grit her teeth. Despite the urge to say something rude, or even throw something at them, she ignored them instead. "I'm okay, Byron, and yourself?"

He lowered his head and peered over his ancient spectacles. "Oh, same old, but there's always news to spread." He removed his glasses and held them between his fingers as if the news held the utmost importance. "Mr. Sherbrook broke his ankle the other day."

She glanced at the women and forced a tight smile. *Maybe his wife pushed him down the stairs.* "Well, I hope he'll be all right."

Mary grabbed a cart and pushed it into the middle aisle. She focused on getting what she needed and getting out of there. The only tranquility in her life was keeping busy at home, and even that got old fast. These days she didn't have much to say to anyone, especially old Byron who was one of the worst gossipmongers in town. He lived for other people's drama and misfortune. Maybe he talked about Mary behind her back too.

When she reached the knife display something new caught her eye. She withdrew a Dexter-Russell skinning knife and eyed the piece. "Hey, Byron. When did you get these in?"

The women exited the shop.

Byron ambled over with a proud smile. "I had a new catalogue shipped to me last month. Mrs. Kipper swears by everything they sell in there and she gets commission on it, you know. Makes it easier for her to care for her dying husband."

Maybe she's slowly killing him while making a little nest egg. "Well, isn't that nice?"

"You bet. Thought I'd try a few items and see how they sell. Always good to help some folks in town."

Mary tried to ignore his attempt at sentiment but failed miserably. Her hands shook at her sides while she tried to be calm. After the way the townsfolk treated her since Tom's death, she'd grown sour to most of them. Even though Byron seemed like such a kind soul, he still talked about everyone.

Lost in her convoluted thoughts, she flipped the skinning knife over in her palm, feeling the weight of it, trying to keep her emotions in check. She didn't like feeling vulnerable in front of anyone.

"This one looks like a real gem. I bet my pelts would be smooth as a baby's butt in half the time with a blade like this."

The doorbell chimed but neither of them bothered to look.

"Wouldn't hurt you to buy one," Byron added, his eyes glistening.

Mary sighed and put the knife back on the shelf. Maybe she should've said yes to Gabe. "I can't really afford it right now. My account—"

"Has been cleared."

Mary and Byron turned to the front door.

Holy shit. Her eyes widened and her heart lodged in her throat. The skinning knife slipped out of her shaky hand and clamored like a church bell on the cement floor. Standing there with a handsome grin was none other than Terry McCoy.

"Hello, Mary."

She blinked, not quite believing her eyes, suddenly faced with the male character in every one of her torrid dreams. She cleared her throat and suddenly remembered dropping the knife. Awkwardly, she bent down to retrieve it, and tried to convince herself that once she looked toward the door again he'd be gone. But as she stood back up and set the knife back onto the shelf, her gaze landed on the six-foot candy bar standing less than five feet away.

Her resolve crumbled. She wanted to rush over and hug him. She wanted him to take her fears away and make these people suffer for making her feel like garbage. They had no idea how much of a powerful man he was, and she knew if she told him how she'd been treated lately, he would do something about it. But she couldn't speak, couldn't move. Apparently both her feet and her tongue were frozen to the floor.

God, he looked good. Tired, but still as handsome as ever with his unkempt hair, sexy eyes, and shit-eating grin. She swallowed the dry lump in her throat, unable to form more than an awkward, "Hi."

He was alone. Terry McCoy never went anywhere alone.

Something must be going on. She knew it like she knew he looked good enough to eat.

Byron stood between them with an odd look on his face. "Can I help you, sir? I don't believe we've met before."

"No, I'm new to town," Terry answered matter-of-factly, and pulled out a wad of cash. "As I said, the lady's account has been cleared." He flattened what appeared to be a fairly large sum onto the counter and casually made his way toward her.

Her pride bristled to have him clear her account, as if he believed she needed him in order to survive. She lifted her chin in defiance. "That wasn't necessary, Terry. I can pay my own bills."

The corner of his mouth tipped up as his gaze swept all over her. "Oh, I know you can. It was only a thank you."

Thank you for what? She eyed him critically, wondering what that was supposed to mean, but decided not to ask in front of Byron.

Terry wore a hoodie, blue jeans, and boots, like many other tourists. Not a fancy leather jacket or crisp slacks. Still, she imagined he had a gun hiding somewhere.

Did Gabe think this was some kind of joke? Why didn't he say Terry was already here? Now she felt completely trapped and forced to babysit him.

She couldn't move, couldn't stop thinking about every little detail since he'd popped into her life almost five months ago. She could only manage to stare at him like a deer in the headlights, unsure how to carry on. After his last visit and no word from him she thought either he was dead, or he didn't give a shit anymore. She often thought about Terry and how he'd blown into her life that day. Every day his face filled her vision, even as she mourned Tom.

How could she miss Terry as if he was an important part of her life? She was a traitor to herself.

Still, she wanted to wrap her arms around him and forget her messed up life, even though she was angry by his lack of a phone call.

Maybe she should take Gabe's money now. It would be what Terry deserved. But then again, that would basically make her a hooker—if her dreams held any weight in the real world. She stared at him, at war with what she should do. How could he show up in her town like this, like he had no care in the world? Were all criminals this casual?

Terry reached a hand out and shook Byron's. "Terry McCoy." He eyed the terrified look on her face and smiled. "I'm an old friend of Mary's. Thought I'd swing by and check up on her, make sure she's doing okay."

"Oh, wonderful." Byron smiled, clueless to how freaked out Mary felt right at this moment, and pumped Terry's hand enthusiastically.

Mary didn't know what to do but plaster a smile. "That's nice of you, Terry." She eyeballed the sexy criminal and said through clenched teeth, "Totally unnecessary, but kind all the same."

"Always nice to bump into an old friend." Byron made his way back to the counter and picked up the bills, completely unaware by the intensity flaring between them.

His eyes widened when he counted the money on the counter. "Friends are a good thing, indeed."

"Is that enough?" Terry asked, not bothering to look at the man.

"Oh, yes. Absolutely." He pocketed half the money and put the rest in the register. No sooner than he cleared her account, old Byron picked up the phone. Mary knew damn well he was calling everyone he knew with the news of the widow Billings' "old friend" with money.

Mary wondered how old Byron would react if he knew who Terry McCoy really was, or what he and his posse were capable of doing. She tried not to think too hard about it and glanced up at Terry with an awkward smile. By rights her shirt should rip open her heart pounded so hard. "When did you get in? Gabriel came to see me, but I—"

Terry pushed her lips shut with his pointer finger. She glared at him, taken back by his audacity, yet powerless to shove his hand away. The heat of his finger sent a little trigger of heat between her legs, and before she could control it, she sighed softly.

He chuckled, his blue gaze soaking her in deep, apparently aware of his effect on her. "I checked in to The Siesta last night." A thick, manly blond brow arched high. "I kinda like the rustic brown paneling and blue shag carpet. I fully expect the bed to vibrate too." His grin was too cute for words. "But I bought all the necessities for roughing it. I plan on pitching a tent in your yard tomorrow, as long as I can survive the bears, wolves, and mosquitoes."

Pitching a tent in your yard. The words sounded so dirty they made her shudder.

"Then after I cook you an amazing city slicker meal, you'll have your way with me—because I know you want to. You can tan my hide any day."

What the fuck did Gabe tell him? Mary blinked rapidly. Unable to respond to his ridiculous statement, she turned away, completely baffled and flustered, and continued putting items from her list into the cart. Terry followed behind, completely silent, yet she felt his stare as if it lived and breathed on her back.

She had made it clear to Gabe she did not want Terry here. What was she supposed to do with him now? Maybe she should drop him off at Mima's doorstep and tamper down the rampant urge to kiss him, to feather her fingers through his hair and demand he make love to her. *Stop it!*

"How long do you plan to stay?" She hated how husky her voice sounded, when she should be ushering him out the door and telling him to go home.

"Maybe a week or two. Thought I'd check out the sights, do some camping, fishing, hiking."

She fought to ignore the way his smooth, deep voice slithered along her arms as if he'd licked her with his words. "Well, you've come to the right place for that." *And after two weeks you'll be gone again. Perfect.*

"I hear there's also a few nice places to eat."

She ignored the insinuation in his voice and continued onward. "Yes, there is." The heat in the shop became unbearable.

Fifty-thousand dollars.

"Mary, put the spaghetti sauce down and look at me."

She spun around. "What?"

He eyed her with blue eyes that shouldn't be so sexy. Shouldn't make her feel naked and unhinged. She wondered what shade they'd be as he looked into her eyes while he pushed into her body.

"I'd like to take you to dinner sometime."

Mary glanced around the shop then lowered her voice, an immediate chill sweeping through her. "I don't think that's a good idea."

"Why?" he whispered back and looked around.

"I can't be seen having dinner with a strange man. It's not done around here."

Terry looked incredulous before his brows furrowed. "Is somebody giving you a hard time?"

"No, no." Mary straightened her shoulders. She certainly didn't need him terrorizing the town, although the thought of it excited her a little. She imagined it must feel amazing to have a man do something that drastic to please a woman. She pushed the cart closer to the back of the store so Byron wouldn't hear what she had to say. "Nobody's said anything to my face, but I see how they look at me. I hear their whispers. They think I had something to do with Tom's death."

Terry moved closer and cupped her shoulder with his big hand then rubbed her back in a slow, torturous fashion. Electricity shot right to her heart—or maybe it was her breast—by his touch. She almost closed her eyes and moaned. Instead she lifted her hand and coughed into her palm, hoping he didn't notice the effect on her.

"The fact is, Tom was respected. He donated quite a lot of his earnings from the trapline to charities in town and the surrounding area. He volunteered his time at events, and he always had a fake smile for everyone." She shrugged, forcing the sting of resentment far away. "I was a loner they knew nothing about who became his wife. Why wouldn't I be to blame for his death? Tom was invincible."

"You are not to blame for anything, okay? I mean it. And who gives a shit what other people think? It's your life. You're the one who has to live it."

"But I have to live *here*."

He shrugged. "Then move."

She released an impatient breath. "It's not that easy, Terry. I don't have millions of dollars to throw around like you do."

He stepped back and chuckled. "Mary, honey. It doesn't take millions to move. Anyway, if you plan to stay here then you have to learn not to care what anyone else thinks. Thicken that skin of yours. Live like you want to live. You're the boss."

But it's not as easy as he thinks.

Mary wanted to smack him and throw herself in his arms at the same time. She wasn't a complete fool. For the first time in a long time, she controlled her future, and she wouldn't let him be the one to mix it up. Besides, she was afraid of what would happen if she did give him such power. He was a friend, nothing more. Even if he did make her insides melt like butter in a pan.

And he hadn't returned her calls. Maybe he enjoyed a handful of other women while she sat at home, alone, thinking about him like some lonely, hick woman.

Maybe I should use him for pleasure then send him on his way. For once I'd be in charge of my own life and do something crazy.

She glanced past him. "Is anyone with you?" She didn't want another repeat of what happened before when Ben and his men tried to hurt her. It wasn't Terry's fault, she knew that, but she was well aware bad things happened in his line of work.

"Nope. I'm alone. Only a select few know my location."

She narrowed her eyes in suspicion. "Why? Is something going on?" Her hackles went up and her gaze sought the skinning knife on the shelf a few feet away. Maybe he had men following him and they'd find her, too.

He shrugged, but his eyes belied his nonchalance. "I just wanted to see you."

She was already an outcast in her town and lately Mima had been too busy with Gabe. But Gabe did say Terry wanted to spend some time with her. What harm would come from a simple dinner with a good-looking man like Terry McCoy? Nobody knew him. Maybe that was a good thing. Nothing else had to happen. Dinner with a man every woman in this town would faint over if he simply smiled at her. But it was Mary he wanted to see.

She made up her mind then and there. "Okay. I can do dinner."

"Wonderful," he said loudly. "Meet me at The Siesta tomorrow night, eight o'clock sharp. Wear something tight."

Byron glanced up from the phone, his eyes wide in complete shock as Terry left her there in the aisle, still holding the can of spaghetti sauce.

Chapter 5

Terry did a double take when Mary walked into the hotel lobby with her face all dolled up, wearing tight black jeans and a snug pink shirt.

He fully expected her to slap on a jogging suit and work boots, or something that screamed she regularly gutted a deer on her picnic table out back. What he stared at right now pleasantly surprised him.

He couldn't help his grin as he eyed her up. All her wavy, chestnut hair touched her shoulders, and framed a flawless, oval face. Full lips tinted pink, bright brown eyes that almost matched her hair, and a pert little nose. She was beautiful. A woman who could be wilderness resourceful yet downtown chic all at once. Terry imagined how she would look in a gown at a gala over a thousand-dollar dinner plate.

Mary Billings would look good on his arm.

He pushed up from his seat on the ratty old lounger by the front desk and made his way toward her, thinking of ice-cold water and Gabe's eyelash curler to settle his erection rapidly going haywire. Since when could he not control himself in front of a broad?

"Come on, honey. I'm starving."

Her awkward silence did nothing to curb his enthusiasm. He'd do just about anything to get into her clothes, and even though their strange relationship got off to a bad start, he was prepared to offer her whatever she wanted. As long as she would have him. He liked Mary Billings. Whether he'd made a bad decision in coming here was another story. He'd take his chances. Life was a chance in itself.

Guilt weighed heavily on his shoulders for many things. He always seemed to reach out for acceptance even when he felt like he wasn't good enough. His father always made him feel inadequate. And here he was, away from the responsibility of the business in order to spend time with a woman. He wasn't there to watch over things even though Colton told him to go away for a short while. He blamed himself for Ben going rogue and causing a shit storm in Mima and Mary's life. Gabe almost got killed because he was blind to what was going on, and he was the animal who took advantage of Mary in her emotional state. He still remembered that kiss and her passionate response in vivid detail.

When he'd first seen her tied up in a chair a few months back, when Ben had kidnapped her, it hit him like a sudden downpour that he wanted her as more than a friend. He wanted something good with a good woman. And he took pleasure in being the one to slit Ben's ankles and slowly lower him into the pigpen.

Colton McCoy's prized pigs could devour a man whole within five minutes. Once those beasts had the taste for blood and raw meat, they'd eat anything put in front of them. Don't go inside the pen if you have a fresh cut on your person, his father had said to him when he was little, before he even had hair on his balls. They'll corner you and eat you in a hot second.

Terry had always been afraid of his father's pigs, and for good reason. Ever since that time he'd thrown an injured rabbit inside, still screaming into the pen, he'd seen the crazy, wide-eyed looks from the beasts before they tore it apart. *That's scary shit for a kid to see*, he remembered. *Exciting but scary as hell.*

He wished he could get rid of them, but he wasn't the boss. Besides, they served a quick and deadly purpose. He'd use them when the need arose.

Nobody fucked with Mary, and if this town kept giving her a hard time, he'd make them burn.

But he had to be careful.

He'd seen how she looked at him, curious but unsure. She just needed a gentle hand from a man with confidence. But he hoped he had enough of it to show her the man he really was. To show her a part of himself nobody else sees.

If Gabe could land a woman and convince her to marry him, then Terry at least had a small shred of hope that one day he could be happy, too.

"Where are we going? There's a nice burger joint down the road."

Terry tipped his head back and laughed. "We're not dressed up for beef on a bun, silly. We're going out in style."

They arrived at the only fine restaurant in town, a bistro-type diner Terry found seriously lacking, but it was his only option. Thank God Mary had said yes because he'd already made reservations at their most private table, and even had them hold a bottle of fine wine he'd brought from home. Wine that probably cost more than their monthly food order.

"I've never been here before," Mary said in awe. "It's too expensive."

He opened the door and guided her through. "Not anymore."

Mary looked up at him, clearly confused. "What?"

He didn't answer. Instead, he gently shoved her inside, ignoring how she glared at him with those stunning eyes.

The hostess, with her dark hair pulled tight at the back and red lipstick, reminded Terry of one of the guitar girls in that eighties music video. She smiled at Terry, but when she saw Mary her demeanor changed instantly.

"Didn't you recently bury your husband?" She looked her over and made a disgusted face. "Kind of early to go out on a date."

Mary pulled back in horror but Terry wouldn't let her shrink away. He put his arm around Mary, keeping her close. He wanted to deck the broad behind the cedar podium, but hitting a woman went against his moral rule. Just because he lived on the wrong side of the law didn't mean he was an animal.

Terry placed his free hand on the podium and leaned closer. "People die all the time. Life goes on. If I were you I'd apologize to the lady. I'm not spending good money in here for her to be insulted." He stroked Mary's lower back and smiled to himself when he felt her body relax. The urge to continue rubbing, and maybe moving further down was an exciting thought, but he pushed the urge aside and gently cupped her hip instead.

The woman swallowed and nodded, her face red. "M-my apologies." She grabbed two menus and immediately guided them to their private booth. Without another word she set the menus down and went back to her post.

Every time she glanced their way Terry raised his brows. She immediately blushed and looked away.

He'd put everyone to shame if it pleased the cute little thing sitting across from him. He focused his attention back to Mary. "You look beautiful tonight."

Her blush made her cheeks deliciously pink. It made the color on her lips brighter. "Thank you. You look pretty good yourself."

Terry glanced up at the stuffed northern pike on display a couple of booths down. A large red and white daredevil hung from its gaping mouth. He almost lost his appetite at the rustic decor reminding him of death. Above every booth hung something killed by somebody.

He turned away from the huge moose head next door and focused on Mary instead. "I'm sorry I haven't called in a while. I had some business to tend to."

"I know. Gabriel told me about Ben." The sad look on her face said much more. Terry wasn't sure where to lead the conversation.

Thank God the waitress arrived right away. He was beginning to think this date would end in disaster before it started.

"Would you like to start with drinks?"

Terry grinned at the waitress. "Bring us a bottle of your best wine, please. I have a woman to impress."

The waitress gave him a knowing smile and winked at Mary before she walked away.

Mary looked like she was completely out of place. Her eyes said it all. Beautiful, sad brown eyes with liquid gold around the iris. They mesmerized him, made him want to stare at her, read her thoughts. Her gaze darted around the room, staring at the animal mounts as well, but she seemed genuinely impressed by the décor, unlike him.

He stared at her while her attention was everywhere else. She was a damaged woman. Maybe she'd never been on a real date before. Maybe she was still scared of him, or didn't trust him, and he deserved it. He knew she needed to be treated with kid gloves, which was a whole new game for him. It was a challenge, and he loved a good game of cat and mouse.

His life had been filled with the type of women who liked bad guys. They wanted the attention, the jewelry, the yacht parties, and expensive wine, and they were fake. Mary Billings would probably be satisfied at that burger joint, and she was real. No fake tits and lips on her.

He leaned back in his seat and stared at the wolf head right above her. The beady eyes reflected a cunning creature ready to pounce. Terry tried to hide his wolfish grin as he returned his focus to Mary.

Being around Mary made him feel good, like he had nothing to worry about. He felt like he owned the biggest piece of earth. "So what have you been up to lately?"

The waitress brought the wine and glasses, and took their food order.

"I don't really have anything exciting to tell. I've been taking care of nuisance beaver in the area, and did some minor repairs to the house. Gabe has helped out quite a bit too. That's about it."

Terry leaned forward. "Not only are you a knockout, you're a handyman, too. Impressive."

Her unladylike shrug made her even cuter in his eyes. "Not really. I just do what needs to be done."

"Anything I can help with?" *Maybe pet you to madness?*

"Well, I do have a wood shed that needs to be filled before winter. I've been busy with nuisance beaver lately and haven't had time for it."

He'd never chopped a piece of wood in his life. "Consider it done."

Mary nodded, and Terry felt a small shred of hope. Maybe this wouldn't be too bad after all, as long as he had cell service to google these wilderness tasks so he didn't look like a total jackass in front of her.

"Look, I know this trip of mine was sort of sprung on you at the last second, but I'd love to spend some time with you. On your terms."

Mary looked up, her smile shy, uncertain. "I don't know what to say. I'm not sure. . . ."

He grinned. "Then don't say anything at all. Let's enjoy dinner and see what happens."

Terry knew right away that leaving things up to her must be a new experience. She began to fidget with her food, making little tracks in the garlic mashed potatoes with her fork. Every once in a while she'd look around the room, perhaps nervous somebody would corner her, but Terry wouldn't let that happen. Even when he'd lifted his arm to take her coat by the booth, and she'd stepped back quickly as if he'd hit her, struck a lethal chord in him. He wanted to show her a good time and prove that some men had good intentions, no matter what they did for a living. And if he ever saw a man raise his hand to her, he'd rip his throat out.

After a while she focused her attention back to him. "What did you have in mind—for us to do?"

Anything that doesn't involve shooting someone. "Whatever you want. You're the boss."

"Anything I want?" Her smile seemed evil almost—something he didn't expect from her. It made him a little uncomfortable, considering he was in the bush and totally out of his element. "How about I take you fishing tomorrow? If you can handle that then maybe I'll let you stay."

If he had to throw a line in the water to prove he wasn't an asshole, then he'd do it with a smile. Her shy nature and pretty face did him in like a bullet to the head, but he knew better than to push her too hard. She'd gone through a nasty time not only from her marriage from hell, but from what she had suffered a few months ago—partly at his doing.

All because he had to find Gabe.

First Ben got her to talk, then Jimmy was ordered to take her outside and kill her. If Terry wouldn't have shown up in the nick of time, Jimmy would've made her suffer things he didn't want to imagine.

A woman like Mary needed to be coaxed out of her shell and treated like a queen, because she deserved it. She deserved better than a meaningless life with an asshole who hurt her, and had the nerve to steal millions of dollars of cocaine. Simply put, Tom Billings was a loser.

Mary deserved to be touched gently and kissed passionately. She deserved what Terry wanted to give her.

"Sounds good to me." Terry lifted his wine glass and clinked it against hers. "Cheers to our little adventure tomorrow. I'll be there with hooks on."

* * * *

Mary stood in her bedroom the following afternoon with the closet doors open and a mountain of clothes on the bed. She placed her fists on her hips and released a pent-up sigh.

Why did she care what she wore to go fishing? She was acting like a foolish girl.

Seeing Terry again with his lazy smile and bright blues gave her mixed emotions. She'd missed him, but she was angry as well. She was attracted to him, but she had to be cautious at the same time. He was part of an organization that set him apart from the average Joe, and he was dangerous. Coming from an abusive marriage, Mary didn't know if she should act on her attraction toward Terry or if she should end their friendship right now and forget about him. She glanced at the cordless phone beside the nightstand, but she didn't have his number to call him and call off the fishing expedition. She took a step toward the bedroom door, intent on throwing on her jacket and heading to his hotel to cancel his visit in person. But she didn't. Her curiosity over why he came here was too strong to ignore.

One thing was certain. He acted like he wanted some kind of relationship. *He looks at me like I'm a bottle of water after surviving the desert.*

But she didn't really have enough time to find herself yet. Not even half a year after Tom's death didn't seem long enough to be spending time alone with another man. Despite Tom's cruelty he'd taken care of her financially. But did he give her a choice? He never wanted her out of his sight, therefore she was stuck at home like a bad pet that needed to be on a leash.

It was easier for a guy like Terry. He didn't have a dead spouse haunting his mind and heart. She was confused by this whole situation. Yes, she wanted to spend time with Terry and see what might happen. At the same time she was afraid to make a mistake.

And if she were to be honest with herself, Terry was completely out of her league. She'd seen the bill for last night's dinner. It was more than what she spent on groceries for an entire month. More than what Tom spent on her wedding ring.

But she couldn't simply stop her attraction for Terry, even after the chaos a few months back. She felt in her heart that Terry wasn't a bad man. Even when those guys terrorized her he hadn't taken part in it. He even tried to stop it. But his friend had betrayed him, and Mary imagined it must be a terrible weight on his shoulders. Still, she had been wrong about Tom, too.

Maybe Terry needed someone to talk to, somebody who had nothing to do with his family business—someone who didn't care that he was a McCoy. According to Mima, Terry had it rough. Harder than most. While she didn't know the exact details of his job or his life, she knew he walked on eggshells every day, and she felt bad for him.

She closed her eyes, remembering the night he'd kissed her. She touched her lips remembering how his felt against hers. How hot it made her. She'd never felt this turned on before.

What the hell am I doing?

She glanced at her reflection in the floor-length mirror. Her eyes were too dull, her lips not full enough, tits too small. Nothing impressive to look at. Why would Terry be interested in her? Was she just some casual bush fling nobody would know about? All of his rich friends and business people would never know anything about her, because she was plain old Mary with seven dogs, a horse, and a shed full of furs.

She lifted her chin and stared at her body again. Maybe she wasn't a model in high places, but she was a strong bush woman. She flexed her biceps. Yes, she had good definition, could lift well over her own body weight. She turned her back to the mirror, looked over her shoulder and grinned. Nice hard legs. Tight bum. Maybe she wasn't too bad after all.

If he wants to be here then he'll have to accept who I am and how I live. She smacked her ass, sauntered over to the bed, and grabbed a pair of jeans.

No sooner than changing into jeans and t-shirt, the dogs howled outside. She glanced out her bedroom window to see a black Suburban pull into the driveway and park beside the house.

She rushed to put her hair into a ponytail as a knock rattled the back door. "Just a minute!"

When Mary opened the door she tried her best not to laugh but failed miserably.

Terry wasn't lying when he said he'd bought all the gear for roughing it, but it made him look like a complete fool and amateur. His moss green, double-breasted shirt and fishing vest, perfectly matched his camo shorts, and every side pocket had a hook hanging from it. Even his fishing hat had a yellow jig hooked to the brim.

On silly impulse she stepped closer and grabbed each side of the hat brim right above his ears, careful not to hook herself. She yanked the cap further down his forehead making his skin crinkle. "Very cute, Terry." She giggled, but when his dark gaze connected to hers and held, the humor died on her tongue. She stared up at him, speechless by the instant swell of heat being this close to him, smelling his spicy cologne and natural manly scent. All she had to do was stand tiptoe and she could feel the mesmerizing heat of his lips again, on hers, like before.

Stunned by the instant change in the air, Mary let go of his hat and stepped back. She laughed, more out of embarrassment than anything, and forced herself to glance down at his boots. They were brand-new work boots without a single scuff mark, rather than good old-fashioned rubbers.

"Are you planning on felling some trees while we're out there?"

"What's so funny?" The sensual sparkle in his eye disappeared before Terry looked down at himself. "The guy at the store said this is what I needed."

"Yeah, and he probably had a good laugh when he soaked you for a few hundred bucks, too."

His grin faded. "It was actually more than that."

Mary cleared her throat to curb her laughter, feeling slightly sorry for him. "Well, might as well put it all to good use. I'm surprised you didn't show up with a portable fish finder, too."

"That would've been a couple hundred more."

She chuckled and eyed the fishing rod in one hand and the bouquet of carnations in the other. "Are the flowers a new trick to lure in the fish?"

"Nah. Just the women," he said, and grinned like the devil.

Terry lifted the bouquet. Mary accepted it and sniffed the blooms. "They're beautiful, but you didn't have to."

The devil-may-care grin faded, and his eyes seemed distant, as if he was looking past her. "Carnations were my mom's favorite."

She eyed him carefully, curious to ask about his mother but thought better of it. Maybe later she could find out more of his story. There was bound to be quite the epic tale from this mysterious man. There was something about him that made her nervous yet excited at the same time. Even though Tom's image still clung to her memory like a bad disease, she had to let him go. And here was Terry McCoy, little more than a stranger, who boldly strolled into her life and turned it upside down. Because of him everything had changed.

"Let me put these in a vase and we'll get going."

"Sure. Take all the time you need."

His smile made her stomach flip upside down. She couldn't be the first woman who wanted to throw herself at him. Maybe he had a whole nest of girlfriends back in the city. The thought made her sad, but at the same time, he was here now and she was in charge.

She was suddenly ashamed of going to bed and dreaming about him last night. Waking up with her fingers between her legs on the verge of orgasm, and not for the first time either.

Needing a distraction from her wicked thoughts, she set out to fill a vase with water and set the arrangement on the kitchen table. The bold mixture of purple, pink, and red, reminded her of the man who brought them. He was bold and colorful, too.

"Do you like them?"

She spun around with a gasp, unaware he had followed her inside. Her nerves jumped to life and her body heated with awareness by his close proximity. Was it a normal thing for him to sneak up on people all the time? She eyed him suspiciously, but Terry simply smiled, apparently content to stand there and watch her, and not try to make any sudden moves.

She turned back to the vase, feeling a little more at ease. "Thank you for the flowers, they're beautiful."

"Not as beautiful as you."

She turned around, her gaze snapping up to his. It was probably just a line, maybe one he'd used many times on other women, but she still liked hearing it. Maybe because she'd never had a man tell her that before.

His crooked grin made her face heat. She cleared her throat and avoided eye contact. She had to be careful with a man like him. She needed to feel safe and secure and know she was doing the right thing. Marrying Tom had been a mistake. What would she be doing with Terry McCoy, a notorious criminal?

"The trail to the river is up the road a little ways." She moved to walk past him, but when his hand touched her forearm and held her, she paused. Every hair tingled where his hand touched her. She sucked in a sharp breath, her gaze downcast.

"Are you afraid to be alone with me, Mary? Do you want me to leave?"

He leaned closer until she felt his breath at her temple. The heated caress made her want to lean in and let him swallow her up in his embrace. A shudder sizzled down her midsection and decided to go right between her legs. "No. It's . . . I'm okay. Just a little nervous, that's all. I don't get much company around here." *Breathe.* She glanced back up, her eyes searching his. Something was happening to her. His touch didn't feel wrong; it felt natural.

Terry nodded, apparently misunderstanding her reaction, and released her arm. "I understand. Remember, you're the boss."

She felt like a nervous girl about to fool around with the bully neighbor. "Well, the fish are waiting for us." She quickly headed for the door, embarrassed by his deep chuckle right behind her, and grabbed her rod and tackle box from the hallway closet.

"Why are we fishing in the evening? Isn't early morning better?" He fell in step beside her as they crossed the driveway to the path across the road.

"Morning or evening. It's basically the same, but I didn't feel like getting up at dawn."

"Ah. I see." Terry chuckled behind her.

They walked in silence along the path, surrounded by the relaxing swish of branches in the breeze. Nothing compared to the natural beauty of her property. Trees pushing sixty feet or more, some with trunks the width of a vehicle. The trickle of water from the river a constant and relaxing sound. The ever-present mountain tips above the treetops. It never failed to amaze her how insignificant she was in this endless highway of nature.

"If we catch anything, will it be on the dinner menu tonight?"

"Sure, if you'd like."

His relieved sigh made her chuckle. "Thank God. I was beginning to think I'd have to shoot a squirrel or something."

Mary paused on the path and turned to face him. "I'm not a complete hick you know. Mima might enjoy frontier living, but not me. I actually own an electric coffee pot, and I blow-dry my hair."

Terry nodded, his lip curling in amusement. "Good to know."

She stepped off the path and parted the brush. "Watch you don't get your rod caught in here. It's a little tricky."

"Want to hold it for me?"

The insinuation in his voice was unmistakable. "I'm talking about your fishing rod—not your dick." Her eyes widened when she realized how terrible that sounded coming from her own mouth.

Terry's rumble of laughter made her cheeks burn. "My, my, you have a dirty mind, Mary. I wasn't even talking about that."

Completely embarrassed, Mary stepped through the brush first and let the branches whip behind her, right in his face. She ignored his curse and his loud fight to get through the brush without getting his rod stuck, and made her way to the river's edge. She'd just set down her tackle box when Terry burst through the trees, violently yanking his pole out of the twisted branches.

"Why don't you trim the brush there?" Terry threw his gear onto the rocks and panted for air. "Jesus Christ, I might need plastic surgery on my face now."

Mary's shoulders shook from laughing. The crumpled mess of his hat barely clung to his head. He looked so cute and out of his element that her smile faltered as she stared at him, realizing this was the first time she'd seen him look vulnerable.

He wanted to come here. The city boy criminal wanted to be here—with her.

Why me?

She opened her tackle box and found the perfect jig. "This is my private spot, Terry. I don't want anyone finding it."

He shook his head and stood straight, stretching out his back. "I don't think that'll ever be a problem. A Smurf can barely fit through it."

Mary turned around and glared at him. "Are you teasing me about my height?"

He cleared his throat and set out to find a spot to fish from. "Of course not." Yet his voice spilled with suppressed laughter.

For a long while they were completely silent, enjoying the trickle of the water, the swish and sway of branches in the breeze, the musical chatter of the birds. Every once in a while Mary would glance at him without making it obvious, and stifle a smile over his struggles. But he managed to get a decent cast out into the river and after a while he seemed to be really enjoying himself. Mary imagined he didn't get much joy in life. How could anyone who lived on the wrong side of the law?

"Have you ever fly-fished?" he asked.

"I've tried it, but I don't have the patience. Less of a headache with a casting rod."

"Makes sense. I've seen fly fishing in movies and it looks tricky." He looked at her over his shoulder. "Can I say something that has nothing to do with fishing?"

Mary cast her line back out and glanced at him. "Depends on what it is, I guess."

"When I first met you, you were very timid. Terrified even. I mean. . . ." He sighed, maybe trying to find the right words. "Obviously what happened with Ben scared you, I know that. But it seemed to me you were already afraid of life. And somehow, right now, you seem stronger."

She looked away and focused on the rushing water. Could she trust him with the truth? She released a shaky breath, her gaze focused on the rushing water instead of him. There were few people in this world she talked to. Mima was wrapped up with Gabe, and her mother was busy soaking up the sun in Florida. They only spoke a few times a year and even then it mostly consisted of the weather and her mother's latest adventures. Would it be a mistake to open up to Terry?

She continued staring at the water. "Before Tom, I was different. I was raised to be tough, like you, I imagine. I didn't have brass balls, but I had a pair of something. He took that away from me—a long time ago."

She didn't dare look at him, because she knew he was staring right at her. "How long did he hurt you, Mary?"

Breathe. "Twelve years."

The silence dragged on for a long while before he spoke again. "And now that he's gone, the old Mary is coming back."

Unwanted tears filled her eyes, and she swallowed. It took a minute to be able to answer without cracking. "I don't know. Maybe I'll never be the old me." It became increasingly difficult to breathe and her vision blurred from too many tears.

"No, no," he said without hesitation. "All he did was put your soul in hiding for a little while, and now she's come back, stronger than ever. This is you. The woman in front of me right now is the real Mary."

She turned to him, *really* looked at him with eyes wide, throat tight. The sincerity written all over his face made her break down right then and there. She barely managed to keep hold of her fishing rod as her knees gave way and she slumped down onto a rock. The tears she tried holding back slipped down her face like the force of the river at her feet.

Violent sobs racked her body as she let go of all the fear, the pain, and the desperation in her battered soul.

Terry was right behind her in seconds and wrapped his arms around her, slowly rocked her against his chest. This had to be the first time she'd ever cried so hard—even right after Tom died. The second time she'd let her guard down in front of Terry McCoy.

She turned and sobbed against his chest until she had nothing left to give. And he crouched there without moving for what felt like hours. He petted her hair and told her everything would be okay. Nobody would ever hurt her again.

If only those words were true.

Terry hugged her tight and kissed her forehead. "Come on. Let's leave the trout to live another day. I've been craving squirrel all afternoon anyway."

She lifted her face and let out a raspy laugh, rubbed her tears away with her sleeve. "Okay."

He wrapped his arm around her, grabbed their gear and walked her home. This time he had no troubles getting through the gnarly brush. He didn't say another word on the walk home, just held her close, a strong wall of protection. The spicy, male scent of him was a small comfort in itself.

When they finally reached the house, Mary was completely exhausted and a little embarrassed by her emotional outburst. But if it bothered Terry, he didn't show it.

Like a man on a mission, he ushered her into the house, straight to the couch. He sat at one end and patted the seat next to him. "Come on." He lifted his arms for her to cuddle up to him.

How embarrassing to be this vulnerable with a man she barely knew. "You don't have to do this, Terry. I'll be okay. I'm sorry—"

"Don't ever be sorry to show your emotions. Come on." He pulled her down and onto his lap before she could argue further. She tensed at first, but finally relented. "Being human isn't always easy."

It felt childish to be in this position as he petted her hair and told her everything would be all right. But it felt good. Maybe Terry McCoy wasn't such a bad man after all.

"Nobody will hurt you when I'm around. I promise you that," he whispered.

After a while of comforting silence, in the arms of a criminal, Mary closed her eyes and drifted off to sleep.

* * * *

He slipped the little blue pill into his mouth and continued down the hall.

The long corridor was unlit as he made his way to one of the bedrooms, but after many years spent in this house, Colton McCoy didn't need light to know where he was going.

Today a handsome deal had been made between the McCoy's and the Montesano family. After receiving his son's finger with the gold ring, his old friend had no choice but to comply or risk losing his other child. Colton still had yet to find out exactly who the other child was in case Montesano went back on his word and they needed a pawn. He had an inkling who it could be, but this night he felt truly blessed and carefree to enjoy himself. Business could wait until tomorrow.

His son was away and safe. The boys were tending business as usual. He was home alone.

Today was turning out to be a good day, indeed.

Without a creek, the door swung wide, revealing a massive bedroom with dark hardwood floors, mahogany furniture, and a canopied bed with sheer, white curtains flowing around it. Lying in the center was a beautiful brunette wearing nothing but a white gown, her captivating beauty glowing in the lamplight filling the room.

Her breasts were magnificent, large and pert with dark, taut nipples.

He swallowed, allowing his hungry eyes to follow the movement of her undulating hips, and what moved in delicious slowness between her luscious thighs. There, crouched on her knees with her long tawny hair touching her perfect ass was his favorite housekeeper, licking his newest pet, Taffy, like a dirty girl.

Ensconced by the torrid scene, he parted his robe and stroked his cock. It would take a little while for the pill to kick in and give him life worth sharing. As he touched himself, Colton quietly closed the door and made his way to the chair beside the bed, careful not to disturb his favorite girls as they moaned and writhed together.

Cassandra, having heard her master approach, moved to the side to offer him a better view of Taffy's wet lips.

"Stay still," he ordered.

With Cassandra's tight bum perched high, he retrieved the glass vial from his robe pocket and tapped a white bump onto her soft flesh. Cassandra giggled but remained still as Colton leaned down and snorted a lift off her fine ass.

Their new shipment turned out to be one of the best yet.

As the blow lifted his spirits, Cassandra went back to business, kneading Taffy's thighs with her expert fingers while her busy little mouth kissed and licked Taffy to shuddering madness. She cried out and arched off the bed, gripping Cassandra's head, holding her there until her climax slowly subsided.

He thickened in his palm. *Yes. There you are.*

Smiling at her master with eyes that spoke of pleasurable things to come, Cassandra licked Taffy's beautiful clit slowly, hungrily taking in all that sweet juice, and motioned for Colton to join them. He pushed away from the chair, his cock hard in hand, and approached the edge of the bed.

"I'm so happy you arranged for this meeting, my sweet. Now you know what I like."

Cassandra looked at him with cat eyes and smiled. "It's all for you, sir." She grabbed Taffy by the hair, yanked her head back and kissed her roughly, making a show of her wet tongue darting in and out and around her mouth.

Colton moaned and stroked harder.

Then, like a cat on the prowl, Taffy crawled around him, massaging his shoulders and kissing his neck, as Cassandra got on her knees in front of him.

Colton smiled with greed, knowing exactly what treat he would receive from his favorite housekeeper. She knew what to do with her bad little mouth. How wonderful his darling wife had been when she hired this special woman with such raw, uninhibited talent.

She crawled to him, swaying her lush bum before his lusting eyes. She took him in hand and pumped him gently. He moaned and closed his eyes, enjoying her warm grip on his hard cock.

As she pumped him, his hips rocked forward, needing the wet hot comfort of her mouth. She kissed his shaft and licked her way from base to tip before taking him right to the back of her throat.

"Yes," he moaned, cupping the back of her head to take him deeper. She was a vixen, and she had skills.

"Enjoy it, Mr. McCoy," Taffy whispered in his ear, stroking his back with her long fingernails. The sharp scrape of her nails gave him instant gratification. He shuddered and released a deep, wrenching sigh.

His balls tightened as Cassandra flexed her throat around him, sucking hard as she palmed his balls and tickled his anus, just as he liked it. He felt the rush, the tingling heat wave right from his toes to the top of his head. He would come soon. He couldn't hold back as long as he used to—not with these talented girls.

She pulled back and whispered, "Let go. You know you want to," and impaled her mouth right to his base as she palmed his balls more forcefully.

Colton stilled and let out a deep grunt as he spilled his seed inside her hot mouth. He leaned forward, needing her body for balance while she milked him dry. His knees buckled and he panted for air. Being able to come sucked any energy he'd had.

When he felt strong enough to pull back, he took her face in his hands to kiss her cheek.

Something sharp and cold wrapped around his neck and viciously yanked him back. Stunned, he whimpered as his body was pulled so hard he rolled back on his heels and his toes lifted from the floor.

He gripped the cord, tried to pull it away from his neck, but he didn't have enough strength.

His eyes bulged. He had no control. No power. He stared down in disbelief as Cassandra wiped his come from her lips, an evil grin on her face. "I hope you enjoyed it," she said. "It was your last."

He stumbled back as the wire cut into his throat. He struggled to remain on his feet, and tried to turn to see who was behind him. *Taffy?* No. She would never hurt him. She was too small to overpower a large man.

The wire cut deeper and deeper, cutting off his air supply, as he coughed and tried to break free. "H-how cou-could y-you—?" His arm swung out, smashing into one of the bedside lamps. It sailed through the air and landed with a smash a few feet away. Still, he couldn't shake off the other man.

A faint vision of Terry and Eliza filled his heart with sorrow. How could he do this to them? How could he betray them all like this? Everything was his fault. His pride and his need for wealth and power would be his undoing.

Did he do everything a father was supposed to do? Should he have sent Terry away to a private school instead of raising him in this business?

The underworld was the only life he knew.

But Colton loved his son more than anything in the world. He should've been a better father. Should've been a better husband. Should've…

Bile stung his throat. Maybe it was his own life's blood.

"Shhh, it'll be over soon," a familiar voice whispered as the breath from his lungs departed.

He blinked in surprise, knowing that voice well. "But, how—"

"This is what you deserve for what you did to my family."

"*N-no.*"

"Once I have your son the power is all mine."

He tried to speak, to beg for his life and his son's, but nothing more than a strangled whimper escaped his trembling lips.

No amount of money could save a man already dying.

Hot tears slid down his cheeks.

The room spun, his head felt heavy as his body weakened. His hands fell to his sides as violent tremors racked his body. He tried to fight it, but he was too frail.

And then he saw Eliza smiling at him, her beautiful face beckoning him. He reached for her, ready to be guided by his loving wife into the grey unknown.

His eyes rolled back as he expelled his last shuddering breath.

Chapter 6

Mary rolled onto her side and hugged her pillow, dreading having to face Terry today. After her little nap on his lap yesterday evening, she'd woke alone on the couch to a house filled with the delicious aroma of homemade pasta sauce.

Finding him standing there over the stove tasting the sauce and making his way around as if he'd been there for years, filled her with comfort, yet she couldn't shake the terrible feeling that this was all wrong. Having a man in her house this soon after Tom's death didn't seem natural.

She wanted company, yet she wanted to be alone at the same time.

They'd eaten in relative silence, only a few words exchanged, and after several drinks, Terry decided to sleep in his vehicle for the night. When she'd asked why he didn't return to the hotel he simply said he wouldn't drink and drive.

She covered her eyes with her forearm, feeling like a total asshole and wanting to shrink away from the world, from him. She should've offered the guest bedroom, especially since he'd taken such good care of her, but she didn't argue with his decision. She'd gone to bed with a full stomach, completely embarrassed and feeling like the worst hostess on earth.

With a big yawn, she pushed up from bed and put on whatever clothes were within easy reach. When she made her way into the kitchen, the scent of freshly brewed coffee was a pleasant surprise. The man was self-sufficient and clearly comfortable despite what happened yesterday. She poured a cup for herself and paused at the distinct sound of wood chopping.

She plodded over to the living room window and stopped dead at the view outside.

Standing with his feet shoulder-width apart, wearing jogging pants and no shirt, Terry lifted the axe and swung it down with deadly precision. The log split in half and tumbled to each side where a decent amount had already piled up. By the looks of it he must've started several hours ago.

She eyed his naked torso. Holy hell, he had a lot of muscle for a tall, thinly built man. But he was athletic and lithe, powerful and sure of himself. As he lifted the axe above his head, she eyed the delicious play of muscle rippling as he swung it back down to split another log.

She took a sip of coffee, content to stand there watching him. After all, she hadn't seen such a splendid, half-naked man for many years. He rested the axe against his thigh and lifted his other arm to wipe the sweat from his brow. His blond hair was soaked, dripping down his shoulders and back. Maybe she shouldn't be watching him like this, but she was a woman, and she had needs and desires like anyone else.

Terry turned at that moment and smiled. Mary stepped away from the window, her cheeks on fire, and the junction of her thighs too hot to handle. How embarrassing to be caught staring at him like this, especially after bawling like a child on him yesterday.

"Good morning," he mouthed.

With a shaky hand, Mary opened the window. "Good morning. Aren't you cold? June isn't usually warm in the mountains."

He grinned. "If it's cold I sure don't feel it. Does showing my skin bother you?"

God yes. Mary's cheeks burned. "Of course not. How do you take your coffee?"

"Black."

She nodded, and retreated from the window to prepare him a cup. A few minutes later she exited the back door and approached him at the chopping block.

Terry took the cup and stared at her as he took a sip. His lips glistened from the brew, tormenting her, reminding her of their long ago kiss. The urge to stand on tiptoe and press against his hard chest and kiss him deadly, made her pulse race.

"How do you feel today?"

Mary tried not to stare at his wet lips and looked down instead, right at the thick matte of chest hair. She swallowed and looked up to his eyes instead. "Better. Sorry you had to deal with that."

She'd never touched chest hair before and the urge to reach out and skim her fingers through it made her face heat. Would it be soft or coarse? Did the hair represent the man beneath? Embarrassed and all tingly between her legs, she set her cup down and proceeded to pile the wood into the shed. She needed to do something other than think about him having his way with her on the chopping block.

"Don't be sorry about yesterday, okay?" Terry picked up the axe again and drove it into another log. The pieces fell to the sides. "It felt nice to comfort you."

Surprised he'd admitted that, she turned around and watched him, at a loss for words as he chopped another piece, having no clue how hard those words hit her. "You didn't have to—"

"Mary, stop it."

She swallowed, automatically assuming she was in trouble. "What?" Her heart hammered as she took a step back.

Terry leaned the axe against the block and strolled up to her. "You're always apologizing." Before she could retreat he put his hands on her cheeks, lifted her face, and brought his lips to hers. She stiffened, completely shocked by his sudden move.

So soft, light, yet he was confident as he explored her. His lips crushed hers, tasting, tormenting, taking all the time in the world. He tasted like coffee and man, passion and danger. And just like in her dreams, he had a hint of stubble to scratch and excite.

Her body shook with nervous excitement. But as quickly as it started, he pulled back.

It took a moment for Mary to open her eyes, and when she did, Terry stared down at her with lust and something else shining in those deep blue depths. "Are you sorry about that, too?"

She swallowed and shook her head. "No."

"Good. Cause as long as you don't push me away, I'll make you not feel sorry every chance I get."

Mary exhaled a shaky breath as Terry went back to the chopping block, picked up the axe, and set another log on the block.

Wow. She touched her lips and stared at him in shocked silence as he chopped another dozen logs, the sweat slithering down his back, making it harder and harder for her to do something useful.

Why, oh why did I let him come here?

Her body still trembled. She felt ridiculous yet wonderful all at once. How could he make her feel this hot without any effort? Was she so inexperienced that a simple kiss made her soaking wet and ready to lie down right there?

He was dangerous. The son of a notorious crime boss. Maybe he killed people daily and snorted cocaine off of women's breasts. She knew so little about him except for these scary things that made her nervous, she literally shook like a leaf in a steady wind.

Maybe now was a good time to discover more about this mystery man who'd wormed his way into her life. She needed some answers to ease the crazy thoughts kicking her frazzled mind.

"Do you like your job, Terry?"

He paused with the axe above his head and slowly lowered it. When he turned to face her, the tilt of his brow and straight mouth made him look different somehow. Perhaps angry yet indifferent at the same time, if that was even possible.

He shook his head. "No. I don't."

"Then why do you do it?"

He looked toward the trees as if he'd find his answer there. With his back straight and his shoulders square he looked completely miserable at that moment. "I guess it's kinda like any family business you're born into. You feel like it's your only choice. And I would do anything for my father."

Mary nodded, understanding the need to please a parent. "Have you ever told him what you really want?"

He sighed, his shoulders slouching. He looked completely lost and tired of life. "No. I've never told him. I wouldn't know what to say."

"You could start with the truth."

He glanced at her then. "The truth is I've always been a little afraid of the old man. I know he loves me, but he expects only the best from me, like I'm just another employee. If I had my way I'd only run the hotel. I'm good at it. I seem to have a knack for knowing what people want."

Not everyone.

"What exactly do you do for him, anyway?"

Like the flip of a switch, gone was his sad and disappointed face, replaced with a sly smile and eyes as deadly as a wolf. "I do anything I'm told."

She swallowed and looked at the house. *So much for reasonable answers.* "Well, how about some breakfast?" She didn't want to hear the details of what his job entailed, having seen enough a few months prior. Maybe that was a bad question to start with.

"You read my mind. Let me finish up here first." And he went back to chopping wood as if their conversation held no weight at all on her fragile soul.

Mary set out scrambling some eggs and bacon and adding slices of bread in the toaster oven. She had just finished setting the table when Terry strolled into the house. He sipped his coffee and stared at her life between these four walls. She tried hard to ignore the sweltering heat his kiss had caused. The house seemed tiny while he was in it.

Terry eyed a bookcase then glanced over his shoulder, his smile teasing. "Historical romance, eh?"

"My favorite."

"So you like the damsel in distress and the noble rogue who comes to her rescue? Only for him to steal her virtue anyway?"

She giggled at his poor attempt at a Scottish accent. "Maybe I do."

"Good to know." He turned his attention back to the bookcase while Mary sat at the table staring at him, intrigued and surprised by his display of humor.

"Are you a damsel in distress, Mary?"

"Uh, no." How could she possibly answer without sounding like an idiot? Yes, she was distressed and unhappy but she wasn't a damsel like in those romance books. She didn't have long, flowing golden hair and bright eyes with tits nearly bursting from her bodice. She was plain old Mary Billings. Shoulder-length brown hair, brown eyes, and barely a handful on her chest. Nothing epic about that.

Terry approached her at the table and leaned down, so close the heat of his breath fanned the ticklish spot below her ear. "Do you need rescuing, Mary?"

She fought to control the sudden and overwhelming electricity streaking through her. "No."

"Are you sure?"

Breathe. "No. I mean, yes." She closed her eyes and shuddered. "Don't toy with me, Terry."

When was the last time she felt this much excitement? She thought he was going to kiss her right there over the toast, and for the love of God, she wanted him to. It terrified her how bold he acted around her. How sensual his words sounded coming from his sexy mouth she should forget about. Why did she feel empty-headed when he looked at her like that?

He was the complete opposite from Tom who was short and stocky with black hair and dark brown eyes, who had no clue how to flirt. Terry was tall and athletic with golden hair and pale blue eyes that seemed to stare right through her into the deepest, darkest depths of her soul. And he could charm the panties right off her over a plate of eggs and bacon.

Maybe she did need rescuing. Maybe she was the poor, hapless girl who needed a strong man to take control.

No. No more doing what a man wanted her to do. She was the boss of her own life now, not trailing behind, terrified of what to do next.

Confused about this whole situation was an understatement, and Mary knew she needed to keep control of herself with a man like Terry. He was probably used to getting his way all the time. Maybe he was a total player and she should avoid him completely. Let him camp out and rest for whatever time he needs then send him home.

Still, she couldn't control the war between her body and her mind.

"How about you show me around after breakfast? I've never really seen the property before, not in detail anyway. Then I'll get to work setting up my tent."

She forked some eggs. "Sure."

They ate breakfast in silence. Every once in a while Mary would look up to find him staring at her. She had a million questions to ask but none of them seemed appropriate at the moment. Maybe some normal time together was all she needed to learn the real man behind Terry McCoy, and to discover what he was *really* doing here. Did he know Gabe offered her money to let him stay here?

He seemed to think she wanted him to be here. Well, she did and she didn't. She didn't really know what the hell she wanted.

She took their plates and set them in the sink, still leery about this whole visit, but determined to keep an open mind. After all, having some company was a nice change. Soon she'd be alone again.

A gust of wind blew into the open window above the sink. She looked out to the stand of pines as she'd done many times before. If only those green guards could tell her what her purpose should be in life. If she were to be honest with herself, *really* honest, she'd want to leave this place, start fresh, make roots in a place where she didn't feel left out. But she couldn't tell Terry that, not now. Probably not ever.

They exited the back door and Mary took Terry around the yard. Behind the house was a small clearing where she kept her skinning station, fur shed, and the smoke house. Everything was kept clean to keep the bears away, although at times her efforts didn't matter. Seven dogs and a gun usually scared them off.

Mary opened the shed door and when Terry stepped inside he seemed surprised at what he saw. "Wow. I didn't realize you could do all this."

Wolf, lynx, and beaver pelts hung on the far wall, all ready to be taken in. On another wall hung batches of sinew. Sometimes when Mary had time she'd make purses and small handbags from deer hide, but she usually just prepared the hides and brought them to Byron. He had his price and she had hers. As long as they both walked away happy, where the furs and hides went after meant nothing to Mary.

But lately all she managed to do was take care of nuisance beaver. The trapline held no importance to her now, not with Tom out of the picture. That was his baby.

"This is my life." She stared at her pelts, proud of her skills yet daunted by her bleak future. She loved the wilderness and the adventure, but many mornings she woke up wondering what else was out there. There must be more to life than this. Sure, she had all the necessities, and sometimes a simple life came by easier, but more and more she became bored of this routine.

Terry walked around and touched the pelts. Watching his hand gently skim the furs made Mary wonder how it would feel if he touched her the same way. But she shook it off and reminded herself that Terry was here as a friend for a quiet vacation. Kissing her as he did shouldn't mean anything, even though to her it did.

"How long have you been doing this?"

She cleared her throat and tried to concentrate on his questions, not how pathetic she was thinking about how hot it would be to make love to him on a bear rug. "About twelve years, I guess. Tom started teaching me a few years after we were married." She looked down at the floor. "When we realized I couldn't have his kids." He didn't need to hear that, probably didn't want to either, but something inside told her it needed to be said.

"A doctor told you that, or Tom did?"

She didn't answer, but she didn't disobey her husband and see a doctor in secret even though she wanted to. There were many things she wanted to do but she couldn't.

When she looked up, Terry was facing her now. She didn't know what went on in his mind, but he seemed sad for her. "Do you want children?"

She shrugged, embarrassed to answer truthfully. "Maybe. One day." She couldn't tell him those motherly urges had bothered her for years now. She wanted to love somebody more than anyone could ever love her. Tom had said it was her fault she couldn't have children. She must be barren and therefore, not a proper wife.

"I'll show you the dogs and my horse now."

Terry nodded without another word and followed her outside. The doghouses were lined up along the side of the house. A few of them were on top of their roofs, others inside their houses. None of them showed any interest in Terry which surprised Mary. *Maybe they were stunned by his good looks, too.*

"They're named after the seven dwarfs."

"You're serious?" Terry chuckled. "I like your sense of humor."

"Thanks." Mary walked over to pet the first one. "They're Samoyed's so they're not big dogs but they have loads of energy. This is Grumpy. I'm surprised you're not getting barked at."

"Maybe he likes me."

"*She* doesn't like anyone."

* * * *

Terry stared at Grumpy, feeling like he'd met a new friend. He reached out to pet her and the dog bared her teeth. He pulled his hand back, grateful it was still attached. The memory of Gabe chopping Adolfo's finger off flashed before his eyes.

"Told you she doesn't like anyone. She barely lets me touch her. She's the dominant one here. They all follow her."

Mary introduced him to Sleepy and Dopey who were, oddly enough, the only others awake and on top of the roof.

"Beautiful dogs. They're so white it's almost blinding."

Mary laughed, walking away from him now. "Not when they get into the muck. It's a job in itself just cleaning them. Good thing for the river being close by."

His gaze wandered down to the jeans clinging to her ass too perfectly. Even though she drowned in her t-shirt he still had a lovely view of her round bum. The urge to grab her by the buns, yank her around and kiss her, bore through him like dynamite. But he kept those urges to himself and followed her around the yard. He knew he'd make another move soon, but he wanted to play his cards right.

Next they visited the barn and a huge horse named Blue. Terry rubbed his muzzle and smiled as Blue nudged his chest and seemed to enjoy his attention.

After a few minutes admiring the big steed, they strolled out of the barn.

"What else do I get to see?"

"That's pretty much it, unless you want to see the equipment. You've already seen the woodshed and chopping block on the other side. The rest of the property is bush and river."

He didn't want to see anything else, only her naked body lying beneath him on the patch of grass they were walking on. "Where should I set up my tent?"

Mary stopped on a flat grassy surface and turned around. "Right here."

"Will I be safe from the bears?"

"Maybe."

"Wolves?"

Her sweet lip curled up at the corner. "Possibly."

"Mosquitoes?"

"No."

He was about to ask another silly question when the phone rang from inside. Mary rushed in to answer while Terry tried to figure out a way to convince her to let him stay in the guest bedroom, or preferably in her bed. He didn't want to admit he was scared shitless to be out here, alone, at night, in the deadly wilderness. He stared at the tree line, so thick he couldn't see much more than a foot beyond, wondering if a fury predator was watching him right now, and licking its lips.

He shook his head. What a pathetic thing to imagine when he was probably safer here than at home.

Mary returned a few minutes later with a rifle in hand. Terry eyed up the gun and then her. "Did I say something wrong?"

She looked confused. "What?"

Terry glanced in the other direction. "Nothing."

"That call was about a nuisance beaver. Apparently a man about ten clicks away has had troubles with it before. His road access is blocked off from the dam and he needs it fixed right away. Care to join me?"

As long as the bullet wasn't meant for him. "Sure. My schedule is clear. We'll take my vehicle."

Mary laughed, eyeing him incredulously. "Are you serious? It looks brand-new."

He shrugged. "It's a rental. I don't care if we put a dead beaver in it."

Terry quickly changed into a pair of jeans and a sweater in the guest room while Mary gathered a few necessities to do her job. He took in the basics of her home, the personal objects scattered about and decided he liked this place. It was quiet and simple, and completely different than home. Gabe was right. Maybe this is exactly what he needed.

They put the gear into the Suburban and headed along a dirt road that looked like it hadn't been driven on in twenty years. The overgrowth crowded the road, making the turns impossibly tight, Terry thought he'd either take off the paint or ditch the vehicle. Mary on the other hand looked happy to be on the road. Maybe getting away from her house was exactly what she needed.

On a whim he reached over and took her hand in his on the center console. Most women loved to have their hand held while out on a drive. He hoped Mary did too.

He felt her tense up, but she didn't pull away. Through his peripheral vision, he saw her look down at their entwined hands, then up at him in question. He sensed her fear at having a man touch her like this, when he knew her husband did no such thing. To Terry, it felt good showing her he was right beside her no matter if they were on a Sunday drive or running for the hills.

After a long while of silence and scenic bush road, Terry slowed the vehicle at the first signs of a wash out.

"This must be it," Mary said. "The guy said he'd be here to show me the pond and to pay me, but I don't see him."

Terry scanned the trees but nobody seemed to be around. He parked the truck to the side and shut off the engine. "Might as well take a look around, I guess. Looks like there's a set of tire tracks before the water, but not sure how old they are. Maybe the guy's stuck back there."

Mary got out and grabbed a couple pairs of rubber boots from the back, and handed him the larger pair. "They were Tom's. Not sure if they'll fit but you'll need them."

The rubbers were a bit tight, but Terry was glad for them considering the pool of water covering the road. They walked along the outer bank, keeping tight to the bushes and even on higher ground the water almost reached the top of the rubber boots. Eventually they came across a fairly large pond, which completely washed out the guy's driveway, but Terry couldn't see a house in the distance.

"Are you sure somebody lives here? It looks like any other bush road."

Mary eyed the pond. "Hard to tell around here. There's a few people who live off of roads like this in the middle of nowhere. Mima's one of them. You'd never know of her cabin unless you came across it by accident or flew over it."

Terry nodded in agreement, remembering Mima's cabin nestled tight in the mountain range. Even by skidoo the place seemed almost impossible to reach.

About fifty yards away Terry saw a mound of sticks and muck. "There's the beaver house."

Mary chuckled. "Well at least you know something about the wilderness."

Her little jab made him shake his head. "Whatever, woman. I may be a city boy but I'm not an idiot. I do read and watch television when I have time."

"That beaver will be here somewhere. We just have to wait." She checked her rifle and walked up to a small hill overlooking the pond. Terry followed, having no idea what else he should do, and knelt down on the grass beside her.

He'd never done anything like this before, and it felt great to be out here like this, in the fresh air without the sounds and smells of the city. A raven sat on top of a mangled-looking spruce nearby, a slight breeze swished the grass around them. It felt like he'd arrived in a different world, squatting beside a woman who lived like this every day.

He stared at her, at the loose strands of hair touching the back of her delicate neck. The urge to trace the tip of his finger along the curve of her jaw, gently cup her neck and force her to face him, was strong. But he also enjoyed simply watching her in her element as she scanned the waterline, waiting for the furry pest to emerge.

"You live for this, don't you?" he whispered.

She turned and looked up at him. "Not really. I do enjoy it, but I'm also tired of it."

He frowned. "Why? You seem at peace out here."

Mary let out a deep breath. "Don't get me wrong, I love the wilderness, but sometimes I wish for something more. More than the excitement of shooting my gun, or even taking the dogs out for a run." She smiled, more at herself, he thought. "I've never gone shopping at a fancy store. I don't even own a dress or a pair of high heels."

He chuckled. "We could change that, you know. I'll bring you to the city anytime you want. Just say the words." He stiffened. The words tumbled out of his mouth before even thinking about it.

She smiled at him, eyes bright with wonder, completely unaware of the turmoil he'd caused himself. Terry wasn't exactly sure what he wanted out of this strange relationship—a real partner by his side, or a friend with benefits? All he knew for certain was that he wanted Mary close to him. He enjoyed her company, her humor, and even the shyness which made her real in his eyes. There was no mincing words or toying with his mind. She said it like it was, and he liked that.

"I'll think about it," she said, snapping him back to the moment. A moment later something caught her eye and she lifted the rifle, aiming it toward the pond. "There he is."

Terry focused where she was looking and saw a tiny spec of brown in the water with a slight wake right behind. He was about to comment on how she couldn't possibly shoot such a small target, but she pulled the trigger and the bullet hit bang on.

"Nice shot—"

A second shot cracked the air. A bullet whizzed by Terry's head and slammed into a tree directly behind him. On instinct, he shoved Mary to the ground and pinned her beneath him. As he tried to make sense of what happened, another shot cracked the air, this time hitting the dirt in front of them. "Please tell me there's hunters around here and we're just in a bad spot."

"It's not hunting season, Terry, and this is private land." She panted beneath him. "This has never happened to me on a call before."

"Fuck." He rolled to her side but kept an arm over her torso. "Don't move." He pushed onto his knees and viewed the landscape from their perch on the hill. Nobody was in sight and the bush across the pond was too thick to see beyond.

Mary stared at him, wide-eyed. "What the hell is going on?"

"I'll explain later. We have to get out of here." Terry lifted his head higher for a better view. Another shot cracked the air. He ducked and put his body over hers again. That shot could've killed him. He felt the air whip across his cheek, but he didn't want to tell her the truth. "We need to get to the truck right now."

They crawled back to the rental. More bullets whizzed past them, hammering at the Suburban and the surrounding bushes. Terry shoved a bewildered Mary through the driver's side door to the passenger seat, and jumped in behind her.

He wasted no more time with talk, and put the Suburban in gear just as a jeep burst through the brush on the other side of the pond.

"Holy shit!" Mary screamed, and gripped the dashboard. "What the hell is happening?"

The jeep plunged into the pond and came straight for them. Pond water spewed over the wheels as it charged ahead full speed. Terry slammed on the gas and spun the truck around, racing back down the road with the jeep right on his ass.

"I'm going to assume that call was well planned," Terry added, as he swerved the truck around a sharp bend.

"What?"

"That call. Did you know the person or get any other information? Because what happened was the perfect setup for an assassination in the middle of nowhere. Probably never find a body out here."

Mary remained silent for a long while as Terry tried to lose the jeep. "Oh, God."

The old gravel road zigzagged around trees and rock cuts, old cut-overs and swamp land. Every time Terry gained some momentum, the jeep would bump his rear end, making him fishtail along the road. He was grateful for the Suburban's heavy weight and long wheelbase. It would take a lot to flip the big beast.

He swerved tight around a corner, narrowly escaping a large boulder on the side of the road.

Holding the wheel with one hand, he pulled out his handgun with the other. Mary's jaw dropped when she realized what he was doing.

He aimed the gun at the back of the Suburban and shot out the back window, before firing two rounds at the windshield of the jeep. The vehicle swerved but never lost momentum.

"Don't forget that hill up ahead," Mary shouted.

But it was too late. The truck barreled over the hill sending them airborne.

Mary held on for dear life as Terry did his best to control the vehicle as they bounced and fishtailed, breaking through overgrowth crowding the road.

"I could use some help, Mary."

"What am I supposed to do?" she shrieked.

"Shoot him."

They swerved around another bend as the jeep touched the back bumper. Terry righted the Suburban and barreled down a short stretch of fairly smooth road. He glanced at Mary, his expression calm as could be. "Do you want to die?"

She stared at him and blinked, her face pale, before she struggled to grab her rifle and aimed it to the back window. He couldn't have been more proud of her in that moment when she fired round after round at the jeep. She bounced in her seat, but every shot hit the driver's side of the windshield.

On the next plateau, Terry saw the Athabasca River winding around the rocky hill, and an idea sprung to mind. At the last possible second, Terry feigned left but took a sharp right, smashing into the rear of the jeep as it tried to pass. The jeep swerved and sailed into the air right over the cliff.

"Oh my God!" Mary screamed in hysteria and covered her eyes. "We're gonna fuckin' die!"

"No, we're not." He slammed on the brakes and skidded to the edge of the cliff. He slammed it in park and left the engine running before he looked at her seriously. "Stay here."

Mary opened her eyes wide and gripped the dashboard again. "No! Don't you dare leave me here by myself, you bastard."

Terry shook his head and couldn't help his chuckle. "You have a rifle in your hands and you shot a beaver over a hundred yards away. I saw a dime-sized piece of its head as it swam in the opposite direction, and you shot right on the mark, woman. You'll be fine right here." He gave her a saucy wink. "I trust you have my back like a good sniper."

She visibly shook, but she held her rifle like a pro. "Why the hell did I agree to let you stay with me? Why the fuck does bad shit always happen with you?"

He chuckled again. Situations like this were a walk in the park for him, but not for Mary. His grin faded at the thought. He shouldn't have come here and put her through this. She had been tossed into his dangerous world—just like that.

He needed to see her, and now Mary could be in grave danger. He couldn't walk away from this thing that had started between them a few months ago, but he had to make sure nothing happened to her. A few months of her face torturing his mind drove him up the wall, and now this.

With Mary sitting shotgun, Terry got out of the Suburban and made his way toward the cliff's edge. About twenty feet below, the jeep lay in a tangled mess against a huge boulder on a lower plateau. Smoke billowed from the crumpled front end.

He found a spot to crawl down the rocks and cautiously made his way toward the jeep, his Beretta cocked and ready.

The door creaked open and the driver stumbled out. Blood covered the side of his face and neck. Terry immediately lifted his weapon when he recognized the man's face. He was a hired assassin, and a good one at that. His father had hired him in the past when Sammy was away on another mission.

This officially ruined his vacation. Without another thought he popped two bullets into his chest.

The gun slipped from the driver's hand as his body slumped to the ground. Terry kicked the man's gun away then checked his pulse. Once he was sure the guy was dead, he grabbed his wallet and cell phone before checking the vehicle for other personal items, making sure not to leave any fingerprints.

As he made his way back to the Suburban, he wondered who was behind this. He found no clues in the jeep to answer that question. First he was poisoned and then a shooter came after him, knowing exactly where he would be. He shook his head as he walked back to the ledge. He couldn't even have a goddamned vacation without something happening.

He got into the truck and slid the Beretta back into his pants. "I don't think it's safe for us to return to your place tonight."

"Why?"

"Whoever sent that man knows I'm here, and they know I'm with you." He put the truck in gear and continued down the road. "We'll stay at a hotel tonight then check your house tomorrow, just to be safe."

Mary looked out her side window and said nothing, but he knew she must hate him right now.

Once again this was all his fault. He couldn't stop thinking about the poison, and now this. Mary was in danger because he couldn't stay away from her.

Terry knew for certain somebody he trusted wanted him dead.

Chapter 7

"I think I need oxygen," Mary choked.

She wanted to scream and cry and punch him, but she didn't think it would do her any good. Maybe he would hit her back. Maybe he would be like Tom.

Fear and doubt was a terrible combination.

Her mind raced with questions and accusations, from Mary allowing him to stay here and of why he really wanted to be here. Considering all the terrible shit that always seemed to happen around him, she should've known his little vacay would end abruptly and violently.

They checked into a small motel on the main street right at the end of town. The room was small and badly decorated, but clean. Mary didn't care what the place looked like as long as they each had a bed. She slammed the door and stood there, fuming and shaking as Terry checked the window locks and shut the curtains.

Suddenly he was standing behind her now, massaging her shoulders while she tried to breathe. "You'll be fine. Just slow your breathing and concentrate. In and out, in and out."

Her chest heaved and her entire body trembled. He probably found her hysteria hilarious. Did he not realize how crazy this was? Not everybody gets chased and shot at when they go to work.

"I don't know how you do it. How can you possibly function knowing people are trying to kill you? How do you get through the day?"

He gently spun her around. "Shh, it'll be okay." Apparently the fear in her eyes turned him on. He leaned down and captured her trembling lips. Her squeal of surprise was lost in his mouth as he darted his tongue inside and tasted her.

Her breathing slowed, but her heart still hammered.

He pulled back. "Want me to show you how to get through the day?"

Mary opened her eyes and released a shuddering sigh. "Maybe."

He smiled. "Maybe yes or maybe no?"

She exhaled a shaky breath. "Maybe—no."

He kissed her again, and her toes curled as he trailed a hand down and gently palmed her breast.

"I think danger excites you, Mary. You're shaking, but you're hot."

She exhaled. "No."

Mary stared at him in complete fear and anger. Flashbacks from the first time she'd met him tormented her mind. But something else lingered there as well: excitement. Good God it felt good to shoot at that jeep. But maybe now she was a criminal like Terry.

She pulled away from him, wide-eyed and shaken. "Should we call the police?"

Terry didn't even look at her. "I wouldn't recommend it."

"Why?"

He pulled his handgun from the back of his pants and checked the clip before tucking it into the back of his pants. "Do you really think that's a smart idea, considering I put two bullets in his chest?"

"You did?" Her face paled. She hadn't seen that part. "Well, it was self-defense! I shot at him too." She paced the room. "Do you expect me to sit here and wait now? This is ridiculous. Maybe we should call Gabe or your father or something. I can't sit here like this."

"Mary, stop." His voice was low and commanding, but not harsh.

She paused and turned to face him. Tears filled her eyes and she took a deep, shuddering breath. "W-what?"

"Do you want me to leave?"

Bang. Bang. Bang.

She gasped and quickly covered her mouth.

Terry put his hand up for her to remain quiet, and in a flash, he had his gun out and ready again. He motioned for her to stay behind as he crept in stealth mode to the door.

Mary stayed close, not wanting to be anywhere else but directly behind him anyway. She grabbed the back of his shirt in a white-knuckled grip and whispered fiercely, "Is that another shooter?"

Terry glanced over his shoulder and chuckled under his breath. "If it is, it was polite of him to knock." He checked the peephole and shook his head.

Mary glared at his back. "This isn't funny."

He slipped the gun back into his pants and answered the door. Mary pressed her back against the wall, terrified he'd lost his mind and was about to get shot, right there in the doorway to room twenty-three.

"Here's your extra pillows, sir. Have a wonderful night."

"Thank you."

Terry closed and locked the door, tossed the pillows onto one of the beds, before he turned around and faced her. "We survived housekeeping."

Mary glared at him. She wanted to slap that shit-eating grin right off his face. "This isn't the time for jokes, Mister McCoy. There could've been a gun or a bomb tucked in between them. She could've stabbed you for all we know."

"True. Now," he stepped closer, closing the gap between them, "you didn't answer my question before we were interrupted."

"What question?"

He stared down at her, eyes dark and sensual, mouth mere inches away. "Do you want me to leave?"

Mary lifted her chin in defiance. "Yes." But her chin quivered. They were already thrust into this—together. And if he left, then what? She'd be right back at square one. Alone. "No." She whirled around, her back facing him as sudden and unwanted tears filled her eyes. "Well, so much for pitching your tent in my yard and having a vacation. Someone will kill you for sure!"

Terry grabbed her shoulders and spun her around, the hint of a smile on his lips. "You're worried about me."

Mary folded her arms over her chest, not wanting him to hold her. "No, I'm not."

He rubbed a tear that had escaped, and traced the pad of his thumb over her cheek to her jaw. The touch was soft, gentle, and it took her breath away. He tilted her chin up, his eyes exploring hers. "Yes, you are. I see it in your face, the way you're standing there like a stiff pole trying to ignore this thing between us."

Mary's chest grew tight. There was something wrong with the air, or maybe this infuriating man knew how to push her buttons.

"I'm going to kiss you, Mary. But maybe I won't stop this time."

She stepped back, nervous and terrified by this crazy situation, yet turned on by his boldness. Her back touched the wall. She was trapped. Trapped between drywall and hard flesh. "I don't think this is the right time to be kissing me when somebody just tried to kill us, Terry."

The heat was unbearable. He seemed taller now, coming at her like a cat on the prowl, and she was a little bird with a broken wing.

"Nobody's trying to kill you. It's me they want."

It was a mistake to rip her gaze away from his and look down.

A hot blush stole her cheeks seeing the impressive bulge pushing out his jeans. Pitching a tent was the least of her worries. Neither was his reference to her being a stiff pole.

Before she could argue, before she could make a smart decision, Terry was against her, that hard piece of male danger nudging her belly like a promise and a threat. He set his palms on either side of her head against the wall and leaned closer, his lips almost touching hers, all she had to do was pucker up and she'd get her wish. Everything made her head swirl.

"Does danger turn you on, Mary?"

She swallowed. "No."

His head lowered more, and before his lips touched hers, he whispered, "Liar."

Mary wasn't sure if she was floating or if he held her up. She felt weightless as his mouth fused hers in a blazing kiss. Maybe it was the danger. Maybe it was the way he gently forced her to give in. Either way her hands were around his neck now, and she wantonly pressed her body against him.

She tingled, burned, yearned for him to be closer, even when her mind screamed to get away.

A hot flush pooled low in her belly, as wicked thoughts of what could happen swirled in her head.

She twirled her fingers in his soft hair while he ground his cock against her, teasing her to madness. Her jeans were soaked. She wanted him to take her, make her feel like he needed her, had to have her.

They both moaned.

His big hand trailed up her ribcage and cupped her breast forcefully, making her ache for more. He pinched her taut nipple through her shirt and bra, and twisted it tight in his fingers. The pain gave her pleasure, made her want more—and then his hand skimmed down to her waist and lower.

She'd never felt such raw passion like this with Tom. It was almost surreal, hot, and torturous.

She let him tear open the button of her jeans, rip down the zipper, and slip his hand inside. He moaned when he discovered she wore no panties.

His finger slipped between her wet lips and—

Terry tore himself away and cursed.

Confused and panting, Mary stared at him in disbelief. "What—what's wrong?"

He shook his head, clearly oblivious to her disappointment quickly boiling into anger. "We can't do this. I have to go back to the scene and burn that jeep."

Mary quickly fixed her pants, still terribly aware of what just happened between them, and the hot wetness between her thighs became a terrible distraction. "I can't believe this. It's like I'm in a relationship with the mob!"

"Not really. We don't have mob connections, not directly anyway."

She threw her hands up in the air. "Whatever! You know what I mean."

The hotel room was in darkness except for the tiny glow of the bedside lamp. They were alone in a fucking hotel room. Somebody tried to kill them. More people could be on their way. She almost gave herself to him like a common tramp.

And she wanted it.

Mary sat on the edge of the bed and watched Terry like a hawk, angry with him, disappointed with her herself, and terribly unsatisfied. "You better explain to me what's going on, or you can go back home and wait for more trouble by yourself then. This whole situation is so fucked up, I can't get my head around it. Why is somebody trying to kill you?"

That was the first time she'd ever said what really weighed on her mind. First time she ever showed her anger to a man. She looked down at her knees, wondering if she had it in her to be strong, to tell him to leave her in peace. But she didn't really want him to leave, not now. Not after knowing the passion that snapped like fireworks between them. Maybe she was wrong thinking they could have something fun if people were trying to kill him. Being in constant fear was no way to live, she knew it now, and couldn't go back to that terror again.

She put her face in her hands and tried not to freak out. Before she met Tom she had a good grip on life. She took care of herself. Didn't let anyone walk all over her. When Tom started hitting her, it was as if the tough part of her shrank away. He'd taken away a piece of her.

Tears filled her eyes and she sobbed. "I won't let you hurt me like Tom did."

Immediately, Terry came to her and took a seat beside her. The old bed creaked in protest. He put his arm over her shoulder and he kissed the side of her forehead. She stiffened, unsure of herself, of him, but he didn't let her pull away.

"I'll never hurt you. And if anyone touches you I'll kill them."

She swallowed, not quite sure if that was the answer she wanted to hear.

Terry let out a deep breath. "The truth is somebody poisoned me a week ago."

She looked up at him and shook her head. This was getting worse with every minute.

"It happened right after we took care of a drug lord Ben was connected with. I guess he hired Ben to steal the shipment." He stared down at her, his eyes searching hers. "That's partly why I'm here. I was told to hide, but I wanted to come here to see you. I thought this would be a safe place, tucked away in the bush. I'd finally have time alone with you. Get to know you. Only three people know I'm here. If I thought for one second we weren't safe, then I never would've come here."

She believed him, but it didn't make hearing the words any easier. "Then you don't even know who's doing this."

"No, and I trust those three people with my life. There's got to be a leak somewhere. I don't know what to think, but I need to get some answers." Terry looked over at the phone on the bedside table. "Which reminds me, I haven't called my father since I got here. So much for a peaceful vacation." He slid across the bed and picked up the receiver.

Mary pretended not to listen as he made a collect call.

"Hello Wanda," Terry said in a hushed voice. "Can my father take a call? I see. Yes, I'm all right. I don't want to say too much. Is dad all right?" His voice cracked. "What happened?"

Terry's shoulders slumped as the woman spoke on the other end. Mary stared at his back, wishing to comfort him somehow, but she was confused and afraid of what happened today that she did nothing but stare at him in terrified silence.

She wasn't used to this. What she knew consisted of keeping the homestead running, not dodging bullets.

"I'll be home as soon as I can." He hung up the receiver and sat as still as a board, staring at the phone, a vacant expression on his face.

After a long while, Mary reached out to touch his shoulder, but when he stiffened she immediately pulled away. "Is everything all right?"

He shook his head. "No."

"Do you want to talk about it?"

"No." He pushed off the bed and grabbed his jacket off the floor. "Stay here. I have to go out for a minute."

Mary didn't get the chance to argue before he stormed out of the room. She stared at the door for a few seconds before she jumped up and went to the window. Discreetly, she fingered the curtain open and saw him pass the bright hotel sign before his body blended into the darkness along the sidewalk. He was heading back to town, pace quick and sure.

Without second thought she decided to follow him.

He seemed fine until he spoke to that Wanda woman. Was she a family member, or his lover? The brief conversation seemed to be about his father. There were too many questions swimming in Mary's mind, she couldn't help following him down the dark sidewalk, stalking him like a crazy woman. If he thought he could walk away without some kind of explanation, then he was dead wrong.

Terry McCoy came to her for a safe haven, and in return they were shot at and apparently now in hiding. *What the hell should she do, sit around and wait to be killed by somebody?*

No more sitting around waiting for anything.

Mary kept a safe distance back as Terry walked past a few buildings then opened the door to a pub. She blew out a deep breath and shook her head. Apparently the news he received made Terry want to lose himself in a drink.

She approached the window and stared inside.

There he sat, hunched over and alone at the bar counter, shooting back one after the other like his life depended on it. The news must be something terrible for him to pound back that many shots in such a short time.

She sighed and looked around the interior. She didn't really want to go in, especially how the townsfolk treated her, but right now it seemed like all they had were each other. Might as well join him and discover what he heard over the phone.

Mary entered the bar and looked around. A young couple sat at a corner table while a group of men enjoyed the pool tables on the other side. She fixed her gaze on Terry's back. He didn't even look at the door when she walked in.

She took another deep breath and approached him. Her chest felt so tight she thought she might crack a rib.

"Can I join you?"

He looked up with the saddest face she'd ever seen. He nodded and pointed to the bartender to serve her the same. Mary pulled out the stool and took a seat, unsure how to talk to him. Maybe silence was best, or maybe he'd talk when he was ready.

He lifted his shot glass and she did the same. With a clink they shot back the booze. Mary's eyes widened as the cheap vodka seared a path down her throat. But she refused to cough or cry or slam her palm down on the counter. Instead she made a disgusted face and tried to ignore the burn of tears in her eyes, never mind her poor throat.

"Vodka."

"I know," she choked. "I think they replaced it with turpentine."

He didn't laugh at her poor attempt to lighten his mood. "A few more of those and you'll be fine," he said without looking at her.

She stared at his white-knuckled grip on the glass. "As fine as you?" *Shit. Maybe I shouldn't have said that.*

He stared at her then, eyes narrow, darker blue. "I guess I deserved it."

Mary leaned close and whispered for his ears only. "Are we gonna talk about your phone call, or get drunk and pretend everything is wonderful and you didn't kill a man after an insane car chase?"

He turned his attention to the row of liquor bottles lining the wall behind the counter. The huge mirror behind reflected the dim atmosphere of two lost people. He responded in a low voice. "I never wanted this life, you know. Too much is expected of me and not once have I ever had time to live and relax and be a normal guy. Every day I have to watch my fucking back. Every day I have to answer to the old man."

Mary didn't know what to say so she simply listened. Sometimes silence is a better answer.

Their glasses were refilled but she decided to wait for this one. Terry shot his back right away, his gaze still focused on the row of liquor bottles. The bartender moved to the far side of the counter to attend other customers. Once he was out of earshot, Terry continued, "My mother died of a heart attack when she saw my father's pigs eat a man."

Mary felt her face turn ashen as her heart sank. She grabbed the shot glass and took it down in one gulp. She grit her teeth and gripped the counter, sickened and disgusted by the image his words portrayed.

"What she didn't know was that man planned to kidnap and torture me to get money out of my father. I was fifteen."

Mary stared at him but said nothing. What could she say? *I'm sorry your mother died but I'm glad you weren't taken?* No words seemed appropriate.

"All this shit is normal, you know. Rival dealers. Kidnapping. Torture. You name it. Even prostitution."

Mary swallowed, not understanding any of it, and not really wanting to hear it. For a short while it seemed they had their own little world at her place. Now she was suddenly thrust into his crazy, shattered life.

What the hell am I doing? She turned her attention back to the two of them reflected in the huge bar mirror. Terry didn't see her watching him. His expression became withdrawn, defeated, that it hurt her physically to see him look this lost. She wanted a normal life, but she was tired of hers. Did it mean she was just like him?

"Gabe's father and my father were old school chums. When Gabe's dad died in a plane crash hauling supplies to a camp up north, my father promised to watch over his boy who never knew his mother. Gabe's been like my brother since I was a teenager. We've done some things for my father that would put us behind bars for life. I'm surprised we're still alive, actually."

"Why are you telling me this?"

He stared down at his empty glass. "Because I want you to know I'm not a monster by choice. I was made this way."

Compelled to comfort him, Mary reached out and rubbed his shoulder. Muscles tensed under her grip. Tears filled her eyes by his heartfelt words. She wanted to say something to help ease his burden. "Maybe you were before, but you can choose to change now."

He exhaled a loud, shaky breath. "It's not that easy."

"Yes it—"

His voice hardened. "No. You wouldn't understand."

Mary stiffened. His demeanor had changed in a flash and now she feared he might hit her.

Terry must have noticed her withdraw and his face softened. "I'm sorry. I . . . I'm just tired of all this. I'll never hurt you—ever."

Mary nodded, not quite sure what to say.

The bartender returned and Terry nodded to refill the glasses. Mary covered the top of hers with her hand. "Can I have a beer instead, please?"

The bartender chuckled and went to grab a cold one. While he was preoccupied in the beer fridge, she leaned close and placed a kiss to Terry's cheek. "You're not a monster, Terry. I know what a real monsters is, and he's dead now. I'm convinced Gabe killed him, and honestly, after everything Tom did to me, I'm learning to accept it." She sighed and sat back on her stool. "I mean, maybe he didn't deserve to die, but maybe it happened for a reason. Maybe he wasn't meant to stay on this earth. I don't think I ever would've had the nerve to leave him."

Terry's eyes locked on hers, but he said nothing. If the timing was right or not, it didn't matter, for when he leaned close and kissed her lips gently, as if she'd shatter, Mary wanted to melt on him. She'd had enough bad experiences not to feel the need for something good amidst all the bad. She knew he felt it too.

Then and there, on that bar stool, she decided she was ready. She wanted to step out of her shell and feel something good. She didn't care if Terry was a criminal.

"Take me back to the room, Terry," she whispered against his lips. "We're going to finish what you started. You can burn the jeep tomorrow."

His eyes widened. "Are you sure?"

She pulled back with a shy smile. "Yes."

The bartender returned with the beer, but she motioned not to bother. Terry stood up and placed a few bills on the counter. "Thanks, man, but we're heading out."

Ignoring the rest of the patrons, Mary hooked her arm in Terry's and they exited the pub. Her heart pounded. Her legs shook. But no matter how terrified she was by her choice, she knew it would happen. It had to. Beyond all reason, beyond all doubt, she wanted him.

As soon as they were outside, Terry turned and pressed her against the outer wall. His lips claimed hers, hard, desperate, while his hands trailed up her sides. The rough exterior of the building scraped against her back, but she didn't care.

The urge to feel him inside her went beyond desperation. Too much time had passed since she felt such passion—such raw need to be taken by a man.

The walk back to the hotel was quick. As soon as they entered the room, Terry threw his jacket toward the coat rack. It landed somewhere on the floor. Neither of them cared as he backed her up toward the bed, both panting and eager to be naked. Once her legs hit the foot of the bed, Mary sat on the edge and wrapped her arms around his waist.

She closed her eyes, soaked in his warmth.

Fueled by something she couldn't control, she pressed her cheek to his stomach. Desperately, she unzipped his jeans as Terry pulled off his t-shirt and chucked it aside. She kissed and licked the hard planes of his stomach as she pulled his jeans and boxers down. He stepped out of them and kicked them aside as well.

This was just sex. Hard, desperate sex between two consenting adults. No strings attached. No hard feelings. Only pleasure amidst the pain.

As his fingers caressed through her hair, Mary worked her way down, trailing her lips around his navel, then further down. She gripped his thick shaft in hand and pumped him gently at first.

He let out a deep moan and pushed his hips forward as she wrapped her lips around his head and tongued the tip.

"Fuck," he moaned, his fingers gripping her hair.

Mary's heartbeat kicked into overdrive as she took him in her mouth and sucked deeply, urgently, loving how he filled her so deep. Back and forth she impaled her mouth on him, enjoying the raggedness of every breath he took, feeling the pulsing rush between her legs every time her throat muscles contracted. Knowing what she did both excited and pleased him, fueled her hunger even more.

She stroked his shaft while she circled her tongue around his head, shamelessly paying attention to the little slit on the tip that made him tremble. Terry's hands slid down her sides as he leaned forward to pull her shirt up. She knew he had trouble keeping control while her mouth was on him, and she liked having that power. As she pulled back and lifted her arms, he pulled her shirt off and chucked it aside. Next he unhooked her bra and flung it away.

With a rough moan, Terry leaned closer and gently pulled her head back to kiss her hard. She moaned as he palmed her naked breast, her nipples becoming hard as stones, tingling with every touch of his fingers while he tweaked and pinched her to madness.

"Lay back."

Mary gazed up at him in a sexual trance and lay back on her elbows, watching hungrily as he unzipped her jeans and peeled them off her legs. Her gaze traveled down to his dick hanging hard between his legs before he kneeled onto the bed and leaned down to kiss her thighs.

He kissed her wet lips. She closed her eyes and moaned, letting her head fall back. It was gritty and dirty and oh, so good. As his big hands gripped and kneaded her soft flesh, she raked his scalp with her fingers, holding him there. Urging him to taste her, begging him to please her. He tongued her slit for long agonizing minutes and when he flicked his tongue over her sensitive clit and further down between her slick lips, Mary's hips arched off the bed.

"*Oh.*"

Her thighs trembled as he sucked her clit while his tongue delved deeper to the very core of her body. Every hot flick of his tongue drove her closer and closer to climax. But as she reached the edge of an exquisite rush, Terry pulled away and positioned himself between her legs. Mary shamelessly pressed against him, wanting him there, wanting that release, while he stared down at her and stroked himself. He nudged her wet folds, parting them, teasing her to accept him.

Her thighs shook and she clenched around him as he entered swiftly and deeply. Mary's eyes widened by the intrusion, yet she perversely enjoyed the pleasure from the pain. Terry must have realized he'd hurt her, and paused. He curved his body over hers, half lying upon her and kissed her deeply, passionately, his hips remaining still.

Then he moved again, rocking her with him in slow, deliberate strokes, lighting her body into liquid insanity. It was amazing how whole yet torn apart she felt in that moment.

She sighed, thrilled by his deep moans as he thrust in and pulled back, tormenting her as she neared the pinnacle of ecstasy again. This time, as Mary clung to him, her body shuddering, her sighs higher and harder, Terry didn't pull away.

He drove into her again, his body in the same position, his warm stomach caressing hers while his cock surged deep, stroking high— and she let go.

Mary cried out, bucking against him, unable to control her reaction. Terry pulled back slightly to watch her face, to see the sex and satisfaction in her eyes.

His eyes darkened, possessive, as if her cries of ecstasy would forever be for him, and him only.

As she clenched his shaft and fluttered around him, Terry leaned back again and wrapped her legs around his waist. He drove deeper, harder, bucking against her, and Mary took everything he gave.

"I want you to come again." He reached out and pinched her nipple, twisting it painfully between his fingers.

Mary sighed and moved her hand down to stroke her clit. The dual sensation of their joining while she played with herself was a wicked feeling.

Terry rocked her body as if she was his lover, not his one-night stand.

He pushed deep and pulled back, circling his hips until Mary thought she'd explode. With every thrust she whimpered and clung to his hip with one hand and strummed her clit hard with the other. She wanted him deeper and deeper and harder. She wanted it all.

Soon the wave of heat washed over her again. She clung to his arms and shrieked hard as the orgasm hit. Terry pushed deeper, faster, and moments later he let out a rough moan and found his own shuddering release.

For a long while in the blissful aftermath, Terry remained on top of her as they panted for breath. He kissed her forehead, her nose, and her mouth. Mary couldn't help being overjoyed being like this with him, something good amidst all the bad.

He rolled over and she nestled into the crook of his shoulder, rubbing and toying with his soft chest hair. It felt right lying with him like this. She felt no guilt, no embarrassment, only contentment. Her lids drifted shut as her hand continued working circles over his chest, until she heard his content snores, and she eventually fell into a hard, fast sleep.

* * * *

What the fuck did I do?

He looked down at her sleeping form.

Tears filled his eyes—something he hadn't had since he was a boy and he'd broken his leg. Even then his father beat him for crying. Real men didn't cry, especially over a woman.

He felt like such a fool. A soft-hearted bastard.

And now he was shedding tears over this sleeping beauty like some teenaged boy who got dumped. Except he was the one who had to leave.

Why did something that felt good be bad? He'd never be good enough for her. Never be able to give her peace of mind like she deserved. He was a fool for giving in and taking her to bed, even though she knew what she was doing. He still should've been a bigger man and said no.

They came from different worlds. Two places that should never collide.

He should've set her at arm's length right from the beginning.

He should've worn a condom.

But they had intensity nailed to a post.

"You better explain to me what's going on, or you can go back home and wait for more trouble by yourself." Her words a few hours ago screamed in his head.

Now he regretted how good it felt to be with her. How soft and supple her body felt beneath him. How she looked up at him and moaned with every thrust. How she wrapped her arms around him with something that felt like trust.

What the hell am I doing?

He pulled the bedspread up and tucked it around her shoulder, covering a body he would love to have beside him every night, and those beautiful imploring eyes that went with it.

"In this business you have to shut yourself off." His father's words repeated in his mind.

He wished he could block out every word his father had ever said, but he couldn't. It was time to be who he was supposed to be, whether he liked it or not.

Terry leaned down and kissed her forehead, gently ran his hand over her soft hair, etching everything about her in his tormented mind. Once he slipped on his jacket, he left the note on the bedside table and left the room. The click of the door behind him felt like the last tick of a time bomb.

He hated himself for leaving her like this. Like some cheap floozy he picked up off the street. But he knew if he waited until she woke up, she'd find a way to convince him to stay. She needed to be safe, because where he was going would be hell for a good woman like her.

If somebody was going to follow him and kill him, then he would do it alone. He would accept it like a man.

It took nearly two hours to finally locate the road and that jeep. He considered himself lucky he didn't take the wrong turn and got lost out here in the middle of nowhere. He'd probably die out here, and he would deserve it.

As the jeep exploded into flames, with the driver at the wheel, Terry wondered why his old man chose this life for them. Maybe Terry could've went to college or university. Maybe he could've made something of himself. Holding a gun in his hand didn't feel exciting anymore—it felt like a meaningless duty.

He felt like a teacher who didn't want to open those books anymore.

He drove all night.

As headlights blurred past him on the highway, he thought about the many mistakes he'd made. He shouldn't have left home. He shouldn't have taken advantage of her. Now his father was dead and a business he never wanted had been thrust into his hands.

Life was unfair at the best of times.

All he wanted was time away with a woman who intrigued him. A woman so different than anybody else, he couldn't get her out of his mind. Well, now he'd ruined what could've been something good, whether it became permanent or not. She made him feel good and now it was over.

After eleven hours on the road and a ferry ride to the island, he was tired as hell and in terrible spirits.

The moment he walked into his father's home, he went straight to the study and took his anger out on anything within reach. He grabbed the filing cabinet, tore it from the mount, and threw it across the room. Documents scattered across the floor.

Furious and shaking and hating his life, he picked up the framed picture of he and his father when he was a little boy, when his mother was still alive. She had taken the picture.

Colton's arm was draped proudly over Terry's shoulder. They were both smiling.

A sob tore from his throat. Hot tears slipped down his cheeks as he remembered, a long time ago, life had been good.

How times have changed.

Tight in his grip, he carried the picture to the liquor cabinet. Gingerly, he set it down in front of him, opened a bottle of fine whiskey and tipped it to his mouth—his gaze still fastened on his father in the picture.

He didn't know how long he stood there, staring at the picture, remembering his life up until now, but it was long enough to polish off the bottle. He stumbled back then forward. His vision blurred.

"Fuck you, Colton," he whispered painfully.

Then he picked up the picture and smashed it into the garbage can.

Chapter 8

Men.

You *can* live without them, and you *can* shoot them—if you want to go to prison.

Right now, Mary wanted to take her trusty old rifle and use Terry for target practice, but she didn't want the orange jumpsuit.

She'd never been more embarrassed in her life when she left the hotel room the next morning, wearing the same clothes as the day before.

She may be a country bumpkin, but she knew what the walk of shame meant.

Even though she'd tried to sneak away, the housekeeper walked by right at the worst moment. But rather than laugh at or be disgusted, the young woman said, "Good for you," and smiled before she walked away.

She couldn't hide. Couldn't shield herself from this town and these people, or their gossip. Hadn't she suffered enough already? Terry had no idea what he did to her when he left her alone. Apparently he didn't listen when she told him how these people treated her since Tom's death. Was he that much of a selfish idiot?

Now she was a husband killer and a whore.

She slammed his note down onto the table under her living room window and screamed out her frustration. Then she picked the note back up, and reread it again, trying not to cry for the hundredth time. Five days had passed since he disappeared, and she couldn't sleep or eat or think of anything but him and what the note meant.

She had been so caught up in her torment she almost phoned every McCoy in the phone book in his city, which would be a complete waste of time and foolhardy. She couldn't imagine criminals being listed in the directory, but Terry did mention he operated a hotel. It couldn't be too hard to find out which one.

Still, she couldn't go through with it.

She was alone again. Even after she'd said he was better off leaving, now she felt truly bereft.

Dear Mary,

I never meant to hurt you, and I didn't come here to use you. Please believe me. Don't let fear stop you from doing whatever you want in life, because you deserve the world. I don't. I only had you for one night, but it felt like a lifetime. I have to do what I was born to do. I have no choice.

Forever yours,

Terry

She set the note back down and stared at the dogs outside. They all stared toward the window, ears perked, probably wondering why their quiet and good-natured master was screaming at them like a lunatic. They had no idea how badly a few words could rip a heart out.

Forever yours.

Yeah, right.

If one night felt like a lifetime to him then how could he leave? How could he make her feel wonderful then take off without even saying goodbye properly?

It was her own fault for thinking it was just sex, because it wasn't. It quickly became far more than that. When he touched her she felt like she meant everything to him. Her body had come alive. Her soul had felt uplifted. And no matter how corny it seemed, she didn't think she'd ever find another man who could make her feel that way.

Terry had branded her. He'd made her his without even trying.

He'd come here to spend time alone with her, and in the process they were shot at, had sex like desperate strangers in a hotel room, then he took off. Could she handle another broken heart?

She may not have been heartbroken over Tom's death, but she still hurt. He hurt her then he left her. Terry made love to her and left her. That was worse.

She hung her head and cried. Really cried. What was she supposed to do now?

A loud rap on the back door made her jump. She quickly wiped her eyes and took a deep head-clearing breath.

Maybe it was Terry. Maybe he changed his mind and came back for her. She ran to the door, but when Mary whipped it open, she couldn't hide her disappointment. There stood Gabe and Mima, holding hands like a perfect, happy couple. She bit back a sob of complete depression.

"Is Terry still here? I have something important to tell him and it should be said in person," Gabe said, completely unaware of her stricken grief. But Mima stared at her hard. She knew something was wrong.

Ignoring Mima's intent eyes, Mary shook her head at Gabe and cleared her throat. "I'm afraid not. He left without warning five days ago. I'm a little baffled and pissed off myself."

"So he knows already." Gabe hung his head and Mima put her arm around his waist to comfort him. "Son of a bitch. He shouldn't have went back without me. I just got the message today because of that pathetic radio."

Mary frowned, confused by the pain written all over Gabe's face. She'd never seen him like that before. "What's going on? He knows what already?"

"His father was murdered five days ago."

All the breath departed Mary's lungs. Her knees threatened to buckle. Immediately she thought back to the night they shared at the hotel. He started acting strange after his conversation on the phone with that woman. Everything made sense now. Why he seemed angry and lost, why he made love to her with such raw passion, almost as if he needed her to love him.

As if he'd never see her again.

Maybe they were fools for letting things go too far. But she couldn't take it back now. She couldn't stop her feelings. After everything she'd gone through, and how hurt she was by his sudden departure, she felt horrible for him.

"Come in. I'll make us some drinks. I think we all need it."

As the three of them gathered around the kitchen table, Mary couldn't help staring at the diamond on Mima's finger. Just a few months ago they had simple lives. Now everything seemed completely different. They were different people now. These hardened men blew into their lives and changed everything.

She didn't feel like the same woman anymore, and after her night with Terry in the hotel, she didn't want to go back to her old self. She rummaged through the cupboards as Mima and Gabe took a seat at the table. "All I have is wine. It'll have to do I guess."

"Wine is fine. Better than nothing," Gabe added.

Once everybody had a glass filled to the rim, Mary looked square at Gabe. "I'm going to show you something, and please don't think the worst of me." She got up and retrieved Terry's note then handed it to Gabe.

She noticed his worried demeanor change to something like curiosity before he set the paper down and shook his head. "I knew he was a softy. What a tard."

"Honey!" Mima elbowed him in the ribs and ripped the paper out of his enormous hand. After she read the note, a knowing smile crossed her cute face. "Oooh. I knew it. I saw the way he looked at you at my cabin. He wanted you." Her dark eyes narrowed, but they gleamed with excitement as well. "And you're upset that he's gone. I knew it when you answered the door."

Gabe's jaw dropped and he fired a warning glance at Mima, although it wasn't mean in nature. "That's enough out of you. You can't know everything."

"You never mind, Mister. I know what I saw. Female intuition is a force not to be argued with."

Mary watched the two across from her, and couldn't contain a smile of envy. They were perfect for each other. Gabe, so huge and dangerous, and Mima, tiny, yet tough as nails, had what Mary wanted. They looked at each other as if that mountain a mile away could crash down around them and they'd never notice its path of destruction.

Contentment. That's what they had. Mary wanted to know what it felt like to be content, to be truly happy, to look at a man and be unaware of the world around them.

And passion. She wanted more passion too.

With her attention divided between Gabe and Mima, and her rioting thoughts of Terry, Mary's gaze wandered around the room. As much as she loved this kitchen and its simple country style with beautiful, hand crafted cupboards, she wanted more than all this simplicity. She wanted to feel excitement. She needed a sense of glamor, to know what it felt like to wear a shimmering dress like in those magazines. Have her hair done in a ritzy salon. To be able to run in heels without breaking her face.

She chuckled to herself over the mental image.

Terry would laugh at her, too. Then he'd offer his hand and help her off the polished tiled floor of an immaculate ballroom and swing her around like a princess.

She shook off the silly idea and faced Mima, whose brow arched high in curiosity.

"What?" Mary took a long pull of the red wine, thinking about her options, and trying damn hard not to blush over Mima's probing stare.

"What are you thinking about?"

Mary looked away from her best friend and halted at her collection of historical romance, remembering how Terry had asked in a deep, sensual tone if she was a damsel in distress.

"I'm thinking about a dress." *And finding Terry and stripping him naked. Baring his body and his soul for me to dissect.*

"A dress?" Mima looked at Gabe before Mary, her expression puzzled. "For what?"

Mary sighed deeply and took another sip of wine. "The fairy tale. But I'm the one who has to do the chasing."

Gabe shook his head, his expression completely baffled and hilarious. "I don't understand you women."

"Maybe I'm crazy, but I'm going to go to the city. Aside from the animals and you guys, there's nothing here for me. At least, not right now."

Gabe looked confused. He glanced over to Mima who gave him a nudge on the shoulder.

Mary shrugged, but she felt her cheeks heat. "I think I need a change in scenery. Well, it's much more than that, but a change is definitely what I need. Will you two watch my babies and the house for a while?"

Mima reached across the table and took Mary's hands in hers. "Of course we will."

"We will?" Gabe echoed.

"Yes. We will," Mima said sternly, then winked at Mary. "Mary has a man to go after."

Mary didn't realize how lost a big man like Gabe acted when Mima was around. Maybe she wore the pants in their little mountain house. Either that or her little mountain buddy constantly distracted him.

Finally Gabe's eyes widened as it suddenly dawned on him what she meant. "Oh, fuck. You can't go there." He took a healthy drink and Mary could see his mind was skipping a mile a minute.

"You know Terry came here to check up on me right after Tom died. Then he suddenly stopped coming. I always wondered why. Then he came back again, and, well, you read the note. Maybe I did something wrong before. Maybe he wasn't really interested. . . ."

Gabe shook his head. "Let me tell you something about Terry. Remember when I first came here and offered you money to babysit? You said he was probably a player and didn't feel comfortable with him staying here, right?"

She nodded, embarrassed by what she'd said that day. She hadn't even given Terry a chance. He was probably as lost as she was in life, except she could decide her actions day-by-day. Terry didn't have the same luxury. He was forced to do his father's bidding, and forced again to run the show now.

"Terry never was a player, Mary. Sure he'd had a few flings, he's a man after all, but he'd never take advantage of a woman—not intentionally. He lost his mother at a young age and he loved her dearly. His entire life has reflected around pleasing his father and doing everything to keep the business in good standing. That shows dedication and loyalty. If he came here to spend time with you, then it meant something to him."

He brought me carnations. His mother's favorite.

"And now his father is gone and he's in charge of something he doesn't want," Mary added, feeling like she was about to climb a mountain without any equipment. But she'd do it if it meant saving Terry from a lifetime of heartache.

But chasing after him when somebody already tried to kill him twice would be like knocking on death's door. She just hoped she had the nerve and the strength to go there, make her peace with Terry, and come out standing tall. She had to. If she didn't she'd go crazy wondering what could've happened. She'd never forgive herself for not taking a chance, because she sure as hell wasn't getting anywhere around here.

"You're gonna be walking into dangerous territory, Mary. I don't think—"

"Nothing you say is going to stop me. He needs me. Now more than ever. I've already shot at a guy because of him."

Gabe and Mima both blurted, "What?"

"You didn't know? I figured he would've told you already. Anyway, I got a call for a nuisance beaver and some lunatic started shooting at us and tried to drive us off the road. Terry killed him. We ended up at a hotel that night."

Gabe released a disgruntled breath and shook his head. "So it's true. Somebody really does want him dead. Fuck sakes."

After long minutes of strained silence, Gabe reached into his inside coat pocket and pulled out an envelope. "Here, if you're going to the city, then you're going to need this."

"What is it?"

He slid the envelope across the table. When Mary tore open the flap and saw a large wad of one-hundred dollar bills, her jaw dropped. "Gabe, I can't take this. I didn't exactly babysit him."

"Well, apparently you did. Think of it as a reward for helping the team." He smiled at Mima who turned pale, then glanced back at Mary, his expression tight with worry. "If things don't work out as you plan, then you'll need some money to go elsewhere. I mean it. Once you show your face, you may become a target yourself."

Mary cleared her throat. She hadn't really thought about that. But she wasn't going to turn back now. She had to do this. "Are you sure?"

He nodded. "Absolutely."

"It's a lot of money."

"To you, sure. To me, not much."

The excitement and fear of the unknown made her whole body vibrate. "I've never really gone anywhere before, aside from college, and that was a long time ago. I don't even know what to do in the city."

Gabe reached over the table and patted her hand. "Don't you worry. I'll have it all covered."

She was really beginning to like this man. "How?"

Gabe glanced at Mima and made an apologetic face, before he focused his attention back to Mary. "Because I'm going with you."

* * * *

Terry stood next to his father's urn, staring hard at the large picture of a younger, more robust man in the gilded frame. Wanda had requested a private service two weeks after his father's death to allow enough time to pass for things to settle and for Terry to take over. Besides, in this business having a funeral too soon after a death risked a mass murder then and there.

He paid no mind to anyone else as he stared at the man who made him. The father who made him into the hardened man he was today.

His last minutes must have been horrifying. Did he see his killer? Did he know him? He'd give anything to take that night away, to save his father, even if they didn't always get along. Even if Terry hated this life he was forced into.

It ripped his soul apart to see Colton McCoy in a container. Nothing but a black ceramic vase as proof that once a strong man had lived on this earth before they burnt his flesh and bone to ash. He didn't even get to see him before he left, and he was ashamed. It didn't matter how hard the old man had been on him. He was still his father, and he loved him.

He swallowed, his jaw tight, his eyes dry. He had no tears left to cry.

A hand touched his shoulder. Without flinching he slowly turned to find two officers out of uniform standing behind him.

"We're sorry for your loss, Mr. McCoy."

He nodded. "Thank you. I appreciate it."

The rookie officer standing further back cleared his throat. He appeared more than a little nervous to be in a room filled with the kind of men that could end his life with a single nod. "Please let us do our job, Mr. McCoy, and solve this case. We understand what you're going through, but let the law handle this."

No. You'll never understand. "Thank you."

Somebody sobbed behind him. It took a moment in his dazed mind to realize it was his stepmother. She leaned back pitifully across one of the fainting couches closest to the picture. Her hands covered her face while her body shook with every haunting cry.

"Excuse me, boys." He took a seat on the edge of the old couch and put an arm over her trembling shoulders. "It'll be okay. I'll take care of you. Whoever did this is going to pay with their very lives."

As he patted her hair and held her to his chest, he glanced around the room to the many people who came to offer their condolences. He recognized many faces. Hardened men who knew well how to navigate this house, and how to conduct business in the McCoy fashion.

But there were a few he'd never seen before. Was the killer here with them? Could he be watching them now and plotting his next victim? Would Wanda and Terry be next? If the enemy was among them he'd rip their throat apart with his bare hands.

Terry's mind raced with so many questions, it took a moment for it to dawn on him that Gabe stood at the entryway to the great room, looking out over the crowd. He watched as Gabe nodded to a few men. Terry raised his hand to wave him over, but when Gabe moved to the side, Terry's hand paused mid lift and his eyes widened in disbelief when he saw who lingered next to him.

What is she doing here? Why did Gabe bring her here?

Dread consumed him. This wasn't the place for her. She should be at home hating him, wishing she'd never laid eyes on him, safe from all the bad people in this world. But he stared at her like his whole existence meant nothing without her.

His heart, filled with sadness for many things, thundered hard in his chest. He took her in, swallowed her up with his searching gaze. He remembered everything in great detail, and it bore a whole into his very soul.

She wore a simple black dress with her hair piled high. No jewelry, little makeup, only her plain beautiful self. No other woman compared to her, and he felt a hard pang of regret if his sudden departure broke her heart. He was an asshole. A lowdown, dirty son of a bitch for leaving her like that. But he believed he did the right thing at the time. This place wasn't safe, especially with her around. Nobody was safe around him and he hated himself for it.

He felt her hold on him right in his groin, as if she'd gripped him right by the nuts and said, *"You're mine, so shut up and accept it like a man."*

"Who's the woman with Gabriel?" Wanda asked, suddenly more alert and sitting upright. "Is she his new girl?"

Fuck. What the hell am I going to do with her?

"Excuse me for a minute." He squeezed Wanda's shoulder and stood up. "She's just an old friend of mine. No worries." But he knew she didn't believe him. He saw it in her eyes, saw the recognition, and surprise.

Wanda's jaw unhinged as she turned her attention back to Mary. She stared hard toward the entryway, but Terry paid her no mind. Wanda only wanted the best for him, and he knew she'd accept Mary once she got to know her.

Terry adjusted the collar of his suit, never more uncomfortable before, as he approached the duo at the doorway. It felt like he faced a judge with a death sentence as his eyes sought hers.

"Gabe." He stared at Mary as he said the words. "I'm glad you made it." Best to not let anyone else realize what this woman meant to him.

Mary stared up at him, blinking rapidly, her mesmerizing eyes boring a hole into his shattered soul. "I-I came to pay my respects."

"Thank y—"

"And to give you shit for the way you left," she whispered fiercely. "Don't ever assume that you're not good enough."

Terry blinked, completely taken back and blown away by her statement. Did she really come after him? He glanced at Gabe who shrugged and made his way over to Wanda.

This complicates things even more.

He blew out a deep breath and nodded at Mary, having no clue what to say. This was a funeral for his father, after all. The details of their frayed love affair would have to wait. He offered his arm, as calmly as possible, and started for the front of the room.

Mary pulled back, her eyes wide. "I'll just sit back here."

"No, you won't." He grabbed her hand and hooked it in his arm and gently forced her to the couch. He'll deal with everybody else later. He knew having her next to him like this could be putting her in grave danger, but there was no way he would let her out of his sight. She was safest right next to him, her hand locked in his, and his eyes locked on her every move. Besides, as soon as he touched her, he was done.

As Gabe took his seat on the other side of Wanda, Terry pulled Mary down beside him. The four of them filled the sofa with no room to spare.

He felt all eyes on them, and even though it made him nervous, he wouldn't let it get to him.

None of his real mother's family attended. Even though the knowledge hurt, Terry understood why. When they lost her, they lost the only innocence they'd had. The only people grieving for Colton were himself, Wanda, and business family. They all were family in one form or another. He grew up around many of the people surrounding him.

It was a shame what his life had become, but it was what it was.

As everyone focused their attention back to the man in the casket, Terry held Mary's hand tight in his. He felt her tremble and couldn't help feeling a spike of hope that she'd chased after him, even if he didn't deserve it.

The timid and terrified Mary Billings came after him.

He had to force himself not to grin during the service.

As a family friend said a few words about his father, Terry glanced over and found Wanda staring down at he and Mary's entwined hands. When she looked up into his eyes, he saw the pain in hers, before she smiled and looked back up at the picture of her dead husband.

Chapter 9

Mary didn't know what to do but stand quietly by herself as the funeral ended and only a few of them remained in the massive parlor. She wondered if they all were roughened criminals or drug dealers or gamblers, or something of the wild sort. Whatever the case, she felt like a complete outcast among them.

A blonde woman—beautiful, probably in her mid-twenties—attended the others with sandwiches, light snacks, and drinks. She couldn't help wondering if she went above and beyond to make these men comfortable, and if Terry enjoyed her as well. Mary may not be aware of what exactly went on in this sort of rich and fabulous and criminal world, but she wasn't a fool. She'd seen enough movies to know that men of Terry's ilk often mistreated women and used them for nothing but sex, or at least some sort of selfish gain. But she knew, deep down, Terry was the good one like Gabe had told her.

She glanced around the room, in awe of the richness of this place, yet feeling more out of place with every passing second. She'd only seen homes like this in magazines for the wealthy and the famous, where homes were passed down generation to generation. The fuchsia-colored settee that held the four during the service must be worth more than her bronco. This wasn't normal in her eyes. Not when she had to work like a dog to pay the bills every month.

Everything in this room was a deep, rich wood, probably mahogany. A floral print covered the walls, along with many large paintings. So much sophistication and class packed into one room.

Vases with beautiful flowers spilling out over the top, and numerous other arrangements attested to Terry's family being well respected. There must be at least one-hundred floral arrangements in this room for the service. It was overwhelming.

When she and Gabe pulled up to the mansion she wanted to ask him to bring her back home. Back to what she knew. A dirt road for a driveway leading to a small house—not a paved driveway circling a fountain that led to a massive mansion. The McCoy home was basically a Victorian museum overlooking the ocean.

This is what Terry knew. He was a powerful man, could have anything he wanted. Now she had entered his element. It took every ounce of willpower and resolve she had to come here and see him, with the hope their brief fling wasn't over yet.

Now what? Maybe she should have planned beyond coming to his rescue. All she knew was that she couldn't let him walk away. Not so easily.

She dared a glance at the urn and the picture, at the face of a man she'd never met. A man she knew was dangerous when he'd walked on this tumultuous earth.

Terry looked nothing like him. Maybe the lovely mother she'd heard about was who he truly took after. If that were true, then she did the right thing coming here.

She tried not to tremble as she stood by herself in this strange place where the only two people she knew were Gabe and Terry, and even they were little more than strangers. She offered a brief smile and nod as the woman who sat with them on the huge sofa, approached.

She was beautiful, with dark hair and matching eyes, and looked much younger than the man who made her a widow. At least she and Mary had something in common. But did she really love Colton McCoy, or was she with him for money and power?

"So you're the one."

Mary blinked. "I beg your pardon?"

"You're the one who caught my son's heart."

The woman lifted her hand and Mary shook it, having no clue what to say to her. This was the woman who gave Terry the news about his father that night. It felt like Mary was speaking to royalty. During her trip here with Gabe, he'd filled her in on some of the details of Terry's family life. Who was who, and did what for the business. Who she could trust, and who to steer clear of.

Wanda McCoy was highly respected and her safety was guarded at all times. The men loved her like a mother figure and always bowed to her whim. Yet another thing that made Mary feel less than adequate. But she didn't come all this way to be treated poorly, after all, she knew Terry cared about her in his own way. He wouldn't allow anyone to mistreat her.

Be strong. Terry needs you. And you need him.

"I'm Wanda. Terry's stepmother."

Mary felt the color deepen in her cheeks. "I'm sorry for your loss, Mrs. McCoy."

"Thank you. Come now, my dear." Wanda put her arm over Mary's shoulder and led her toward an adjoining room. Mary stared back at Terry, unsure if she should go with her, but when he nodded consent, she blew out a breath of relief and gladly followed. At least some female company might make her feel more at ease.

"Let's have a strong drink," Wanda added. "It's custom in this family to celebrate the life of a loved one when they leave us."

"Okay." Mary looked around the room, which seemed like another big living room but more private. This room was painted a deep burgundy with accents of white and light grey. More exquisite paintings adorned the walls, and the floor-to-ceiling windows were dressed with lush white curtains. She imagined they must have many drinks in this room celebrating another dead person. "You have a beautiful home."

"Thank you. Colton's first wife—Terry's mother—had good taste. She designed this home, you know." She smiled as she poured their drinks. "Eliza was a dear friend of mine. I was heartbroken when she passed. Such a beautiful woman with a kind, loving heart. Colton and I grew closer as we needed each other's support to get through such a trying time in our lives. Falling in love with him came quite naturally."

Mary nodded, not quite sure what to make of her statement, and accepted the drink. Wanda seemed to be overselling herself, but maybe Mary was overreacting. She tipped the glass to her lips and nearly moaned aloud by the sheer flavor of ecstasy. Whatever it was, it tasted like it probably cost a mortgage payment.

Wanda gestured to a nearby loveseat. Mary took a seat, her posture stiff and awkward as Wanda sat right next to her, so close their thighs touched. Mary felt trapped. Her heart pounded and her palms grew sweaty. It seemed like now would be interrogation time.

Terry's stepmother raised her chin regally as she regarded Mary, her dark eyes as dark and as foreboding as a black hole. "Tell me. How did you and Terry meet?" She stared at her, unflinching, as solid and bright as a diamond.

Mary tried to pick the right words. "Well, we met by accident, literally. When Gabe crashed near Silver Creek where I live, I happened to be there when Terry . . . picked him up."

"I see." Wanda chuckled under her breath. "There's no need to hide anything from me, my dear. I know everything." She patted Mary's knee, her long fingernails gripping her flesh. "Don't be afraid, child. You're quite safe here with me."

Mary smiled despite the fear of this overwhelming place and the people within it. Terry's father wasn't safe, how could they protect her? "Thank you."

The guys strolled in at that moment, and Mary breathed in relief to see Terry's face. When he took a long, thorough look over her, it felt like she would be all right. He would make sure she was safe.

"Mary, this is John Covington, he handles the books, and this is Buck Johnson, the estate manager." Both men came forward, all smiles, and she gladly shook their hands. Another gentleman walked in behind Terry and he commanded attention unlike the others. "Mary, this is Sammy Hayes, a dear friend of the family. Sam, meet Mary. She's the one with the ace shot I told you about."

Mary blushed under the intent stare of Sammy's dark eyes, as well as his contagious smile. He had mocha skin and short black, curly hair. She guessed he was of mixed race, and he was gorgeous. He walked over, leaned forward, and took her hand, flipped it over and kissed it. "It's a pleasure. Always nice to meet another shooter."

Trying not to laugh, Mary cleared her throat and took another sip of her drink. "Thanks. I'm not really a *shooter*, I just do what needs to be done."

Sam grinned, displaying a single gold tooth that gleamed in the light. He reminded her of a pirate. "So do I."

He sure knew how to make a woman feel like she was the brightest light in the room. She caught herself staring at him and quickly averted her gaze.

"Terry, sweetheart, you must show your girl one of the spare bedrooms. She might as well get comfortable after coming all this way," Wanda said as she stood up from the loveseat. "I too feel like I need to rest. Gentlemen…" Wanda nodded and gracefully swept toward the doorway, her black silk dress billowing behind her.

"I'm taking Mary to my place," Terry added before she left the room.

Wanda turned in the doorway, frowning. "Nonsense. I want to get to know her. We should all stay here. It's safer that way."

Terry gave his stepmother a stark glance, daring her to challenge him. "Mary and I need to talk. You'll be safe with the guys here. Can our visit not wait till tomorrow?"

Wanda sighed loudly. Mary guessed the woman wasn't used to not getting her way. "Fine. Tomorrow it is." She turned her attention to Mary. "We'll do lunch as a family and then we'll go shopping in the afternoon. It will be wonderful. I've always wanted a daughter." And she blew out of the room before anyone could argue.

Mary sat there in quiet misery, staring at the hallway where Wanda disappeared, wishing Mima could be there to offer support. She felt so out of place maybe this was the wrong time to come here, especially during his father's funeral. Now she was being forced to have lunch and go shopping with a woman she didn't even know. She may seem nice but Wanda made her feel beneath her, as though Mary should be washing her feet not looking for a new wardrobe.

Thank God for Terry. She felt his eyes on her even though he spoke quietly to the guys. She felt his intensity and his strength right across the room.

Then she saw it. A painting of a beautiful blonde woman who looked exactly like Terry. Mary stood up and wandered over, hands clasped behind her back. The blue eyes were as beautiful as they were haunting. The artist perfectly captured the sadness behind all her beauty. No matter where you stood in the room, those eyes followed your every move. She wondered if his mother had ever been happy in her marriage. Was she a victim long before she saw Colton's pigs eat a man?

Mary shuddered and ripped herself away from the painting and stared hard at Terry, unable to hide her trepidation.

When his eyes met hers he immediately ended the conversation. "Okay guys, let's talk about this another time. Mary needs to rest." He stood up and put his hands on her shoulders. "Are you okay?"

She forced herself to smile. "I think so. I'm just—tired."

Gabe and Sam stayed behind as Terry led Mary out of the house to his car. He opened the passenger door and closed it behind her. As they sped out of the driveway, she couldn't help wondering if she'd made a huge mistake in coming here. This rich man in a rich house wasn't what she expected. She knew he had money, but she didn't realize what his daily life consisted of, or what exactly he was capable of. And here she was, a bush broad who didn't belong here.

Country hick storms the criminal underworld. That's what the papers would say if they knew what was happening. Maybe they already did and were taking snapshots from the bushes right now. She had no idea what to expect in Terry's fast world.

Now she was in his element. Maybe she should've brought her rifle.

Soon the quaint and tailored countryside changed to buildings and sidewalks whizzing by. Mary felt more and more ill at ease. Now they were truly in the city. Away from anything familiar.

Everyone and their dog filled the sidewalks. Action surrounded them as Terry veered around traffic and turned down so many different streets, Mary was already lost. Put her in the middle of the bush with an axe and she'd be fine. Here she was nothing but a body in the concrete jungle.

When they arrived at the Sea Scape, she was bedazzled as Terry guided her through the lobby of the majestic hotel. Right away the enormous plants caught her eye.

"Those dieffenbachia's and palms are huge," she commented. "They must be over ten feet tall."

Terry shrugged. "I have no idea what they are but Dad loved them. Everything you see here he picked out himself, right down to the lampshades. But the palms were his favorite." He took her over to an aquarium filled with a variety of colorful fish. "Here." He passed her a jar. "Take a pinch and toss it in."

Mary tossed the flakes of food into the water, and watched, fascinated as they all rushed to eat.

"When I'm in town I feed them every day. It may sound funny, but these little guys are kinda like therapy for me."

Mary glanced up at him as he stared into the water, seemingly lost in the glass box. He seemed different, then. Like a whole other man, not somebody who had a gun shoved into his belt. She knew it had to be there somewhere. But knowing he took the time to feed the fish seemed normal. She never imagined any part of his life being normal.

He turned to her then, his eyes dark, searching hers as if he wanted to know her secrets. "I guess I should've asked if you wanted your own room, or if you're staying with me?"

She blushed. "Well, I think it's pretty obvious why I came all this way."

"To rescue me?"

"Maybe."

For a long while, they stood there staring at each other. But the tension was as hot and uncertain as a blazing fire.

"I didn't think I'd ever see you again." He seemed so lost. His tormented expression sizzled the tiny hairs on her body.

"I know. I decided you needed me. Let's hope I won't regret the decision."

His sudden smile would put the sun to shame. "Then I'll be damned if you're staying anywhere but in my bed." He grabbed her hand and led her to the elevator.

Her entire body trembled as he pressed the top button. She hugged herself, rubbing her arms absently, and imagined this must be what the hooker in *Pretty Woman* felt like heading up to the penthouse for the first time.

Terry put his arm over her shoulders and drew her close. His comforting strength and the pure male scent of him set her more at ease.

But when the doors opened right into his apartment, Mary couldn't help her gasp of utter surprise at the view.

"Holy shit."

She stepped inside, forgetting about Terry, completely stunned by the view before her. Nothing but a wall of glass covered the south side of the apartment with the most beautiful view of the harbor and the endless ocean beyond. Far more spectacular than his father's home. She wandered over to the window and looked out.

Beyond the bay the ocean spanned as far as she could see. A great highway of blue.

Hundreds of boats lined the docks in the harbor beneath. Several were out on the water. She could see everything from here, like she stood on top of the world.

"Not bad, eh?"

"Not bad?" She let out a baffled laugh. "It's awesome. I've never seen anything like this before. Not in person anyway."

He stood behind her now, and placed his hands on her shoulders. "Imagine how I felt when we went for that drive through your woods." He kissed her shoulder and made his way to the sensitive spot below her ear.

Mary trembled from the sheer ecstasy of his warm lips on her cool flesh. "Do you mean the scenery or the car chase?"

He chuckled, and the vibration on her neck made her shudder. "I'm glad you came here, and I'm sorry for how I left. I would never intentionally hurt you. I was afraid of—of everything, I guess."

She closed her eyes and exhaled. "I know. When you left that note I read between the lines." A fierce tingle curved along her spine from his busy fingers. "But don't worry, I'll make you pay for that."

"Mmm." He rubbed his hands up her sides to her ribcage, and pressed his hard body against her back. "You changed everything when you walked into the room today."

"I didn't know if I had the strength to do it, but I couldn't live with myself if I didn't at least try."

"Told you I was right. The real you is a tough cookie."

Mary pressed her palms against the window while he continued kissing her neck and rubbing around her curves with his hands. Every touch lit her fie. Her breath fogged the glass as he held her hips and pressed his erection against her bum.

"I want to be inside you, Mary. Two weeks away from you was two weeks too long."

She closed her eyes and exhaled. "Yes."

Terry trailed his hand down to the hem of her skirt and raised it above her ass. "I promise to be gentle later." He unzipped his slacks, and when she felt the hot, hard shape of him nudging her, Mary sighed and pushed her bum back against him.

He guided his cock between her legs and rubbed himself against her panties. She pushed back, needing him there, needing him inside. The intensity was like a living, breathing thing surrounding them.

"Do you want me to use a condom?" he murmured urgently.

Then he pulled away before she could think to answer. Mary released a pathetic whimper, feeling painfully bereft and desperately turned on. "No, I mean, we didn't use one before." She blushed, beyond embarrassed by their previous indiscretion and her desire to not use one now. Maybe she should've thought about it harder before acting on her red-hot needs.

"You're the only woman I've done that with. I promise."

She swallowed hard and nodded. She wasn't the kind of woman who played the field or had experience with multiple partners. Using a condom wasn't a new experience for her but it certainly had been a while since she'd used one, or needed to use one.

"I trust you. Now get back here." Mary turned her back to him, waiting for him to make the decision. She didn't have to wait long, as he moaned in pleasure and rubbed his hands up her sides again.

"You have no idea what it means to me to hear you say that." He pressed his hard-on against her back, teasing her mercilessly.

Everywhere he touched her, her body felt singed by fire.

They both panted in unison. Maybe it was the intensity of their relationship, maybe the pain of death around them, or maybe they just missed each other that much, but when he pulled her panties down and entered her from behind, tears filled her eyes from the sheer ecstasy.

"You're mine now," he moaned, and pushed in deep, nearly lifting her off her feet.

Terry gripped her hips, rocking her with him, and took her hard against the window. Even though his loving became rough, Mary wouldn't have it any other way. She felt his passion, his desperation, his need for her with every thrust.

She rolled with him, crying out with every hard pump, on the verge of orgasm as tears filled her eyes.

She reached down and circled her clit as he relentlessly filled her from behind. As her body shook and the orgasm crested, Terry pushed in deep, biting her shoulder, making her scream, but he didn't find his own release.

He leaned against her back, still hard inside her as she trembled and gripped him in delicious aftermath.

"I'm sorry if I hurt you," he murmured.

"You didn't, and we're not done."

He pulled away as she pushed off from the window, and turned to face him. As Mary stared down at his beautiful cock, naked and hard and glistening wet, she wanted more. She wanted him deep and slow. She wanted him to come inside her. She wanted to feel his control snap and make her his completely.

Terry cupped her face in his hands as he kissed her, tasted her; explored her with unrestrained hunger. He stepped out of his pant legs, she wrapped her arms around his neck; he picked her up to carry her to his bedroom.

With a gentleness she didn't think a rough man like Terry could have, he undressed her, taking the time to tease, tickle, and tweak. She melted, burned for him to take control of her body, as he'd done only twice before.

As he laid her on the bed, Mary knew this was it.

Nothing would be the same after this night.

A new tension simmered between them as he slid off his jacket, tossed it aside, and unbuttoned his crisp white shirt. Mary stared up at him with wonder as he peeled off the shirt, unveiling that furry chest she'd come to love.

"I never realized until I met you how much of a turn on chest hair can be," she said, her eyes drowsy in lust, cheeks rosy in embarrassment.

Terry chuckled. The muscles in his arms bulged as he chucked the shirt to the side. He stared at her with hunger and possession as he stripped. She stared back at him, but her gaze faltered and traveled down at the dangerous weapon hanging between his legs, before she looked back up into his eyes. What she saw there was a promise for much more than a hard and fast bang against a window.

"Sometimes I want to rub my face against your chest."

"Like a pussy cat?"

She grinned. "In heat."

She lifted her arms for him to come to her, and he knelt on the bed and laid down beside her, his lips finding hers for a long, passion-filled kiss. His hard, powerful body pressed against hers, desire flaring hot.

It couldn't get any better than this. And if it did, well, she'd probably explode.

Mary brushed her hand through the soft curls of his chest hair, lightly raking her fingernails down his rib cage to his navel. Then with a boldness more invigorating than ever before, she stroked his thick cock.

A low sound of pleasure rumbled in his chest while his tongue danced with hers.

With agonizing slowness, Terry peeled himself away from her and trailed his tongue over her chin and down to her chest. He took her taut nipple in his mouth and rolled it with his tongue, the sound of his sucking powerfully erotic, she gripped his hair and ground her hips against him.

Boldly, she reached down and stroked him.

"Fuck," he whispered, and bit into her nipple, while his hands slid down her hips.

No. I'm in control.

Mary shoved against his shoulder, pushed him onto his back, and straddled him.

With his mouth all over her breasts and his hands reaching round to cup her ass, grinding her over him, she wanted to shout her pleasure. Wanted to scream as he filled her deep.

She ground against him, hot and heavy, then reached down and guided his hard cock where she wanted him.

"Everything's different now," he moaned and sucked her nipple hard. "I'm not letting you leave. I'm not letting you go anywhere without me." His shoved his pelvis up, his hot, hard cock sliding torturously between her wet lips.

With a high whimper, Mary sank down, greedily taking him in deep.

She moaned and sighed and rode him slowly as he murmured hot words of passion and dazzled her with his lips and tongue. He touched her everywhere, his fingertips gripping; his palms rubbing her to madness.

He filled her. Stretched her. Made her want to come all over him.

This was the side of him she needed. The loving torture his body gave her. The real man behind the mask.

She bit her lip in exquisite pleasure as he nibbled on her nipples, biting and sucking while that wrenching, hot pressure of release drew near.

She lifted up high and slammed back down, bucking against him in raw ecstasy.

"Yes," she whimpered, and leaned down to kiss him. She felt the tremble, the hot surge gripping her.

Then suddenly she was flipped onto her back.

Mary moaned and feathered her fingers through his soft hair. She gripped him hard, holding him there as he teased and tweaked and bit her nipples. She'd been hurt in the past, but as she lay there beneath the solid weight of Terry's body, she knew without a doubt he wouldn't hurt her. He touched her as though she were the only sunshine in his dark life. As though she held the key to any shred of happiness he could grasp, and she wanted to make him happy. Wanted to make him love her.

Terry knew she was close. He pushed deeper, harder, and when he wrapped her legs around his shoulders and rolled her hips with him, Mary let go.

Wet heat trickled down her thighs as Terry continued pumping her.

Mary's mind became a hot mess of satisfaction as she trembled and whimpered, numb to everything but their bodies clinging together.

She closed her eyes and moaned as Terry released a rough moan and found his own shuddering climax.

"Yes."

Terry lay atop her, panting; she remained still, perfectly numb and content. She didn't think she could move even if she tried. After a few minutes she managed to roll to his side and put and arm and leg over him. He kissed her forehead and held her close.

Neither said a word.

They didn't need to talk. Not tonight. Right now she needed to feel him next to her, holding her, making her feel like she made the right choice. She fell asleep with her cheek to his chest, feeling more at home then she'd ever had before. Yet her dreams were plagued with visions of a masked killer, out to destroy everyone in his path.

Chapter 10

The cello resounded a beautiful solo through the Tail Wind Lounge, located off the lobby in the Sea Scape Hotel. Terry tapped his fingers on the table, in tune to the jazzy beat.

He loved the music almost as much as he loved his restaurant. The Tail Wind was decorated in a deep and luxurious navy blue with silver accents on everything. The hundred-plus mirrors adorning the walls reflected smiling faces, the glow from chandeliers, and shimmering crystal dancing off of each other. Everywhere you looked something glimmered and dazzled under the lights.

Terry sipped his drink while he waited for Mary and Wanda to join him for a quiet family dinner, remembering as a young boy how those many mirrors intrigued him. How could he look into one and see the side of his head in another? Or the back of his head from another one at the same time? The mystery and magic of those mirrors bedazzled him as a child. If his parents couldn't find him, everyone knew he'd be hiding in the lounge.

He chuckled and sipped his drink again. As an adult those mirrors were a great benefit. Nobody would dare stand up and try to surprise him from behind. He watched everything. He saw everything. He knew everything. His table had the best view.

Wanda strolled in first wearing a beautiful red gown with her dark wavy hair hanging loose off her shoulders. No wonder his father loved her instantly. She was gorgeous, and smart. He watched her discreetly as she graced their floor, the trail of her gown billowing behind her.

His stepmother smiled and nodded to a few regulars, as well as the staff, then took her seat opposite Terry on one of the plush high back chairs. "Hello, darling." She smiled wide, almost as if she had an excellent secret. "Wait until you see her."

He eyeballed the doorway but Mary wasn't there. "When is she coming?"

"Tsk, tsk, boy. Never question a woman's arrival."

Terry chuckled at his stepmother's haughty remark and lifted his hand to beckon their waiter. "Champagne, please, Johnathan."

A short moment later, Johnathan arrived with a cask of ice and set it on the table. "If I may, sir?" At Terry's nod, the young man poured two glasses for each of them and gently set the bottle of Krug Clos du Mesnil, a Côte d'Or Chardonnay, on ice.

"Everything is going well tonight, Johnathan?"

The young man nodded and smiled. "Absolutely, sir." He folded his hands in front of him, his stature stiff and sure. "I'll return when your lady arrives."

Not only was Johnathan the best waiter in this city—as far as Terry was concerned—he also took charge of the lounge. The Tail Wind ran smoothly at all times because of Johnathan's quick wit and charm, and Terry respected the man.

"He's such a good boy," Wanda said, staring after him.

Terry watched, amused as Wanda's eyes drifted to lower places as she watched him walk away. A hint of color touched her cheeks before she turned her attention back to her stepson and smiled.

"How is it that you treat your staff so well? You're polite to them. How do they do their job with such efficiency when you're soft on them?"

Terry pursed his lips to halt his laughter as Wanda stared at him with wide, incredulous eyes, as if treating people fairly seemed foreign. "I believe in treating *my* employees with respect, and paying good wages, they in return do their job well. In that circle, my guests are happy, and I'm happy."

Wanda sighed deeply. "Your father wasn't like that."

His good mood dimmed slightly. He knew his father could be tough, but hearing her say it aloud made him shift in his seat. "Dad wasn't always easy, especially on me."

She leaned closer, elbows on table, hands clasped together. If her dark eyes could slice open an already festering wound, they looked at him like that right now. "I always wanted to do something. Something more for the business, but Colton never let me." She leaned back, her chin lower, lips pouting, the expression on her face softened almost instantly. "He wasn't always nice to me."

Terry reached across the table and patted her forearm, hearing these words for the first time. He hadn't realized until now that maybe his father had been hard on more people than just his son. But why would she tell him now? His father was dead, and he couldn't turn back time. "I'm sorry." He truly meant it. "But what would you want me to do? Everything is taken care of, as it always has been."

"But I can do many things. I know people—"

Terry's gaze drifted to the doorway, and his mind went blank.

He blinked, not quite believing who stood there looking like a flower rising in the desert, surrounded by cacti.

Terry didn't even feel Wanda pull her arm away as he stared in complete shock and awe at the beauty walking toward their table.

Her hair was piled high with a few ringlets framing her face. Silver earrings shimmered under the lights. A frothy white gown, tied around her neck and tapered down, barely covered her pert breasts and flowed like water down to her heeled feet.

He pushed up from his chair and pulled out hers. "Wow," was all he managed to say as Mary gracefully took her seat. *Holy flying fuck.*

"Thank you."

Johnathan arrived within seconds of Mary taking her seat. Terry had a hard time containing his disappointment that he couldn't comment more on her beauty before the goddamned waiter arrived. He sat in pouting silence as the girls fussed over each other like a couple of hens.

"Champagne, Mrs. Billings?"

And that fucking name.

Mary glanced at Terry, an odd expression on her beautiful face, before she looked back up at Johnathan. "Please, call me Miss Lector."

Terry shoved forward, suddenly interested to speak. "Lector? As in the serial killer from those movies?"

Wanda gasped in outrage and Mary chuckled. "Sorry to disappoint you, but I'm not one in the same. Lector is my maiden name. My new driver's license, health card, and other documents arrived two days before I came here. Right in the nick of time. I'm officially a Lector again. It feels good." Her smile was simply stunning.

Terry pushed his seat back. "Excuse me for a minute, ladies. I need to make a quick call." He walked away from the table, heart pounding, as he pulled his cell out of his pocket and dialed her number.

He held his breath as the answering machine kicked in.

"Hi. You've reached Mary Lector. I'm out at the moment, but please leave a message and I'll get back to you when I can. If this is a wildlife emergency please notify the ministry immediately. Thank you."

Terry returned to the table, smiling like a man who just received the best blowjob ever. He took his seat and listened in as Wanda asked Mary a few personal questions.

"Tell me about your family, sweetheart."

Mary fidgeted with her napkin, a sign he knew she must be nervous. "Well, let's see. I'm an only child. My parents divorced when I was a teenager, and Mom moved to Florida for the weather."

Wanda smiled in wonder. "Florida is beautiful. I especially love the beaches in Miami. And your father, did he stay in this...Sliver Point?"

The troubled expression on Mary's face worried Terry, as well as her stiff body language. Her father must be a sore spot, as Terry's was for him.

But like a trooper, Mary lifted her chin slightly. "Silver Creek, not Sliver Point. And yes, my father is there."

"How is he? What is he like?" Wanda asked, totally unaware that her questions were quickly becoming too much for Mary. Terry was about to put a stop to it, but Mary reached under the table and put her hand on his knee.

"He lives deep in the bush away from any human contact. I haven't seen him since I was a young girl." She cleared her throat and took a healthy sip of champagne before she continued. "He lost his marbles after Nam."

Terry stared hard at Mary. He had no idea about her family life. Why hadn't he asked her these things before? He was so caught up in wanting to take her to bed, he never considered finding out about these important facts about her life. He felt like an asshole. A horny dog who couldn't see beyond taking her clothes off.

Wanda seemed bent on getting to the bottom of the woman who'd captured Terry's interest. "Ah, I see. Your mother left when he went crazy?"

"Wanda, that's enough," Terry warned. "This is supposed to be a nice family dinner, not an interrogation."

"It's okay." Mary squeezed his knee, and turned back to Wanda. "No, she didn't leave him then. The voices didn't get really bad until the eighties, shortly after I was born. One random fall day he took his rifle and we never saw him again. My mother may as well have been a widow all those years. As much as I love my dad, I will never try to find him. His only peace is quiet, and I respect that."

Terry took a deep breath and stared at Mary with new eyes. Even though she'd lived a rugged lifestyle, he thought her upbringing must have been relatively easy. Who would've guessed small town life wasn't a stroll in the park? Now he knew better. Now he understood her more.

"My mother was granted a divorce several years after his abandonment. But enough about me." Mary pulled her hand away from his knee. "Tell me about your family, Wanda."

Terry's lip twitched in amusement as Mary put her elbows on the table and rested her chin on her fist. The view from his seat was simply stunning, and cute all at once. He imagined she felt awkward as hell, sitting there in a five star restaurant, wearing a beautiful gown and high heels, in the company of powerful, and very rich people.

And she was a trapper.

A mountain woman.

His little minx who shot a beaver in the back of the head.

For the first time in a long time, Terry felt at ease. He settled back in his chair, content to simply watch her, not really listening to Wanda's story. He casually sipped his champagne, enjoying the atmosphere and the company. Despite the depressing turn of events, he sorely needed a nice, quiet night with the people he loved.

". . . difficult for young women . . . most of my brothers are gone . . . many poor people in my country."

He frowned and sat straighter. "I thought you were from Los Angeles."

"I am, darling." She winked. "But I wasn't always a rich girl."

Terry settled back in his seat again, watching in silence until their dinner arrived. He never realized Wanda lived a poor life in her younger years. As far as he knew, she was a spoiled rich girl who knew his mother from back in the day. Now that he thought about it, he didn't know much about Wanda at all, or that she once had brothers.

His stepmother had always treated him like her own son, and no matter what fell into her lap in this crazy family life of theirs, she always held her head high and made him feel loved. But hearing her speak of a past he knew nothing about alerted him to the fact that maybe Wanda wasn't who she claimed to be.

Why bring these details out now?

He had always been overworked and overtired to pay much attention to his father's second wife, or anything that had nothing to do with business.

As dinner was served, he quietly contemplated digging up her background, but shook off the notion. Wanda was a good woman and loved Colton very much. If not for her his father would've died of loneliness after his mother passed away.

Wanda was the string holding them all together.

As they finished dinner and Wanda took her leave to return home, Terry ushered Mary back upstairs and made urgent love to her on the couch, with that sexy dress shoved up around her neck.

* * * *

Thick clouds blanketed the sky with the sun peeping out now and then as Mary ventured down the hotel steps and headed toward The Bay Centre around the corner. After leafing through several guides Terry left for her to browse, she'd discovered that Victoria had some of the best shopping around. The Centre covered an entire city block with over ninety street front shops and many more inside.

As much as she wanted a walk along the water she also craved an entire day spoiling herself in these shops. When she finally had the nerve to count the money Gabe had given her, she was overwhelmed and flattered that he'd handed over ten-thousand dollars to her for doing absolutely nothing. Would she ever get used to that much money kicking around? Even Gabe had acted as if that much coin meant nothing at all.

Still, she couldn't help her excited grin at finally being able to do something she'd never experienced before—real shopping.

Maybe later she'd take a stroll through the market since Terry's fridge was filled with beer and a few plates from the restaurant, wrapped in foil. He clearly needed proper food instead of constant room service or takeout from a fast food joint.

The sidewalk teamed with locals and tourists. Half the people who passed her by had cameras at the ready, and all smiles. She couldn't help one of her own as a pudgy little boy with chocolate smeared all over his face, ran up to his mommy and yanked at her skirt.

"When do we get to see the killer wales, Mum?"

"Maybe you should be watching the water instead of packing in all that sugar," the mother said, and rustled his white-blond hair.

Mary stared at the little boy and imagined a younger Terry.

He was an innocent boy at one time too. When did everything change?

She contemplated this as she continued onward, wishing Terry could join her instead of all these meetings he had to attend.

She'd left home to be with him, only to be alone anyway. But she didn't let that cloud her mind. She was in a new world, free to enjoy the scenery unlike her own back home. Besides, he'd lost his father and inherited an empire. She understood he had business to tend to. She just needed to keep busy as well until he could spend more time with her.

She passed a cart filled with freshly caught fish. She chatted briefly with the owner of the booth and decided on the way back to Terry's apartment she'd purchase a salmon for dinner.

Mary was overwhelmed by the constant hustle and bustle around her. From fresh food to jewelry to every style of art. Carvings, crafts, clothing, music in the streets, you name it, and she hadn't even reached the mall yet.

She weaved around people, lost amidst the crowd, before she saw a familiar face dashing across the street. A handsome face she'd never forget.

Not having anyone else to chat with she picked up her pace and followed him. What harm could come from asking him to join her for coffee?

He moved stealthily through the crowd, his crisp black suit stark amidst the colorful tones of everyone else. Mary almost had to run to catch up to him as he disappeared between two buildings.

She reached the narrow walkway between two shops and paused.

Maybe I shouldn't follow him back there if he's on a secret mission.

She hesitated, then looked back at the crowd. Many people filled the streets, but nobody paid any mind to a young woman who had no clue what she was doing or where she was going. Still, if something happened a scream would bring everybody around.

And she was curious.

She took a deep breath, squared her shoulders, and stepped into the walkway. The back of his suit disappeared from view around another corner. Heart pounding, yet anxious to see what he was doing, she picked up her pace again.

Voices and music filled the air. The distant sound of a boat along the water blended happily with everything else. It was a beautiful day despite the clouds, not too hot, the breeze rustled her hair. She gasped as a flock of starlings suddenly burst into the shaft of sky between the two buildings. In a tight formation they soared above the buildings, zigzagging like a black cloud across the sky.

Mary shielded her eyes and watched, fascinated by their skyward dance and smiled at the beautiful view.

But as she stepped out into a small parkway behind the buildings, she froze. The smile on her face faltered, her eyes grew wide in disbelief.

There, with arms and lips locked passionately together, stood Wanda McCoy and Sammy Hayes.

Mary shifted back closer to the wall, stunned by the intense and highly inappropriate scene before her. Her mind raced a mile a minute. They hadn't noticed her. They probably didn't notice anything, entranced as they

NEVER GIVE YOU UP   121

were in each other. To Mary it seemed they only had eyes for each other, as if they'd been lovers for many months, or maybe even many years.

Embarrassed, and a little worried, Mary slunk back around the corner of the wall and rested her back against it. She closed her eyes and breathed deeply. She should call Terry right away with the news. She should burst around the corner and scream that she'd seen them.

But she didn't.

Instead, she walked back the way she came and went straight back to the penthouse, her day of shopping completely forgotten.

* * * *

She had always been a jeans and t-shirt kind of gal.

Tonight she chose comfort with a touch of sexy in a white tank top and black jeans, with roman-looking sandals. She kept staring down at her glowing tank top as they all sat beneath the black lights in Terry's favorite club the following night.

Apparently this place was another business the main business owned and operated. Numerous well-dressed people came up to the table to talk to him, whisper dark secrets in his ear. He was kind to all of them, and only denied a few who seemed messed up on something. Those people were hauled away by the bouncer and chucked outside.

Mary felt overwhelmed by the attention, even though none of it was directed toward her. She sat right beside the big boss, and she felt so out of place she had no clue what to do with herself, for more reasons than one.

This was not her world. She was just a guest. What she had to say probably didn't matter, even if Terry always tried to make her comfortable. How could she tell him what she saw? Would he believe her? Should she stay out of it?

Keep your nose out of it. Maybe Wanda reached out to Sammy in her grief. She knew what that felt like, needing a warm embrace. Needing a strong man. What business was it of hers that Colton had been murdered only a couple of weeks ago? Still, it seemed wrong that Wanda would have a relationship with one of Terry's close friends.

She sucked in a calming breath, leaned over and whispered, "Are you going to give me a tour in town? I'd like to see some attractions…if you have time."

Terry smiled and rubbed her hip, holding her close against him. "What would you like to see? What interests you?"

"Killer whales. I've never seen one up close and personal. And museums. Castles. Are there any castles around here?"

Terry chuckled. "Slow down. You can see all of that. Whales and sea lions at Fisherman's Wharf. Craigdarroch Castle. The Maritime Museum, among numerous other things. Don't worry, honey, you'll get your fill of everything. But right now. . . ."

He stood up and offered his hand, his eyes twinkled danger under the black light.

Mary reluctantly put her hand in his. "What?"

"I want to dance with you, that's what."

"I-I don't—" She stood up, trembling, feeling all eyes on her as Terry led her to the dance floor.

"Don't worry. I'll take care of you," he murmured for her ears only, and wrapped her up in his arms.

She didn't even notice the music had changed from funky hip-hop to a slow song as she easily fell into step with him. She'd never danced with Tom before. He never took her out on the town. Only when she was young did she ever let loose on the dance floor.

Terry smelled of spicy cologne as she rested her cheek to his chest. She closed her eyes, enveloped in his powerful arms and confident stride. Nobody else existed as they swayed and turned and clung to each other.

His hand curved around her back to nestle just above her bum. She felt the heat of him through her clothing, felt the steady thrum of his heartbeat against her cheek.

She needed this. Needed to know that he wasn't embarrassed to bring her out here like this, a country girl completely lost in the city nightlife.

He made her feel like she belonged.

When the song ended and he led her back to their seat, only then did she realize how different she was from the other girls. Their slow dance lasted only a few minutes, and once again she felt out of place, as if somebody simply flipped a switch.

She felt like a ragamuffin around the young women wearing tight dresses barely covering their breasts and skirts revealing too much ass cheek. She had to admit they were gorgeous: curves in all the right places; hair dyed and cut in the latest fashion; long colorful fingernails.

Mary stared at her own hands and frowned. They were dry and her nails needed a serious filing.

What the hell did Terry see in her? She glanced at him discreetly, and felt a gut-punch as his eyes followed the other girls on the dance floor. She followed his gaze and stared at the women.

It was painful to watch as they jiggled and grinded on the dance floor, the music once again back to its fast pace. Many of the girls switched from one man to another, apparently eager to take any one of them home for the night, or perhaps they shared each other.

What ever happened to being content with one man?

"Don't be jealous, Mary. You're more tempting than they are," Terry said in her ear as he lightly stroked her hip.

She blushed, looked away from the girls and lifted the cocktail to her lips. Thank God for the dim lighting as the patrons basically had sex on the dance floor with their clothes on. She didn't want to be caught watching, but she couldn't help herself either. The fact that Terry had seen her staring was bad enough. Now she felt even worse.

Back in Silver Creek they had a couple of small pubs, country music or classic rock ruled the radio, and women dressed respectably. They didn't grind their box or shake their ass, leaving nothing to the imagination, and if they did they were labeled a slut and would never live it down. Silver Creek had a few of them, as every town did.

Mary took in the club and its people from her seat beside Terry, Gabe, Sam, and a few others at the VIP booth. She tried not to stare at Sam and give away her secret as the cocktails went down like water and her buzz grew rapidly by the minute. As much as she wanted to dance to a fast song, she didn't think she'd look sexy out there. With her luck she'd be the one to fall and she wasn't even wearing high heels.

"Excuse me. I need to use the can—I mean—ladies room," she said, squeezing between Terry and the table. As she passed him, Terry planted a hand on her ass cheek and winked when she looked down in surprise.

As she made her way toward the restrooms, she noticed a man watching her from the shadows. He appeared to only have eyes for her, even though another woman stood at his arm. Mary lifted her chin and paid him no mind.

While in the stall, a group of women walked into the bathroom.

"See that broad with Terry? She looks so plain my grandmother could pick up faster than she could."

"I know. I'm disgusted with him right now. I know what he likes, and that's not what he likes."

Mary's heart pounded, but she remained silent.

"He probably feels sorry for her. Last time he took me out I wore my best and tightest and he still took it off me in less than thirty seconds." The women laughed. Mary's knuckles tightened. "She looks like a nervous hillbilly."

"She probably wouldn't know what to do with him anyway. Maybe she's a virgin and he's just testing her out."

"Don't be jealous, Louisa. You're better and sexier than she will ever be. He'll go back to you once he's finished with his pity fuck. You know he will."

Mary heard enough. She flushed the toilet and stepped out of the stall. When the girls saw her they all shut their mouths, eyes wide. They were city girls, like Terry was a city boy at heart.

Her composure faltered. Maybe she had been wrong to think he really cared for her, and that he was happy she came here to be with him. Perhaps she didn't really know him at all.

But those girls didn't chop wood every day. They didn't care for a horse and seven dogs either. She probably had more muscle than all of them combined, and she was proud of herself for being in solid shape. Yet her heart sank thinking that maybe they were right about Terry.

Mary leaned over the sink with all the confidence she had and washed her hands quickly. She had no use to plaster on more makeup. Once she dried her hands then walked to the door, she said over her shoulder, "I'm sorry. I didn't realize looking like a cheap hooker was sexy."

She walked out the door of the restroom and found the nearest exit. What she really needed was to get away from his type of crowd and get some fresh air. She didn't care if Terry didn't know where she had disappeared to, she knew how to hail a cab and find the Sea Scape on her own. She wasn't that much of a hillbilly idiot.

If they were the kind of women he preferred then maybe she should go home and forget about her feelings. Shut herself off from the world. Get lost on the trapline and become like her father. Right at this moment she had more doubts than ever before.

Why did I come here? Does Terry even want me here?

She shoved through the side exit and breathed a sigh of relief. But when the heavy metal door slammed shut behind her and locked her out, she realized with a cold clinch of dread, the door had led her out to a dark alley running parallel with the building.

The stench of piss and garbage hit her forcefully, nearly making her vomit. She covered her mouth and headed toward what looked like a main street up ahead at the front of the club, where the light was brighter.

Club music pounded inside the old brick building as she made her way toward the street.

A glass bottle smashed somewhere behind her, followed by a faint rustling sound. With her heart pounding and nerves jumping, she spun around. Nothing but a garbage bin and a street light beyond the darkness were in view. Taking a shaky breath, she turned back toward the street and continued, holding her purse tight.

She should've stayed in the club. No matter how upset those girls made her, this situation was much worse. Anything could happen out here.

Right at that moment two men walked into the light at the main street, a few yards ahead of her. She paused when they paused. They stared at her with a gleam in their eyes that would make any sane woman want to run. Facing a grizzly bear would be easier for Mary then what the look on their faces meant.

"Perfect timing. We were wondering when you'd show up."

Mary sucked in a sharp breath, her heart pounding. She looked behind her, terrified there were others with them, but still only darkness and that one street lamp was behind her.

If anything she'd read in the papers about city life should be believed, then being alone in an alley with two strange men staring at her was the worst possible place to be.

The men stepped into the alley and inched their way closer. One of them was the guy she saw standing by the washrooms.

She clutched her purse. "W-what do you want from me? I don't have any money."

The other one chuckled. "We don't want your money, honey. But you're coming with us."

Mary took a step back. They stepped forward.

Having no other options, she spun around and ran back toward the side door she had exited, screaming at the top of her lungs.

She heard them behind her, so close they would reach her any second now. But she refused to give up. Just as she reached the streetlight, somebody's hand grabbed her shoulder and viciously yanked her back.

Both of them grabbed her arms preventing her escape. She screamed and kicked, trying to break free, but she wasn't strong enough. As they tried to pull her back into the darkness beyond the streetlight and the club side door, Mary heard Terry's voice.

She pushed against one of the men and saw the club door held open and Terry looking outside. "Mary, are you out here?"

"Over here," she screamed, before a hand clamped over her mouth.

His face turned toward her voice, and when he saw the two men holding her down, he immediately ran toward them. The club door slammed shut behind him. "Get your fucking hands off her."

While one man held her back, the other charged at Terry. She held her breath as Terry was blinded by the sudden light of the street lamp and took a hard shot to his jaw. He stumbled back, but shook it off and managed to block a second punch. He grabbed the man's arm, twisting it hard behind his back. A bloodcurdling scream echoed through the alley as Terry yanked his arm out and jabbed his hand up under his elbow.

Mary cringed at the disgusting sound of bone snapping. She watched, stunned by Terry's quick moves and his strength.

As the guy stumbled back, crying, and holding his arm, Terry smashed his fist into his face and shoved him to the ground. The guy jumped back up, his face white as a sheet, and took off without looking back.

Terry turned around, shifting his gaze to the man holding Mary.

"Stop right there." Her captor pulled out a knife and Terry halted.

He lifted his hands. "Okay. Okay. Let her go and we'll forget about this."

Mary whimpered as the man lifted the knife and pointed the tip to her throat.

"Oh, there's no forgetting, Terry McCoy. This is just the beginning."

Terry's eyes narrowed. "What did you say?"

The club door burst open again. This time Gabe and Sam hurried out. Obviously the boss had been gone too long.

"Stay back!" The knife pinched her skin. Wet heat slithered down her neck as he pulled her back with a rough jerk.

Gabe and Sam made their way closer despite his warning. Mary knew she had to try and do something. It didn't matter if it was three against one. He had a knife to her throat and she knew, without a doubt, that he would use it.

She shut her eyes tight and hoped to God she would make it through this. As fast and as hard as she could, Mary jammed her foot down on the toe of his shoe. The knife slit along her throat as he stumbled back. But before he could grab onto her again, Mary threw herself onto the ground and watched in horror as Terry lunged at him.

"Be careful," she shouted, terrified he'd be stabbed trying to save her.

Gabe and Sam rushed up and helped her to her feet as Terry danced around the man with the knife, narrowly escaping the sharp blade.

Mary clutched her neck to stop the blood flow. Already she felt weak in the knees and faint.

The bloody knife sliced through the air. Terry jumped back, moving his head to the side as it slit through the air an inch away from his cheek and eye. As the man rushed forward, Terry gave him an uppercut and sent him flying backwards. He hit the ground hard. The knife flew out of his hand, landing near Terry's feet.

The raw animal hatred in Terry's face scared her, but Mary knew he wasn't a monster. He was doing what he had to do, and he had to protect her. Hope swelled in her heart. She grabbed Gabe's arms and held onto him tight, unsure of her trust in Sam, as Terry picked up the knife and walked over to the other guy.

Blood seeped out of his nose. He crawled back and lifted his hands in defeat. "Please. Please don't kill me. I was just doing what I was told. I swear."

Terry set one booted foot onto his ribs and put his weight on the guy's chest. He rested one elbow on his knee and held the knife in his other hand. "And what were you told to do?"

The man whimpered like a scared little boy. "If you promise not to hurt me, I swear I will tell you."

"Okay. I won't hurt you."

"It was Montesano," he blurted. "We were hired to kidnap your girl. That's it, I promise. Please, let me go. You'll never see me again."

Terry glanced over to Gabe and Sam and gave a single nod before he turned back to the guy beneath him.

"You're right. I won't."

Mary shook as Gabe turned her around, held her close, and guided her back to the club.

"You promised!" She heard him scream.

Mary released a startled cry when she heard the man beg, "Please!" His next words abruptly ended.

* * * *

Terry eyed the four men surrounding him in the study. Their first official meeting since Colton's death was somber but necessary. They needed to form a plan and end this bullshit before Mary or somebody else gets killed.

Terry, for one, was already doing his part, and he hated every minute of it.

He strummed his fingers on his father's huge and highly polished mahogany desk. One of the few things that survived his tirade when he first returned home. Broken bookshelves, shattered glass, and scattered books still remained, along with a few broken pictures of Colton McCoy in his younger days and various business acquaintances. The only picture which remained untouched, unmarred, was a picture of Terry's mother. She was the only whole piece in a room of broken promises and dreams. For now this room was off limits to housekeeping.

Terry probably looked like he hadn't slept in days, and it sure felt that way. Every night he had been plagued by dreams of how his father was strangled to death and of his faceless killer. No matter how hard or soft or how swift or slow he made love to Mary, he still couldn't get a decent sleep.

"How's Mary?" Gabe asked.

"Shaken, but okay. She's not to go anywhere by herself until this mess is cleaned up."

Everybody nodded in agreement.

Having everyone gathered around the famous McCoy desk while he made decisions, brought back many memories for Terry. Memories they all had in their own way. More times than he cared to count they'd held meetings here—some good, some bad. Now it was Terry's turn to run the show. He knew he could handle it, but from the beginning he never wanted this life.

"So we know the Montesano family is behind this. I suspected as much, but I'm confused why the old man would risk a war between us. He may have more money, but we have more reach. Adolfo's death was strictly business, and he knows that. Is there another family member we don't know about? A cousin, a brother?" Terry ran a hand through his hair. He wanted to walk away right now. "Whoever this other person is could be in the goddamned house for all we know."

John Covington, the moneyman, glanced up from his notes. "I'll look through the records today, Terry. See if I can make a connection somewhere."

"Considering how Colton was killed, right here in the house, it has to be somebody from the inside," Gabe added. "Somebody who knows where we are at all times, and how to get around without being noticed."

Buck Johnson, the estate manager, shrugged. "I haven't seen anything out of sorts. The usual people have come and gone. The housekeeper does her job as usual from nine to five. Wanda sleeps all morning and shops all day. I'm as confused as everyone else."

John looked at Terry directly. "Your father discovered some information recently, but as far as I know he hadn't yet told anyone. It was good enough reason to consider changing his will."

That got everyone's attention. "Change his will? Do you know why?" Terry asked.

John shook his head. "I'm not his lawyer, just the bookkeeper, and his longtime friend."

Terry nodded although inside his hackles were screaming. His father hadn't mentioned at all wanting to change his will. "I guess we'll have to find that out ourselves, or maybe we'll never know." He paused. "What about the housekeeper? Does anybody know anything about Cassandra?"

"Wanda hired her over a year ago. She was recommended by a family friend." Buck chuckled. "Your father took a real shining to her, and especially the escort Taffy."

Terry shook his head in disgust. "Really? I don't think I want to know any more." How could his father do that to Wanda? After all these years of her taking care of him, he had the nerve to sleep with other women. Did he cheat on his mother, too?

Sam cleared his throat and spoke up. "Taffy was already found dead by a single stab wound to the chest. Her death came across as most others would in her edgy field of work—according to our police sources."

Terry shook his head, feeling more weight on his already-taxed shoulders. "Jesus Christ. As far as I'm concerned, everyone is a suspect around here," he concluded.

Sam shifted his gaze around and Terry watched him sharply. He should've informed him immediately about this Taffy broad and what role she had played. As far as Terry was concerned, his men should tell him every goddamned thing.

"Make sure my stepmother is safe, Sam. I don't want anything to happen to her, especially since Mary has already been attacked. Both of them have been through enough already."

Sam nodded. "I'll keep an eye on her. No worries."

"Where were you when Dad was killed?"

Terry's fingers rapped on the desk, echoing through the room like a ticking bomb.

Sam shifted on his feet. He looked very uncomfortable. "I was sent on a job. You'll have to trust I'm doing it right, like I always have."

Terry sighed heavily and rubbed his forehead. "Okay, Sam. I'm sorry." Fuck he felt beyond tired and disoriented. Sam had always been his dear friend. He'd never betray his trust.

Sam cleared his throat, his gaze burning into the closed study door. Terry knew he was itching to leave and he felt a sharp and sudden sense of foreboding. He eyed him sharply. Something wasn't right with his longtime friend.

"You guys go ahead and finish this meeting without me. I have shit to do." Sam left the room, unaware of all the suspicious eyes trained on his back.

Terry and Gabe shared a glance, and he knew he was right to be suspicious.

Chapter 11

The Montesano's ranch spanned across a small valley in Southern California, although Terry knew the family had emigrated from Columbia over thirty years ago.

Terry and Gabe set down on the private airstrip south of the ranch, ready to put an end to this rivalry. Having met the old man, a long time business acquaintance and friend of his father's, Terry was sure Antonio Montesano would listen to reason.

Although he didn't have it planned out perfectly, Terry was willing to risk his life to make a deal with the old man. If he didn't call off his tirade, then they would kill everyone in his family and burn this ranch down.

He was here to talk, but ready for a fight.

Terry pulled the rental car up to the guard house and chatted with the armed man keeping post. He knew he was entering dangerous territory, but he had no other choice.

Adolfo's death wasn't personal. It was business.

Once he was approved entry, Terry drove past the armed guard and up the long driveway toward the main house. He glanced through the rearview mirror and blew a sigh of relief as Gabe took out the guard and continued on foot.

Gabe had strict orders that if anything went wrong, he was to burn this place down with everyone in it, whether Terry got out or not. Gabe almost punched him in the mouth when Terry had given the order, but when it came down to the safety of Mary and Mima, Terry's death would be worth it. He didn't want to leave her, but he wouldn't risk her life for his. He wouldn't let her die for his father's business, because Mary was worth far more than any amount of money.

He pulled up to the house, parked the car and patiently waited as another man checked him for weapons. When they found him clean, a man led him into the massive mansion, straight to a private sitting room.

He paused on the threshold, took a deep breath, and stepped inside the lion's den.

Antonio Montesano turned from his liquor cabinet, his dark eyes emotionless, his expression passive, as he glanced at Terry.

"You have grown much since last we spoke, young man."

Terry swallowed, nervous and a little scared to be in the same room with such a powerful man, but he wouldn't let him see it. "And you look healthy, Tony."

"Thank you. My wife insists I drink vegetable shakes every morning. They taste like goat shit, but I feel good. She enjoys my vigor in the privacy of our bedchamber. Once again she's expecting my child." Antonio filled two glasses and gestured for Terry to take a seat.

Terry couldn't believe the old man's boys still worked. "Congrats."

Once again his thoughts drifted to Mary, particularly her believing she was barren without having it confirmed by a doctor. Terry would bet his left nut her husband was to blame but felt the need to blame her anyway. That must be hard for her to bear when she was still so young and Antonio should be kicking up dirt.

He accepted a glass of brandy, Antonio's favorite, and tried to focus on the Spanish kingpin—not Mary's sweet face and aching heart.

Antonio Montesano was pushing eighty and you'd never know it. Only a few streaks of white highlighted his jet-black hair, framing a tawny face with few wrinkles around his calculating eyes. To a stranger he could be fifty.

Terry looked away from Antonio and glanced around the room, nearly blinded by the endless glint of gold on every surface. Gold statues and figurines. Gold-leafed ceilings and walls. Old paintings framed in gold. This family was ten times richer than he could ever hope to be. Even the rim of his glass was tipped in gold.

"You took my son away from me, Terry. Consider yourself lucky you're not already dead."

Terry took a sip, needing the alcohol. He knew he would be safe in this room despite his nerves and the armed guards all over the property. One thing his father taught him that he'd never forget—a true businessman would never harm another while making a good deal. "He tried to kill me." Terry rolled his shoulder, feeling the usual nasty ache as he said the words. "Three inches lower and you would've had a war on your hands."

Antonio nodded. "Yes. Your man, Hayes, said as much."

Terry frowned. *Sammy?* "You've spoken to Hayes recently?"

"Oh, yes. Your father sent him here to make a new deal." He looked thoughtful for a moment. "But I was confused why he would ask about my children."

Children. "I thought you had one son."

Antonio smiled. "I'm a Spaniard, and I've had three wives, Terry."

His eyes held a gleam that made Terry nervous. He cleared his throat, determined to stay focused. Whatever his father had sent Sam here for, could be the key to something big. "I would like to propose a deal I'm sure you don't want to refuse. I'll make you even richer than you already are."

Antonio's dark eyebrow shot up. "Oh?" He sat forward, elbows on knees, curiosity in his eyes. "This deal will make me feel better about Adolfo?"

Terry cleared his throat. "Your son disrupted business and tried to steal from me. Now my father is dead as well, and my woman was attacked."

Antonio shrugged, and lounged back in his chair. The conversation obviously bored him. "Business is business. What do you propose?"

Terry took back the rest of his drink and set the glass down on the mahogany side table. He stared at Adolfo's ring on Antonio's baby finger. "A recent scuffle landed some information that you are behind these threats. I want you to call off this crazy mission and put a stop to this rivalry. Nobody else needs to die."

Antonio frowned. "As much as I would take the credit, I didn't make that call. As much as I loved my son, his greed is what killed him. I am a man of business, and I would never risk that for anything."

Terry's heart lurched as Antonio looked away, his expression immobile. To Terry, it felt as though the kingpin was ready to end the conversation. "If you didn't make the order, then someone did under your name. Nobody blurts out a lie when they're about to die."

Antonio's eyes narrowed as he returned his attention to Terry. "I see. Yes, you're right." He lounged back and clasped his hands over his knee. "Then I must tell you, all I have left is one young son in grade school by my current wife, and an older daughter from my first wife. She's very beautiful, and highly intelligent. If it is she using my family name, then she will pay the hardest price. In her dishonor from the past, I have washed my hands of her."

An older daughter from his first wife. Fuck.

"Now tell me of this wonderful proposal before I lose my patience."

It took every ounce of his control to keep his expression blank while he fought to come up with a decent plan. He didn't expect another child, especially not an older daughter. All along he thought a man killed his father. But a woman could sneak around easily. The housekeepers, his stepmother's friends, even his own female staff at the hotel could've walked right into the house and never be questioned.

He nearly jumped out of his chair as a crazy thought entered his mind. With his heart about to burst through his chest, Terry looked him square in the eyes and didn't bat a lash. "In exchange for your compliance and your partnership, I'll give you my Bolivia connection."

That got Antonio's attention.

The old man sat forward again, his expression full of surprise. Terry knew his mind was going a mile a minute. His Bolivian manufacturer had the best product. Nobody could beat it, and Antonio knew that, as Adolfo did. Only Terry and his father knew the location of his maker, and that secret would never get out—not while Terry lived.

He didn't give two shits to keep Bolivia or not. After all, he never wanted this life. He was forced into it. Now he had other plans. Nobody could tell him what to do anymore.

"Tell me the name of your daughter and I will send her home without harm. You have my word." He held his breath as Antonio considered the request.

They sat in silence for a long while. Terry sat with as much patience as a dog with a bone sitting atop his snout. He just wanted to go home and be with Mary. He wanted to offer her the world. But he needed answers more than anything.

Antonio stood up, retrieved Terry's empty glass and proceeded to pour them another drink.

"Daniella disgraced me when she got with child out of wedlock, and then she aborted my grandchild. I haven't spoken to her in many years. I will never speak her name in this house again. She didn't know her place." His smile seemed forced. "But, you have a deal, Terry. I will find her and bring her home on my own terms. No other harm will come to your family. You have my word as a gentleman."

As they shook hands and clinked glasses—a promise between men—Terry knew he'd be calling upon Antonio very soon.

* * * *

With a big stretch, Mary sat up in Terry's enormous bed and stared at her surroundings. The sun shone high in the east, blaring bright through the floor to ceiling windows in Terry's bedroom.

One week had passed since those men tried to abduct her. She touched the scab on her throat, thankful the cut hadn't been deep enough to need stitches. What a terrifying night. But what a rush to watch Terry beat the hell out of those guys. If he wouldn't have suspected something was up and wondered why she'd taken so long in the washroom, who knows what could've happened. They would've kidnapped her, and then what? Rape or murder, or both?

She didn't want to think about it. She only wanted to imagine how she could help Terry achieve what he really wanted. The kind of life that didn't require looking over his shoulder every minute, or having to kill people when she knew he didn't want to do that.

When Terry burst through the club door, he'd changed everything. He'd taken away her doubts about those women and what he truly wanted. The fact that he worried about where she was spoke more than any words. She had seen the terrified look in his eyes as those men pulled her further into the alley. And she'd seen the fury as well as Terry came after them like a feral beast, without a thought to his own safety.

He was her savior. Her criminal angel.

She sighed deeply and sunk back against the pillows, a content smile crossing her face.

I'm in love with a crime boss.

Chuckling at herself, she whipped her legs over the side of the bed, grabbed her new silk robe, and headed to the window.

She had become the lover of a criminal. Not long ago she lived a simple life in the wilderness. Every day consisted of feeding the animals, routine runs to keep up their exercise, household chores, and taking care of nuisance beaver. Mucking out Blue's stall and hauling hay every day had been a chore in itself, sometimes more consuming than taking care of hundreds of pelts.

Now she was being cared for like a princess while Mima took care of her homestead. She felt guilty, but at the same time she didn't want to go back. Not yet.

It almost felt as though she was a traitor to herself for enjoying this pampering. Was it such a bad thing to enjoy being wined and dined and having Terry open doors for her, or slip her coat over her shoulders before he kissed her cheek? Did this change in her physical life mean she'd changed as a person too?

Her steps faltered as a sudden wave of nausea filled her stomach. Her cheeks heated as she rubbed her upset stomach. Before she could get back to the bed and rest a moment, get her wits about her, her eyes widened as she realized she needed the toilet not the bed.

In a panic, she burst into the en suite just in time to be sick.

A short while later, after washing up and drinking a glass of water, Mary managed to drag herself to the kitchen, her stomach empty and rumbling for food. But somehow this morning everything smelled disgusting. She decided on toast and managed to keep a few bites down even though it tasted like cardboard.

That's when it hit her.

She was late.

Oh, God.

Happiness and dread filled her all at once. Could this really be possible? She'd been too preoccupied with Terry lately that she didn't even notice the change in her body. Sore, fuller breasts, queasy stomach, lack of or massive appetite. The urge to puke whenever she smelled chicken. Those were big warning signs for a pregnancy.

A triumphant smile curved her mouth. After years trying to make Tom happy, she still couldn't conceive and she'd truly believed Tom had been right when he said she must be barren. She believed him enough not to see a doctor about it.

A few weeks with Terry and she was royally screwed.

She wandered to the living room window and looked out, blinking away the sting of oncoming tears. They hadn't used a condom the first night, or any other night since then. How could she be so stupid? She closed her eyes and banged her forehead against the window.

What have I done? What if he thinks I'm setting him up?

Would he kick her out and never speak to her again? One thing was certain. She needed to get a test—right now.

In a torn state, she whipped on jogging pants and a sweater. Her entire body trembled in fear and excitement as the elevator jerked to a stop on the main floor. The doors opened. Guests looked her way, appalled as they took in her rumpled state of dress. She squared her shoulders, held her chin high, and proceeded past the front desk to the huge double doors.

"Excuse me! Miss Lector? Miss Lector!"

Mary froze and turned toward the voice. A pretty redhead stood behind the front desk, staring at her with huge green eyes, behind the thickest black-rimmed glasses she'd ever seen. But she looked cute as hell in them.

"Uh, yes?"

The girl smiled and it made Mary breathe a little easier.

"Mr. McCoy doesn't want you to leave without an escort. Shall I have Ezra go jogging with you?"

Mary blinked, wondering why—oh, right—the jogging suit. She cleared her throat and approached the front desk. "I'm not going jogging.

I—ah—it's a female thing," she whispered. "I didn't have time to dress properly."

"Oh!" She blushed and whispered back, "You could've phoned down. I can help you." She reached for her purse. "I'm Sal by the way. I'm the dayshift girl and a good friend of Mr. McCoy's. You can ask me anything."

The girl would've went on and on, but Mary put her hand up. "No, no. Thank you, Sal—I—ah—appreciate your help, but I prefer to purchase my own. I—have a special brand I like to use." Tampons were of no use to her now, but Sal didn't know that.

Sal smiled and Mary liked her right away. "Okay, hon. Ezra will walk with you in any case."

Mary sighed, her shoulders sagging. "All right then."

This was the second most embarrassing point in her life. First, leaving a hotel in Silver Creek after banging Terry the night before, and now walking in sweats next to a man in a business suit to get a pregnancy test.

Thankfully, she found a pharmacy only a block over. And wonderful Ezra didn't say a word, or even ask what she needed to buy so desperately.

Once she was safely back in Terry's apartment, away from prying minds and busy eyes, she locked herself in the bathroom.

When she walked back out three minutes later, with a positive reading in her shaky hand, she went back to the window and bawled her eyes out. Life couldn't get much more complicated than this.

Can I do this?

But she smiled through her tears, almost as though no matter how scared she felt in this moment, the news was a good thing. Tom couldn't give her a child but Terry did. It wasn't her fault. She wasn't barren. After all this time, now it finally happened.

Something came over her in those terrifying moments. She'd finally gotten what she'd always wanted—a baby to love. Someone to love her back unconditionally.

Could she switch to this new life with a baby in her arms, too? It was one thing to be wined and dined every night, and have a housekeeper to clean the place, but did she really deserve all of this? Maybe it would be better to walk away from this insane world and raise the baby on her own, in the safety of her boring mountain town.

Her thoughts drifted back to when she'd first arrived here.

The Sea Scape was a grand, beautiful hotel, and the city of Victoria a wondrous place as well. No wonder many people lived and vacationed here. It wasn't just the gorgeous views of the ocean, the laid back atmosphere, or the happy faces on the locals. Above all, to Mary, the

Victorian architecture simply stunned her at every turn. Summertime on the island was an exciting affair as well. Music in the streets. Every style of art imaginable, fresh fish and produce. This place had it all.

But those things were simple perks to having Terry in her life.

She stared down at the harbor. Hundreds of boats lined the docks, shining as brilliant as the sparkling water under the bright morning sun. She wondered which of the fancy yachts belonged to Terry. She'd never been on anything bigger than a fourteen-foot aluminum fishing boat.

Again, she laughed. Her life had changed so quickly and drastically it seemed surreal. Maybe this was all a dream. How long would she stay before she had to return home, back to her regular life?

I don't want to go back.

She glanced around the room at Terry's things. Few pictures covered the utilitarian walls. The only pops of color in the room were a few throw covers and pillows on the low back leather couches. A couple abstract paintings. A red-handled set of knives on the kitchen counter. Everything else was a bland grey, white and black.

What she really wanted was to be right here with him. She wanted to put color in his life. There was more to this existence than handing somebody a briefcase and having to look over your shoulder.

But what if he didn't want the same thing? Maybe this was only an exciting fling for him and soon he'd send her on her way. *What would he say about a baby?*

He needs you as you need him. She rubbed her flat stomach and glanced at the note Terry left for her every morning on the coffee table. Today he would pick her up at noon for a special lunch. Until then, she could do whatever her heart desired, and if she had any questions, she could trust Sal to help her with anything.

Terry had been the first man to make her feel comfortable, and wanted. More and more she was beginning to like it. Was it possible a bad guy could be this wonderful? Tom did nothing but accuse her of not being good enough. Not looking good enough, and not doing anything right. Terry seemed happy to just have her around. He touched her with gentleness while he possessed her body with rough possession. He made love to her as if the world didn't matter, as if nobody else mattered. She loved him for that. But was it real love, or fascination by the way he treated her so different than Tom had?

Thinking about all these confusing things that had suddenly changed in her life, she took her time getting dressed, and being thankful for what she had.

Since her arrival, Wanda had taken her shopping on several occasions and she actually enjoyed herself. Every time Mary reached for her wallet to pay, Wanda insisted on buying for her. Hush money perhaps? Despite her initial embarrassment, Mary finally caved and allowed Wanda to pay the bill. After all, nobody had ever done that for her before. It was a whole new world and she liked it.

Wanda didn't treat Mary as though she was beneath her, and she chided herself of her immediate reaction that Terry's stepmother was a snooty bitch. Still, she'd never forget what she saw in the parkway that day with Sammy Hayes.

Whatever the case, the amount of clothes and accessories piling up in Terry's apartment was getting a little ridiculous. None of this stuff would be suitable at home in Silver Creek. Not when she lived in the bush.

But she shoved the thought aside. Silver Creek held no importance here, even though she knew she'd have to return one day. Now they would have endless gossip knowing the widow Billings came home from an unknown vacation, fat with child.

With a heavy heart, she chose a snug but stretchy burgundy pencil skirt and loose-fitting beige top that hung a little off the shoulder. Cute with a hint of sexiness. She teased her hair into a loose wave and applied some makeup.

The view in the floor-to-ceiling mirrors along one hallway wall was impressive, she thought to herself, and adjusted her pose. With a critical eye she gazed at her reflection. No more faded jeans and oversized shirt, no rumpled Stetson or wool toque. No mucky work boots or hip waders here. Staring back at her was a smart looking woman who may be small, but she had a big heart and only the best intentions. And maybe she had a cute face. Maybe. She winked at herself.

I hope you see me for me, Terry McCoy. Because I see you.

As she dabbled some perfume under her ears—a flowery vanilla scent Wanda said Terry loved—the buzzer rang.

When she answered the door, Sal stood there with a warm and highly contagious smile. "Hello again, Mary. Did you find what you were looking for this morning?"

Mary's lip twitched as she smiled. "Yes. Thank you."

"Oh, good. I tried calling but you didn't answer."

"Sorry, I didn't hear the phone ring."

The charming woman smiled. "No worries. Your ride is waiting downstairs, and you look lovely, by the way. I'll escort you down.

I know it must be frustrating being watched at all times like this, but it's important."

"I know." She tried to hide her excitement over this special lunch with Terry, and to share her news with him, but failed miserably. If Sal noticed her perma-grin, she didn't say anything. "Let me get my purse."

As the elevator descended toward the main floor, Mary checked her watch. It wasn't quite noon yet, but she was excited to get out of the apartment and spend some alone time with Terry. How would she tell him of the news? Just come out with it, or dance around the subject? Wait until she had a bump or she outweighed him?

Considering the chaos these past few weeks, they sorely needed privacy to have a really good heart-to-heart.

She glanced at Sal under the cover of her eyelashes. She was a beautiful girl, voluptuous, the stark red of her hair a perfect match with such bright green eyes. Mary felt envious, and maybe a little jealous of the beautiful woman. She would give away her best chainsaw to have more than a handful on her chest and such a curvy frame. The men must fall hard and fast for Sal.

She wondered if Terry looked at Sal as a potential bedmate or just an employee.

Why do I have so many doubts all the time?

The elevator opened and Mary made her way through the grand lobby to the huge double doors. Sal returned to her post at the front desk as Mary approached the black limo waiting outside.

The driver opened the rear door and Mary stared in puzzled disappointment at the person waiting for her.

"Hello, darling," Wanda purred. "I'm sorry Terry couldn't make it, but I have a special surprise for our lunch today. Come in now." She patted the seat next to her.

Mary glanced back at the hotel doors, wondering if she should speak with Sal first, but decided not to be a bother. It was only lunch with Wanda after all. Maybe Terry would be able to join them later on. She offered a smile and stepped in, taking the seat beside Terry's beautiful stepmother.

"Have some champagne."

Mary shook her head, still feeling ill. "No thank you, I don't think—"

"Nonsense. A little champagne never hurt anyone."

Mary reluctantly accepted the glass. *Would one glass hurt the baby?*

"We have cause to celebrate, darling. Terry has made a wonderful deal."

He has no idea what he's made.

Despite her disappointment that Terry couldn't make it, and the fact that she didn't feel comfortable drinking, Mary learned after several outings with Wanda, the woman always had good champagne within reach. Saying no would raise questions she didn't want to answer until she'd had her talk with Terry. He should be the first to know—not his father's second wife.

The limo pulled out of the parking lot and headed downtown. As she'd done before, Mary stared out the window at the beautiful architecture of the city. She sipped the champagne slowly, careful not to overdo it, barely listening to Wanda's endless chatter as they passed numerous buildings and shops.

After a while she didn't feel normal. Didn't seem like the car was driving straight. She blinked and stared out the window, realizing the buildings were blending in with each other. Elongated shapes and bright colors filled her hazy vision.

She cleared her throat. "Um—I'm—"

"Yes, darling?" Wanda's voice didn't sound right.

Her face felt clammy and pale. "I don't think—the champagne. . . ."

"Don't worry. Everything is going to be fine. I'll take good care of you."

And the world around her suddenly vanished.

* * * *

Mary opened her eyes and groaned. Her head throbbed and her throat felt so parched she couldn't swallow properly. She moved to rub her eyes and realized with a start that she couldn't move. She pulled hard, but her hands were tied behind her back, secured to something cemented in the floor.

Fully awake now, she looked around, blinking rapidly to see through the dim room. "Hello?"

She was trapped in a dingy basement or cellar of some sort. Only a small window ten feet off the floor allowed a sliver of light into the room.

She tried her hardest to remain calm, to breathe and keep her head on. *What happened?* The last thing she remembered was sitting in the limo with Terry's stepmother. Was Wanda trapped in here, too?

"Wanda?"

"Ah, you're awake, darling. That's good."

That's good? Mary turned her head toward the voice, confused why Wanda sounded calm. A chair scraped on the cement floor somewhere behind her. She glanced up and swallowed as Wanda stepped into the shaft of light and looked down at her. This was not a good situation at all. In fact, seeing Wanda look so cool felt very, very wrong.

"How do you feel?"

Mary pulled at her restraints. "I don't understand. What's going on? Why am I tied up?"

Wanda's smile was pure evil, but she sounded calm. "Because I need you."

Mary's heart slammed in her chest and she desperately yanked at her restraints. *No.* "For what? What did I ever do to you?"

Wanda chuckled before she nodded to someone in the shadows. A man appeared with a chair and set it down in front of Mary. She tried to make out his face but it was too dark to see him.

Wanda smoothed her skirt, took a seat, and crossed one leg over the other. She appeared calm and completely in control. So she really was a bitch after all.

"Are you thirsty, sweetheart?" Wanda took the offered glass of water from the shadowed man and attempted to press it to Mary's lips. But she turned away, refusing the water, especially after what the champagne did to her.

"Suit yourself." Wanda handed the glass back to the man, who returned to the shadows.

She was in a whole heap of trouble and she couldn't do anything about it.

"What do you know about this business, Mary? Has Terry ever explained it to you?"

Mary felt sick to her stomach as she tried unsuccessfully to free her hands. Tears filled her eyes as the realization sunk in that this may be the end for her, and for the baby. "No. I don't know anything." Her voice sounded weak, hollow.

"I see why. You're a scared little thing, aren't you?"

She trembled with fear, but something else boiled in her blood. Anger and resentment. Pure rage. After everything she'd already suffered through in life. Now she had to be kidnapped. She lifted her chin in defiance, ignoring Wanda's snarky laugh. "What the fuck do you want from me?"

"I want you to sit there and look pretty. Don't worry. Nothing will happen to you as long as Terry comes to your rescue." Wanda leaned forward and eyed Mary from legs to eyes. "Oh, he'll come for you, I'm sure. He likes your type. Small and vulnerable."

Mary spit in Wanda's face. "Fuck you."

Wanda laughed hard.

For a few tense moments, silence filled the air, before Wanda wound her arm back and struck Mary hard across the cheek. As she whirled from the hard slap, Wanda pushed up off the chair and wiped the spit from her cheek. With all the calm of a woman in charge she walked around the room, hands clasped behind her back.

Mary was seriously beginning to think that Wanda was very messed up. *How can I get out of this? How can I make her let me go?* She looked around the room, but there was only one way out. Even if she could convince them to untie her, she'd never make it to that door.

"Did Terry ever tell you about his mother?" When Mary refused to answer, Wanda continued, undaunted. "She was beautiful. Sweet. Naïve. I wanted what she had. More money. A beautiful home. A husband who loved her more than the world. And there I was, raised in a land where women had only what the men chose to give them. Eliza took me into her world, exactly as I had planned." Wanda stared up at the tiny window. "She had no idea what her precious husband did when she wasn't looking. But I did." She turned around, her eyes wide and crazy. "I just wanted her to see what the pigs could do. How was I to know she'd die of a heart attack? I only hoped she'd leave him, then I could take her place. She made it quite easy for me."

Mary's stomach turned in disgust and her heart ached for Terry and his mother. She couldn't help but imagine a dark and dreary day with the sound of bone crunching in the pigpen. Bile slithered up her throat. She had to swallow hard not to puke. "You're crazy."

"Crazy? Do you know what crazy is? Do you know what I've gone through? Do you know what they did to my brother?!" she shouted. "He was trying to bring them down. Trying to make things better for our family. And your sweet little Terry cut off his finger and dumped his body into the ocean."

Mary cringed at the ugly image. She didn't want to know what they did. She didn't want any part of this, and now she was trapped in a basement with a mad woman who was going to kill her. If she could lure Terry's unsuspecting mother to her death and laugh about it, then she was truly sick.

"When Terry showed me my darling Adolfo's finger with our family ring, I knew what I had to do. It was time to do what he couldn't after all these years."

Mary glared at Wanda, wishing she could get out of her restraints and strangle the woman herself. Not only for herself, but for Terry's mother. "You killed Terry's father didn't you?"

Wanda tipped her head back and laughed. "If you knew what kind of man he was, you'd understand why. Adolfo is gone because of Colton."

"Are you going to kill Sam, too?"

The laughter died in Wanda's eyes. She glared at Mary, her mouth a tight line. "What are you talking about?"

Mary fixed her with a deadly glare. "I saw you with him. You were kissing him in a parking lot."

"Ooh. I remember that." Her expression immediately switched from anger to wonder. "What a beautiful afternoon we shared." She looked thoughtful for a moment, before she fixed a curious, maybe even nervous glance at Mary. "Who did you tell?"

Mary shrugged, hoping it gave her an edge, although inside she trembled. She had nothing to bargain with.

"Terry doesn't deserve this."

"They all deserve this you stupid bitch! They're all the same!"

An image of Tom flashed before Mary's eyes. If Colton was anything like Tom, then yes, she could understand why Wanda would want to kill her husband. But it didn't make Wanda any less insane, or give her the right to take someone's life.

"Did Terry tell you what he did, Mary? Do you know what he did to you?"

Mary frowned, confused by this crazy woman. She wasn't making any sense. "What are you talking about? Terry didn't do anything to me." Wanda couldn't possibly know about the pregnancy.

"Oh, yes he did." Her laugh grew loud and irritating. Then she looked Mary square in the eyes. "He killed your husband. He was the one who pushed him into the river. I overheard him and Gabriel talking about it."

The world stopped turning. An image of Tom flashed before her eyes. *No.* Mary's jaw dropped as instant, hot tears filled her eyes. *No, it can't be. Terry wouldn't do that to me.*

She lifted her chin in defiance, although inside she was falling apart. She wanted to scream at them all and disappear. But she wouldn't give Wanda that much pleasure. "If you think your lies are going to make me turn against him, you can go fuck yourself."

"Ha!"

"Terry's going to make you pay for this."

"That's what I'm hoping for, darling. When he finds out where you are, he's going to fall right into my hands. Don't worry. Soon the Montesano's will have no competition at all." She pointed to Mary. "Tape her mouth shut. He'll be here soon."

A single, sharp knock banged on the door. Mary tensed and looked up.

Wanda stood, her smile beaming, and answered the door. "There you are, my love. See my surprise?"

Mary's eyes widened as Sammy Hayes strolled into the room. Her heart sank. Tears pricked her eyes as Sammy's betrayal struck her with brute force. There it was right before her. Sam wasn't an unaware lover. He was Wanda's accomplice all along.

When he looked down at her, he seemed surprised at first glance, before he leaned over and kissed Wanda's cheek.

Mary hated him. Wanda was a madwoman and Sam was a traitor.

"You've outdone yourself, my sweet. What is your plan?"

Mary's shoulders slumped while her mouth was taped shut by the other man. She dropped her chin. Staring at the floor, she hoped to God Terry would know what to do before it was too late.

Chapter 12

As soon as Terry arrived back in town he made a mad dash for the hotel. He needed to make sure Mary was safe. He bounded up the front steps to the hotel, eager to see her beautiful, smiling face and hold her in his arms. Once he was sure of that, he had a wonderful date planned for them out on the yacht. Steak and lobster roasted to perfection by his most trusted chef. The best champagne money could buy, and a bed covered in the richest silk sheets. A day in the sun and a night under the stars on the open ocean.

Nothing gets better than that.

Maybe we could discuss the future. Decide how to run the hotel, together. Sell the estate and keep her house as a quiet vacation home in the mountains. He had all kinds of ideas.

He whistled a snappy tune as he headed for the elevator, paying no mind to the guests milling about. Gabe was looking into Montesano's older daughter, and would soon discover a connection. He was sure of it. Right now he needed time alone with Mary.

"Excuse me, Mr. McCoy!"

He paused and glanced over to Sal standing behind the front desk. "What's up, Sal?"

"An envelope came in for you—"

"Can it wait until later? I'm picking Mary up for lunch."

Sal looked confused. "But your limo already picked her up, sir."

"What?" Every muscle in his body tensed. His worst fears came to fruition.

Sal's face paled and her big green eyes seemed to double in size. "Did I do something wrong? I was just following orders. I'm so sorry, Mr. McCoy."

He blew out a frustrated breath and opened the envelope. There, in bold letters on a tiny piece of paper, was something no man ever wanted to read: *If you want your woman back, come alone, or I'll kill her slowly.*

He slammed his hand down on the front desk. His curse echoed like metal on metal through the lobby. The small crowd grew silent. Whispers filled the air.

With blinding tears, Terry stared at the address beneath those frightening words, knowing the place as an abandoned industrial lot they'd used in the past, and crumpled the paper in his hand. "Fuck." He looked around the room. Maybe somebody was watching from the shadows. Maybe he was being set up, but he couldn't ignore the note, and cursed himself for getting Mary into trouble. She came after him. After he left her like a scared little boy, she had come after him. And now she could be suffering at the hands of some asshole who wanted revenge against his family.

Now he knew why his father shut himself off from his emotions. Perhaps that's why he'd cheated on Wanda. Maybe he didn't really love her. Maybe he couldn't. She was a body to turn to when the one he truly loved was dead.

He tried hard to be smart, to not let his emotions get the best of him. But with Mary they did. She had become the only peace in his fucked-up life. But he wouldn't—couldn't—shut himself off from her. And now he had to get his woman back.

Only a few people could use his limo. A very select few.

This was his burden to bear—not Mary's.

He forced a reassuring smile for Sally. "You did nothing wrong, Sal, don't worry. But please, don't ever assume I'm around until you see me with your own eyes, especially at a time like this."

She nodded quickly. "Of course, Mr. McCoy. Will Mary be all right?"

"You're damn right she will be. Remember what I told you over the phone?"

Sal nodded immediately.

"Good."

Without another word he ran out of the lobby and whipped out his cell phone. He punched in the number Gabe used while in the city and breathed a huge sigh of relief when his best friend answered on the first ring.

"Somebody took Mary."

It took a moment for Gabe to answer. "What? I thought Montesano agreed to your deal?"

"He did, but apparently he can't control his daughter."

There was a short silence before Gabe spoke again. "What do you want to do?"

"The only thing I can do. I've been instructed to go there alone. I really need you to go to the house and check on Wanda. They may come for her next."

"I'll head there right now. Are you sure you don't want backup?"

"I can't fuck this up, Gabe. I don't want to lose her." He hung up the phone and shoved it back into his pocket. He knew what Gabe would do once he was sure of Wanda's safety. It didn't take much to retrieve his location through the cell phone with a little help from their friends. But that wasn't important right now. He needed to get to that address and get Mary back no matter what it took.

He got into his Camaro and made one more call before he smoked the tires and sped out of the parking lot.

Ten minutes later, Terry pulled into the abandoned industrial lot, past the old tractor-trailer yard where rows of trailers and cargo bins, rusted from years of neglect, spanned across the massive yard. Everything was covered with graffiti. Remnants of squatters littered every building corner and alleyway.

A forty-five-gallon drum still smoked next to the road. Terry wondered if somebody was scared off or permanently silenced.

This place had been abandoned over twenty years ago. Lately it served as a means for under aged kids to party, drug deals to be made, or a quiet place to kill somebody.

Soon this site will become state of the art condominiums.

Horrific images of Mary hanging from a beam with her blood dripping into a pool on the floor flashed in his mind as he parked the car and turned off the ignition. He closed his eyes and repeated in his head that Mary needed him. As much as he wanted to step away from this life, he knew what he had to do. He had to get her back, no matter what it took. No matter if he had to trade places, because he'd gladly die for her. He got her into this mess, and he was sure as fuck going to get her out.

He got out of the car and gently closed the door. As he made his way around the back bumper, he pulled out his Beretta and twisted on the silencer, praying for a steady hand and perfect shot. He took in his surroundings like a sniper eyeing the scene. Carefully, he peered around the corner of one of the buildings and spotted a man he didn't recognize guarding a door. No vehicle was in sight, but they could have it hiding anywhere around here in this concrete and metal jungle.

He crept around the machinery, carefully making his way closer. Once he got into range, he lifted the Beretta and fired one shot. The guard's knees crumpled and he hit the ground.

Terry glanced around the vicinity again. Once he was sure the coast was clear, he made a mad dash to the door and checked the guard. Blood oozed from his chest, and when he touched his neck, he found no pulse. Quickly, he pulled the body away from the door and hid it behind an old neglected loader.

Again, he inched his way to the door, carefully eyeing all directions, weapon ready.

His heart pounded. He fought to control his breathing as he twisted the doorknob. The hinges creaked in protest as he slowly pushed open the heavy metal door, and slipped inside.

He entered a long narrow hallway shrouded in darkness. His cell vibrated in his pocket and he quickly checked the message from Gabe: *Wanda is missing. House is empty.*

Fuck. Now what the fuck was he supposed to do?

Prepared for the worst, Terry continued down the hallway to a set of stairs leading underground. He took them slowly, trying to make out any strange noises or voices as he descended. Nothing but silence met his ears.

Then he heard it. A woman's laugh, and it was painfully familiar.

No. Not her. Please don't let it be who I think it is.

He reached the last step, approached the end of a short hallway, and made one last promise to himself before he burst around the corner at full speed.

Stunned by the sudden attack, the guard barely had a chance to raise his weapon before Terry fired two rounds into his chest.

The guard flew back and hit the wall as Terry burst through the door. The second he stepped inside a fist came out of nowhere and smashed into his cheek. His head snapped back, but he quickly corrected himself and blocked an uppercut from a second man, then another from the first, before somebody kicked the back of his knee and took him down. They rolled on the cement floor. His knuckles connected hard to the cement floor, but he felt nothing. He needed to get to Mary and get her out of here.

A muffled cry resounded from somewhere in the room, but Terry had other things to worry about. He rolled over, barely avoiding a kick to the head, and managed to get back on his feet. He prepared for another round and held his fists high to protect his face. But when the click of a hammer being drawn echoed through the room, he knew his fight was over.

He rubbed the back of his neck and looked around the dim space for the first time. A small window maybe ten feet above shone little light into the vast room. A few crates were piled into one corner.

One of his attackers wiped blood from his face, while his gun pointed to Terry's head. Another man stood to his other side, his gun trained on Terry as well. He was totally outnumbered and his weapon was on the floor.

Then he saw her. In the middle of the room, on the floor, with her hands tied to a post and duct tape over her mouth, Mary stared up at him with utter fear in her eyes. Her cheeks were wet from tears and it was all because of him.

"Right on time, Terry."

Sammy Hayes stepped out of the shadows.

Terry expelled his breath, not quite believing his eyes. *This can't be happening.* How could Sam do this to him? He'd never felt more betrayed in his life. He tightened his fists, hoping to get a shot at the man who'd been his good friend for years.

"Jesus Christ, Sam. How could you do this?"

Sam shrugged, his face void of emotion.

"Fuck. I should've known there was something up with you. Why, Sam? Why?!" He shouted, almost on the verge of tears. How could he betray him like this? "I suppose you killed my father, too? How could you do it after everything we've gone through? Everything he's done for you?"

He couldn't believe Sam would bring Mary here to lure him in. Why not kill him before Mary even got involved? He should've let that poison kill him instead, before he fell in love with her. Before he realized what he truly wanted in life.

"Sam didn't kill Colton," said a lilting feminine voice. "I did."

Terry's heart tripped as his stepmother appeared out of the shadows and stood next to Sammy. He'd never felt angrier with himself, and everyone else, before. He shook his head in complete disgust and raw hatred.

"Nice to meet you, Daniella. Why not stick with your real name? I didn't even know you were Montesano's daughter."

"Nobody did."

He grit his teeth. "I can't believe you had us fooled all this time."

"Men are stupid when they're in love, Terry. You're just like your father, pathetic and weak."

He grit his teeth. "I'm nothing like my father."

Wanda tipped her head back and laughed, before she strolled over to Mary and grabbed a handful of hair, yanking her head back. Mary whimpered behind the duct tape, her eyes wide and wet in terror.

"I suppose it was you who poisoned me then, you sick bitch." He wanted Wanda's hands off of Mary. *Come here and hit me if you want.* Any way to keep her attention off of Mary was better than nothing. He'd take Gabe's eyelash curler with a smile if it meant Mary wouldn't be touched.

"Everyone knows your love for Finlandia Vodka, Terry. It's the first thing you touch when you come home."

Her snarky smile really set him off.

"Cassandra had difficulty at first. Colton nearly caught her, but my precious girl knows how to distract a man very well, and your father loved her little ass—"

"That's enough."

Wanda laughed at his obvious disgust. "Cassandra was such a lovely creature. She'd do anything for me. And when I say anything, I mean *anything.*"

What a disgusting broad.

"Everything worked out perfectly, didn't it, Samuel? Aside from a few hiccups, I'm happy with our progress. Soon everything will be mine."

Sam's eyes drifted over Terry briefly, before he nodded at Wanda. "Yes, my sweet. Anything you want."

What a fucking idiot. Doesn't he realize he's being used? "Sam, don't let her get to you. You're nothing but a means to an end. She'll kill you too, like she did to my father."

Wanda strolled over to Sam and kissed him passionately. "I would never hurt my Samuel. He means everything to me. Soon this empire will be ours." She turned and stared at Terry. "And I'm going to kill you next, right after Gabriel arrives."

Terry shook his head. At least he had some hope that one of them would survive this mess. "Gabe isn't coming, so go ahead and kill me if you want, but don't hurt Mary. She has nothing to do with this."

Mary shook her head and mumbled under the duct tape.

"Oh, but she does. In order for me to succeed with my plan I need all of you gone. With your father and you out of the picture, all of this will be mine. The money. The business. Everything. But I have to tie up all loose ends. I know Gabriel won't quit until he sees me dead, which is why he's on his way here right now. I left a little prize for him in the parlor."

Fuck.

No wonder his father had mentioned to Buck about changing his will. He must've learned something about Wanda and wanted to take her out of it. Now he was dead, and Terry next. Antonio was right. His daughter was a smart cookie. She got rid of her rich husband just in time and now his successor would be next.

He turned to Sammy again, hoping he'd listen to reason. "Sam, listen to me. She isn't worth it. She used my father. What makes you think she won't do it to you?"

"Shut up!"

Wanda stormed over to Terry and backhanded him hard across the face. "You stupid little boy. For years I took care of you and that old, ugly father of yours."

Terry grit his teeth. If he ever wanted to hurt a woman, it was right now.

"All I wanted was to prove to my father that I was smarter than him," Wanda shrieked, flailing her arms in the air. "I can run this business as well as any of you. But at every turn I was pushed away because I'm a woman. I had no rights, and no power. Well look at me now." She stood tall and proud, and Terry realized with dread that Wanda was completely insane. All this time she never cared for any of them, she only wanted power. Power drove people over the edge. It killed them, just like it did his father.

Now Terry knew for certain he told Sal to do the right thing.

"You really think you can run the show? Do you think your father will let you be his new competition? He'll have you slain in your sleep within days, daughter or not."

"Ha! You don't know anything about my father," she spat.

A wicked grin played across his face. Every muscle in his body tensed. "I know him a lot more than you think."

Wanda frowned, and he detected a hint of fear in her eyes, on her face. Maybe her plan wasn't perfect after all.

"What do you mean?"

"Let Mary go and I'll tell you."

Mary shook her head in disagreement, but Terry ignored her. He only wanted her to be safe. Trading his life for her was the only bargaining tool he had, and he'd gladly take it.

"A vehicle just pulled up."

"Perfect. Gabriel is here to save the day." She smiled triumphantly at Terry. "Maybe I'll let your girl live, for a little while, as long as I get to see you two boys dead. Then all my worries will be gone like the wind. Right, Samuel?"

Sam nodded again. Terry wanted to kill him. But right now all that mattered was coming up with a plan and getting Mary the hell out of here.

* * * *

Mary stared at her lover a few feet away. He looked beyond angry and broken. To learn how his friend betrayed him, yet again, must be hard to swallow. First Ben, and now Sam. Would Gabe do the same? Mary had no idea what to think. She was a hard-working bush girl caught in the middle of this scary world of crime.

And she was pregnant.

What else could possibly go wrong? She stared at Terry. She wanted to tell him now, before it was too late, before they all die. Would it make him fight harder if he knew he would've been a father one day?

But she couldn't utter a word with the tape on her mouth. There was nothing she could do. No warning she could give.

Suddenly the door burst open and two men dragged an unconscious Gabe into the room. They dropped him on the floor and left him there, his face bloody and bruised. Mary guessed they'd taken him off guard and although he did his best to fight back, it wasn't enough. At least now she knew Gabe wasn't working for them. Gabe was on the right side.

She looked over at Terry again. He stared at her with such stark emotion it hit her both physically and emotionally.

"Terry, darling, why don't you tell your little girlfriend what you did to her husband? I'm sure she'd like to know," Wanda said, and smiled like a snake. "She doesn't believe me."

Terry's head jerked up and his eyes widened. "What? What are you talking about?"

Wanda chuckled and crossed her arms over her breasts; her pose casual. "Don't ever underestimate me. I've overheard many conversations in my husband's study. One of them involved a Mr. Tom Billings and his deadly swim in the river."

Terry looked down at the floor for long, heart breaking minutes before he faced Mary, his expression defeated.

So it's true. She wasn't lying.

Tears filled Mary's eyes, but she didn't look away from Terry. She wasn't afraid anymore. She was angry and lost, and didn't know what to believe with these people. She was just an innocent woman, living her life in peace, doing nothing to nobody, and now this. All these lies and competition, for what?

Greed. Nothing good came from greed.

Wanda nodded and Sam cocked his gun, pointing it at Terry's temple.

Hot tears slid down her cheeks. She wanted to beg for Terry's life. She wanted to beg for her and her baby's life, and go back home.

But she wanted to know what really happened to Tom. She needed closure.

Wanda raised her voice. "Tell her, or I'll have Sam shoot her first."

The gun turned to Mary now. Her body trembled in fear and outrage as Sammy pointed his handgun to her temple. A slight squeeze and she'd be gone—just like that.

"Okay! Okay!" Terry looked Mary straight in the eye. "Tom was already into the blow when we found him. He said he'd sold some of it to some people he knew. But that wasn't the reason why I lost my shit on him. I saw the bruises on his knuckles. Mima said he'd beaten you two days before. She said he'd be at his trapper's shack."

Mary's throat tightened. She remembered that night like it happened only yesterday. She couldn't chew solid food for a week.

"So I hit him, over and over again, until I couldn't close my fist anymore. He said you weren't good enough, and soon he would've cashed in the money from the blow, and left you for some other broad he was having an affair with."

Mary whimpered beneath the duct tape.

"I dragged him down to the river and held his face under the water until he stopped shaking. Then I shoved his body under the ice and he disappeared. Two weeks after that I started checking up on you. I felt sorry for you, but that's not—"

"You're a widow because of this man, Mary," Wanda cut in, her voice loud, daunting. "How much do you want him now? He was only using you for an easy fuck like every other greedy, heartless bastard."

Mary cringed as the duct tape was violently ripped from her mouth.

"Mary, I swear. I'm not using you," Terry blurted, his voice desperate. "I felt ashamed about what happened. That's why I visited you, to make sure you were okay. I didn't plan to care about you, it just happened."

But she had nothing to say now that the tape had been removed. Too much to think about. She hung her head and tried not to break down in front of these people, in front of Terry. She'd suffered enough already. Crying wouldn't bring her any peace. *No. No more crying.* She was sick and tired of nothing but heartache. If she died today, she'd die with her head held high, knowing she didn't do anything wrong, and only did everything she could.

At that moment Gabe groaned and opened his eyes.

"Wonderful," Wanda said. "Let's get this over with so I can return home."

"That's not your fucking home, it's my mother's," Terry said through clenched teeth.

Something Wanda had said before entered Mary's mind. She looked back up at Terry, her resolve stronger now. He deserved to know the truth. "Wanda led your mother to the pig pen, Terry. Your mom is dead because of her. She planned it all along so she could marry your father."

"Shut up!" Wanda shouted.

Terry glared at his stepmother. If the look in his eyes could kill, they were ripping Wanda apart right now. "I'm going to kill you with my bare hands. My mother was an innocent woman." He struggled against the men holding him down, but he wasn't strong enough to take them all.

"Untie his little fruitcake," Wanda shouted. "I'm bringing her with me."

Mary struggled as Sam untied the rope from the post and roughly hauled her up. She hauled back and punched him hard, but Sam grabbed her as if she weighed no more than an empty bucket and shoved her into the arms of another man. She kicked and struggled against him, but he was too strong. As the man pulled her back toward the door, she dared one last sorrowful glance at the man she loved.

"Where are you taking her?" Terry struggled against the men once again.

"Kill them," Wanda ordered Sam. "I have a special treat for Mary. She's going to meet those hungry little pigs."

Mary gasped as Wanda and one of the men dragged her from the room. She saw Terry staring at her with pure fear in his eyes before the door slammed shut behind them.

* * * *

Terry glared at Sam as he took a deep breath, lifted his hands, and cracked his neck. "Stand them up," he ordered the three remaining guards.

Terry and Gabe were yanked onto their feet and forced to stand side-by-side. "You're going to pay for this, Sam. I swear to fucking God," Terry warned. "My father trusted you. I trusted you."

"So did I," Gabe added, his voice seething with rage.

Sam's smile was almost comical as he shook his head. "You boys have a lot to learn, and we don't have a lot of time." He lifted his gun and shot one of the guards clean between the eyes.

Terry blinked in stunned confusion, his eyes wide. "What the fuck—"

Before Terry could comprehend what was happening, Gabe spun around and elbowed the other guard right in the eye. As he stumbled back, Gabe took him down to the ground as Sam shot the last man three times in the chest.

Terry lunged for his gun. "What the fuck was that?" He lifted his weapon and pointed it at Sam's face.

"That was me saving your ass," Sam said, as calm as ever.

Terry's hand shook as he stared Sam down, his weapon still trained on him. "But I thought you were with Wanda—"

"I was." Sam slipped his gun back into the waistband of his pants, trusting Terry not to shoot him.

While Gabe broke his attacker's neck, Terry and Sam stood face-to-face in the middle of the room. "Colton ordered me to return to base a couple of months ago, but I don't think he knew how far she would go to get what she wanted. Even *I* didn't know the extent of her greed until today. Your father would've given her anything. Money. Jewels. A house anywhere in the world. He asked me to watch over her, and to take care of her, and I mean I did *everything* she want—"

Terry trembled with so much rage he almost pulled the trigger. "Please, spare me those details."

"Fine. Anyway, your father became suspicious of her when large sums of money went missing soon after your mother's death. Turns out, Wanda—Daniella—was forming her own empire to take over yours. Then she was going to take out her own father. Colton was catching on to her."

Sam stepped closer and put his hand on Terry's trembling shoulder. "I'm sorry how things happened, buddy, but I had to do what I had to do, and I feel responsible for your dad's death too. He may have been a hard man to love, but he took care of all of us. Now let me finish my job and help you avenge him. You have no idea how long I've waited to kill that bitch without you shooting me first."

Terry released a hard, pent-up breath. Everything happened so fast he couldn't get his mind around it. How Sam could sleep with Terry's stepmother—even if he had been ordered to—went over the edge of reason. But that was the kind of man Sammy was. He'd do anything for the old man, no matter how insane the job would be. He had to give him credit for that. His father must have known Sam would do the job without fail. Even though Colton lost his life, at least the truth was out.

He lowered his gun. "You had me fooled, Sam. I almost shot you."

Gabe stood up and dusted himself off. "Will you two shut up? We still have shit to do."

Mary. "We have to stop them before they reach the estate."

"I swear I didn't know about that part," Sam yelled as Terry shot out of the room and bolted up the stairs.

He had his woman to save.

Chapter 13

Mary slunk in the back seat of the limo as it raced toward the McCoy Estate. Beside her, Wanda held up the mirror of her makeup powder and freshened her lipstick. She could be going out to a luncheon, the woman was so calm and cool that Mary shook her head in complete shock.

What the fuck is wrong with these people?

She eyed the small handgun peeking out of Wanda's purse as she stared at her reflection in the mirror. Wanda was dumb enough to allow Mary to be untied, which gave her an advantage. If she could manage to talk to her, and distract her, maybe she could get the gun.

"Why are you doing this, Wanda? Why go to all this trouble?"

The woman glanced at her with a bored expression on her face. Her right hand settled on top of the gun, makeup now forgotten. "*Ugh.* Good thing you're cute, because you certainly are not smart. I told you already. They killed my brother."

Mary shook her head. "It's more than that, and I'm not an idiot. If you're going to have me killed, what harm can a few questions make? Humor me in my last hour." She was really getting tired of all this drama and bullshit.

Wanda sighed and settled more comfortably in her seat. "Very well. What else do you want to know?"

Mary was careful not to look down at the gun, but she was ready to pounce when given the opportunity. "How old are you?"

"Thirty-eight."

Only a few years older than me. "Do you have any children?"

"No." Her demeanor changed then, and she shifted uncomfortably in her seat.

Mary knew immediately she had something to work with. "Do you want kids?"

Wanda shrugged and looked out the window. Mary discreetly reached for the gun but Wanda turned her head and Mary stopped short. Wanda noticed the change in her demeanor and took her gun in hand.

Mary pretended not to notice and forced her attention to the window. The beautiful landscape with its mansions and summer cottages whizzed by. She wanted that gun. She wouldn't kill Wanda, but she would use it as a threat and a way to get out of this car. Killing a person was different than shooting an animal for its pelt and its meat. But in her heart she knew she would pull the trigger if given no other choice.

They were almost there. Only a few miles away from the end of her chapter. She had to come up with something and save her baby.

"With my luck I would have a daughter, and she would be worthless. Only boys get what they want in my culture."

"If I told you I was pregnant, would you let me go?"

Wanda's eyes widened. "What?"

Mary blew out a shaky breath, not quite sure how to say it. She forced herself to look back out the window, and pretend there wasn't a gun aiming at her. "I took a test this morning, right before you kidnapped me. I've been sick every morning for nearly a week now, but I hadn't told anyone." She glanced back at Wanda, her expression tight. "Terry doesn't know he's going to be a father. And you know what? I'd be happy if I found out I was going to have a girl."

Wanda's eyes were still wide, maybe unsure if Mary was lying, or that female instinct to protect a child warred in her mind.

Driven now, Mary kept going. "My husband, the one Terry killed, said I'd never be good enough because I couldn't get pregnant. He said it was my fault, and then he'd hit me. So you see, Terry did a good thing by killing him." She looked down and rubbed her flat stomach, in awe something could actually grow in there. Too bad it had to happen in this fucked-up situation. "I guess Tom was wrong." *Come on. Let your guard slip. That's all I need. One little slip up from you.*

A slight smile curved Wanda's lips. Her chin quivered. She reached out tentatively toward Mary's stomach with her free hand. "Can I?"

Mary nodded, and a look of wonder crossed Wanda's beautiful face as she lightly rubbed her palm over Mary's stomach. Her eyes shimmered.

"I always wanted a baby of my own, but my first love was killed before we could marry. I aborted the child because I couldn't handle it alone. I couldn't bear to look at my baby's face and see my dead lover."

Tears glistened in her eyes and slid down her cheeks. "My father is a bad man, just like Colton was. They only care for power, not of their wives or their children. Only power. When I married Colton he couldn't give me a baby. He already had his family with his first wife." She dried her tears with a handkerchief. She looked sad, but that didn't change the person Wanda had become.

"Then you'll understand why I have to do it," Mary said.

"Do what?"

In a desperate move, Mary smacked the gun out of Wanda's hand. The weapon flew onto the opposite seat. Before Wanda could react, Mary grabbed the back of her head, and smashed her face into her knee. Wanda's body fell unconscious to the limo floor. "That."

Mary grabbed the door handle, prepared to jump from the vehicle, but it was locked. Frantic, she looked around the back seat. Nothing was large or heavy enough to break the glass.

There was only one option left.

Mary grabbed the gun and slid forward, rapping hard on the middle window separating them from the driver. As the dark tinted window rolled down, she quickly jumped back and grabbed Wanda, jabbing the weapon against her neck.

"Stop the car or the bitch is dead."

Still holding an unconscious Wanda, Mary jolted forward as the driver slammed on the breaks, and unlocked the doors.

She had no time to waste. Mary shoved Wanda's limp body toward the other seat and opened the door. There was no time to form a plan. She heard the man exit the vehicle with a curse as Mary made a mad dash straight for the bush, still holding the gun.

She was free.

Crouching behind a thick stand of red willows, she waited, not daring to make a sound, keeping a keen eye on the vehicle. The small handgun shook in her hand.

Moments later, Wanda staggered from the limo looking like a disheveled and pissed off cat. The distinct smudge of mascara marred her usual perfect face. Her pristine bangs stood slightly on end as if whipped by a strong wind. She stared at the bushes, with a look to kill, right where Mary was hiding.

"What do you want to do?" The driver asked. For some reason he seemed oddly familiar to Mary, but she'd met so many people lately, she couldn't tell for sure.

"There's no time to go after her. Besides, the boys will be dead by now and Sam will make it look like they killed each other."

"And when he returns?"

Wanda smoothed her bangs and grinned up at him. "The pigs can still have their dinner. I never intended to keep him anyway. Let's go."

Mary released a wretched sob as the limo sped away. *Terry.* She fell to her knees in the grass and covered her teary face with her hands, haunted by Terry's image. Now she was truly alone, and pregnant, stranded on the side of a road she wasn't familiar with. She'd tried hard to be strong in the face of danger, but this was too much to bear.

She lifted her face to the sky and thought of everything they'd shared in their short time together. He would want her to be strong, to move on and be safe. She could be safe in her little mountain house away from all this insanity.

She could raise her baby. Far away from this insane world.

I saw the bruises on his knuckles. I held his head under the water until he stopped shaking.

Terry took the real monster away from her.

He said he felt sorry for her, and that he'd never expected to care. She didn't expect to care either. She didn't want to fall in love with him. She didn't plan to get pregnant.

Nothing was the same anymore.

Still hiding behind the bushes, she looked down each end of the road. A few vehicles passed in either direction, without a clue to what happened outside of their perfect little worlds. They were clueless to the lives of the others in the shadows. The bad ones. The criminal ones. The ones who were made into monsters without a choice.

Tom had a choice—Terry did not.

Her mind made up, Mary tossed her heels aside and headed toward the McCoy Estate, keeping tight to the trees with Wanda's gun tucked into the waist of her skirt.

Wanda was going to pay for what she did to her baby's father.

* * * *

Terry, Gabe, and Sam entered the driveway to the McCoy estate with dust kicking up behind them. Terry held his breath when they found the limo parked by the front steps with two doors still open.

Nobody was near the barn and his father's prized beasts were all outside to play in their massive enclosure. Something wasn't right. Where did they take Mary?

The silence haunted Terry as Gabe shut off the engine. Not a single bird chirped from the trees. Not even a gust of wind swept over the grass. Every hair on Terry's body pricked with uncertainty and fear that this could be another trap.

"Where are they?" Terry scanned the yard. Nobody was around, not even the estate manager. Buck should be outside at this time of day, usually playing around with his numerous flowerbeds or mowing the lawn.

"You two go around the house. As far as she knows, I'm still on her side," Sam said, stepping out of the car. "I'll go in alone."

Terry pulled him back. "What if she saw us with you already? When she sees we're still alive, she'll have you killed."

"It's a chance I'm willing to take." Without another word, Sam rushed up the front steps and entered the main house. Terry stared after him, suddenly ashamed of himself for doubting him. In his eyes, Sam was a true hero for putting his life on the line even after Terry threatened to shoot him.

When the time was right, Terry vowed he'd make it up to him.

He crept around the right side of the building as Gabe took the left.

Memories of Wanda crept into Terry's thoughts as he made his way around the house, Beretta cocked and ready. How could they not see she was a psychopath? His mother died because of this woman. The same woman who then tricked his father into marrying her. Not once did Terry ever have ill feelings for Wanda. Not once did they ever argue. He had been a fool for not seeing what his stepmother truly was.

Regret was a terrible burden to bear, and he regretted many things. But maybe Mary was right. Maybe he could tame the monster he'd become and live like a normal man, as he'd always wanted. Live without all this chaos, and take care of a good, honest woman.

He had few good memories in this house, but many bad. This estate meant nothing more than that to him. A piece of a memory.

He glanced through the window into the parlor, his rapt gaze immediately landing on the body of the housekeeper. Blood pooled on the hardwood floors all around her. It was Cassandra, the young woman his father had apparently taken a shining to. *Poor thing, she certainly didn't deserve to die.*

The faint hum of a chopper resounded in the air. Terry looked up toward the north to find the family chopper slowly descending toward the helipad.

Voices, barely audible over the whirring blades came from the front of the house. He retreated his steps, keeping tight to the wall and peered around the corner.

Two men dragged Sam's limp body toward the pigpen. He must have been knocked around hard to be unconscious, or maybe he had another wound on the front of his body Terry couldn't see. Either way, he was in deep trouble as the pigs swarmed the fence in a frenzy. Terry had to stop them. Sam had willingly risked his life for him.

It sickened Terry to see the wild hunger in their eyes. A hunger his father had created in those otherwise harmless beasts.

He couldn't tell if Sam was dead or only unconscious, but he couldn't assume the worst. He inched his way closer and aimed his weapon toward one of the men dragging Sam. If he could get a clean shot off, he could buy Sam some time to save himself.

Another movement caught his eye and he faltered. Wanda ran toward the chopper carrying two suitcases.

Mary wasn't anywhere in sight.

Just as Terry stepped around the corner to go after her, something cold touched his temple.

"Drop it, or you're dead."

This can't be real. He knew that voice all too well. This was getting worse by the minute. "Buck Johnson," he said, and dropped his Beretta.

"Let me guess. You were fucking her, too?"

Terry stared after Sam and the two men. They were getting close to the pen and Sam still wasn't moving.

"I was always her favorite." Buck shoved the gun harder against his temple. "Move it."

Terry walked slowly ahead of Buck, completely blown away by how insane this family had become. Power made people go crazy.

"Where's Mary?"

Buck snickered and pushed against his back, making Terry stumble ahead. "If it makes you feel any better, she wasn't with them. She's dead in a ditch somewhere." He leaned close and whispered in a menacing voice, "She's dead because of you, Terry."

Terry's blood ran cold. On raging impulse, he spun around and decked Buck before he realized what hit him. He stumbled back and gripped his bloody nose, but he still managed to hold his weapon. Shaking, Buck lifted the gun again and pointed it at Terry's face.

"You're not gonna win this time, buddy."

Terry lifted his arms out to his sides. He didn't care if Buck ended his life right now. "Go ahead. Put me out of my misery."

Shady Grace

Buck laughed but didn't take the bait. "Keep walking." Terry continued toward the chopper with Buck right beside him. "There's no such thing as love in this business, boy. You know better than that."

As they neared the chopper, Buck shouted to Wanda, "Look what I found."

She spun around. Her eyes widened in shock when she saw Terry, then she turned her attention to Sam being dragged to the pen. "Serves him right for betraying me," she said loudly. "I wasn't going to keep him anyway."

"You're going to get everything you deserve, *Daniella*."

She turned back to Terry, her smile like a snake about to strike. "Kill him, Bucky, honey. Then we can leave. We'll return when the action dies down and get a clean-up crew." She smiled in victory. "Just think, Terry, darling. Soon this house will be exactly as I envision."

Terry closed his eyes, ready for the darkness to take him. Maybe he'd see Mary and his mother there.

He jerked as a shot cracked the air.

When he opened his eyes there was no darkness. No white void. No Mary. Only Wanda, staring down at the ground next to his feet. He glanced down, his ears ringing from the shot, to see Buck lying there with a hole in his head, his eyes wide open.

"Move!" Gabe shouted, clutching his bleeding arm. "Don't let her leave!"

Terry looked back at Wanda, his heart in his eyes. She had betrayed them all. She had destroyed everything that ever mattered to him. But he couldn't do it. He couldn't make himself reach for Buck's gun and end her life. He didn't know why, but maybe he was just tired of this same game, and maybe he couldn't handle seeing the only other parent in his life die.

She lifted her tear-streaked face from Buck's dead body. He thought he saw pain in her eyes, pure fear, but it didn't change anything. It wouldn't change what she did to his mother, his father, and now Mary.

Wanda proudly raised her chin and climbed into the chopper.

Terry stood frozen to the ground as the chopper lifted off the pad and flew away.

Nothing mattered to him anymore.

Mary was already gone. The only peace in his life was gone.

Gabe halted beside him, panting for air, and slugged Terry in the shoulder. He didn't even feel it. "Why the fuck did you let her leave? She doesn't deserve to live—"

"She'll wish she was dead when she realizes who's flying our chopper."

Gabe shook his head, clearly pissed off that she'd gotten away. "I don't understand. Who's flying it?"

A slow smile crossed his face as he focused on the chopper. "Her father, and he's one pissed off man."

"Oh. Right. How exactly did you get him to come here?"

They stood side-by-side, both staring as the chopper faded into the endless sky.

"I got Sal to call him. I knew he couldn't say no. Not with the deal I made him."

A hair-raising scream came from the area of the pen as Sam regained consciousness. Gabe checked his gun and swore. "Fuck. I'm out of bullets." He shot off toward Sam, not even seeing Buck's gun at Terry's feet. Terry stood numb in the same spot, unable to do anything of use. He watched as if through a tunnel as Gabe rushed the two men while they lowered a screaming Sam over the top of the railing.

The pigs gathered in a tight little formation waiting for their dinner like many times before.

The wind picked up with a sudden force as Gabe grabbed the arm of one man, violently twisting it until the bone snapped. As he dropped to the ground, shrieking in terror, Gabe ripped the gun out of the guy's holster and shot the other man in the face.

He reached for Sam and ripped him down from the top rail as one of the pigs lunged for his foot, missing his ankle by mere inches.

As Sam composed himself from his near brush with a terrorizing death, Gabe strolled over to the man with the broken arm, shot both of his legs with the man's own gun, before he fired a single round into his forehead.

The violence was over.

Terry's chest tightened and he couldn't breathe as he turned his attention to the water. He didn't want to think but he couldn't stop the images of Mary's face before his eyes. Maybe he should walk to the shoreline and just keep going until the water swallowed him up.

His father would tell him to suck it up and move on. If only it was that easy.

Gabe and Sam came toward him. They had no idea what happened. He would have to tell them what Buck said about Mary.

It was only the three of them now, and John Covington, the moneyman. If Wanda scooped money soon after his mother's death, then John was either a total fool or he was fucking her, too.

Tonight, he'll be getting a visit.

Tomorrow everything will change.

But first he was going to get off-the-wall hammered, maybe he'd forget who he was. Maybe he'd be able to forget her beautiful face after a while.

Terry glanced around the yard like a stranger stepping onto the lush green grass for the first time. The huge Victorian mansion, surrounded by beautiful gardens, seemed like a monstrosity amidst this serene landscape. He wasn't in awe anymore.

Everything had been built from lies and betraying hands.

It was time to make a change, if only Mary were here to see him do it. Because she had faith in him, he wanted to make things right for her. He wanted her to be proud of him from wherever she was.

Gabe and Sam dusted themselves off as they strolled over, Sam limping from the cut on his ankle, Gabe cradling his bleeding arm. Terry tried to smile as they stood in a circle on the helipad, but he couldn't. He should be dead, not his sweet Mary.

"Better get your arm looked at," he said to Gabe without any emotion. He was dead to the world.

"What do we do now?" Sam asked. "Where did they take Mary?"

Terry's heart lurched as he cleared his throat. "Buck said something about a ditch. They already killed her."

"I wouldn't underestimate that woman of yours," Gabe said with a smile.

Terry ran a hand through his hair, frustrated with himself, and angry that he couldn't contain his tears in front of them. Pissed off that Gabe actually smiled at him.

"I couldn't save her, Gabe! She's gone. The only woman I've ever fucking loved is gone." He put his hands on his hips and looked down at the concrete pad. He felt like that slab of cement. Cold and hard and alone.

"Look behind you, you idiot."

His head snapped up and he stared hard at Gabe, who was looking over his shoulder.

When Terry turned around his lungs emptied of breath. His heart pounded and his hands shook at his sides.

There she stood, his beautiful Mary, standing there panting, as if she'd walked through the bush for miles, and apparently with bare feet.

"Loved, eh?"

His upper lip twitched. He cleared his throat, embarrassed his feelings were out in the open in front of two of the deadliest criminals in the country—and a trapper. "Something like that." It took every ounce of will not to laugh and cry, he was beyond relieved she was alive. He rushed over and grabbed her, held her tight, afraid to let her go. He ran his hands up and down her sides, over her back, needing to assure himself that she was real, and that she was unharmed.

His hand slid over a familiar object tucked in her skirt. "What's this?"

"A gift from Wanda."

"Whatever," Gabe cut in. "We need to settle—"

Terry put his hand up to silence him, every fiber of his being only focused on Mary. He held her back and looked down at her in awe. *What a woman.* "What happened? How did you get away? And where are your shoes?"

Her perfect little eyebrow arched as she grinned. "I convinced them to let me out, with a little help from this." She waved the gun in the air. Gabe and Sam mirrored Terry's look of surprise. "And I threw those goddamned shoes in the ditch. How am I supposed to walk here in heels?"

"I'm impressed," Gabe said. Sam's gold-toothed grin reflected the same.

Mary glanced around the property, unaware of the carnage that had happened only minutes before. "What happened to Wanda?"

"She's gone. You'll never have to worry about her again, I promise."

"Oh, for fuck sakes. Come on, Sam. I need a fucking whiskey," Gabe blurted.

Terry didn't care what they did. Not with Mary standing there looking all tired and content, her hair all windswept and beautiful. He stepped closer, took her head in his hands and brought her lips to his.

She tasted like his dark days were finally over.

Now that he had his second chance at life, he wasn't going to waste any more time. He pulled her into his arms again and held her tight to his pounding heart, grateful she survived this insanity. She nestled her cheek to his chest. "Now what?"

Terry put his arm over her shoulder and held her tight as they followed the guys back to the house, but they weren't rushing. "They're going to have a drink, and we need to talk about the future."

Mary sighed. "I think you're right."

"Maybe we should go straight to bed. I should check every inch of your body and make sure you've come to no harm, *my damsel in distress.*"

Mary giggled and playfully slapped his chest. "I do feel tired, you terrible Scottish rogue." She paused at the door and looked up at him. "But we're not really going to sleep, are we?"

"Nope. I'm going to take you to a room far away from the parlor. Then I'm going to make love to you until one of my boys lays claim in that womb of yours. We'll make this shit legit."

Mary made a disgusted face. "That doesn't sound very sexy, Terry. Besides, you already did."

It took a second for her words to register before his eyes widened and his jaw dropped. "What? Are you sure? How?" His entire body shook, he was so terrified by the news. He was going to be a father. That scared him more than having a gun to his head. But it was awesome terror.

"Well, it all started when we had unprotected sex in a hotel room. And several more times after that."

He started laughing before he let out a manly holler. "Yes!" Then he scooped her up in his arms. "Told you it wasn't your fault. You just needed a real man with good swimmers."

Surprised but obviously relieved by his response, Mary hugged him tight and squealed as he burst through the door with her in his arms. "Why can't we go near the parlor?"

"Never mind."

She yawned and stretched, her smile teasing. "Maybe a nap is a good thing for me in my condition. A real nap where I actually sleep."

"Not unless you want to sleep with a gun against your bum."

She giggled and smacked his shoulder. "I already have one there."

"Yeah, you have a point. But I really need to empty *my* chamber." He shoved through the door and went straight to the nearest bedroom down one of the hallways.

He shut the door with his hip, went straight to the enormous bed and dropped Mary on it. "Get naked, woman. It's time to check you for injuries."

She looked at him with love and sex in her eyes. "Terry?"

"Yeah?" He pulled his shirt over his head and chucked it on the floor.

Mary struggled to get out of her bra in record time. "Are you sure this is what you want? I mean, am I what you really want?"

He crawled onto the bed and crowded her against the pillows. His little mountain woman wasn't going anywhere. She could keep her house in Silver Creek if she wanted, but they'd only be going there once in a while for some serious relaxation and some of that wild outdoor sex Gabe talked about. Maybe he'd take her inside the tanning hut on one of her furs. The possibilities were endless.

No words could ever describe how happy and relieved he felt right in this moment. "You're damn right you are. You're mine, and I love you. Don't ever question that."

Her content sigh when he settled over her was music to his ears.

"I love you too, Terry. Business can wait till tomorrow, right?"

He growled against her neck and ground his erection against her. "Yes, Boss. Anything you say."

Be sure not to miss Jannine Gallant's thrilling Who's Watching Who series!

Every Vow She Breaks

A Promise Can Follow You To the Grave...

Claire Templeton is drawn to the majestic beauty of the California Redwoods in the hopes of capturing an unexplained phenomenon on camera. What she doesn't expect is to run into her first love, Jed Lafferty, the boy she worshipped as a child, the man she's never been able to forget.

Carefree, fun-loving Jed doesn't believe in fate, preferring to make his own luck. But when he runs into the little girl who used to follow him like a shadow, now an irresistible woman, he can't help feeling the odds are turning in his favor. Letting Claire walk out of his life the first time might be his single biggest regret. But when strange gifts and cards left for Claire turn sinister, it's clear someone else from her past isn't ready to let go . . .

"Jannine Gallant is an exciting new voice in romantic suspense."
—Mary Burton, *New York Times* **bestselling author**

"Well developed, realistic characters. Entertaining family dynamics. Jannine Gallant gives you a satisfying read."
—Kat Martin, *New York Times* **bestselling author**

Visit us at www.kensingtonbooks.com

Chapter 1

The scent of burgers and fries drifted through the diner as the swinging kitchen door slapped against the wall. Claire Templeton's mouth watered. With a sigh, she poked through her salad, stabbed a tomato and popped it into her mouth. Given her petite frame, eating fries wasn't an option unless she wanted to look like the portly waitress. Not that the woman, who dwarfed the taxidermy bear in the restaurant's entrance, was doing too badly at the moment.

Her ample bosom swayed as she set a plate loaded with a double-decker cheeseburger and onion rings on the table in front of the customer in the booth across from Claire. *Customer* didn't do the man justice. Supreme specimen of manhood came close. Those naked Greek statues had nothing on this guy. Sun-streaked brown hair crowned a tanned face with bright blue eyes and a killer smile…which he was currently using as he requested extra mustard.

"I'll get it right away, hon." Augusta—if her nametag was to be believed—put one hand on her padded hip to lean in close. "You have to be the best-looking man ever to walk through that door." A jerk of her head toward the bear set graying wisps of hair fluttering around an age-creased face. "If I were thirty years younger—"

"They'd arrest me for soliciting a minor."

A robust laugh drowned the chatter of a family with three young children two booths down. "What a charmer."

The linoleum floor shook as the woman rounded the end of the counter and disappeared into the kitchen.

Claire rolled her eyes. "She didn't move like that when I asked for another slice of lemon in my iced tea."

Her hunky neighbor met her gaze and grinned. "Didn't your mama ever teach you you'll catch more flies with honey than vinegar?"

"I didn't want to catch flies. I wanted lemon."

Something about his smile nagged at the back of her mind.

Nope. I'd never forget crossing paths with this man.

Augusta returned and plopped a bottle of yellow mustard on the tabletop. She gave Mr. Ruggedly Handsome a toothy smile. "You planning to be in town long?"

"A couple of days. I want to do some hiking in the redwoods around here."

"Be sure to come back for breakfast. No one makes pancakes like Ralph."

"I'll do that. Can you recommend a campground? I drove by quite a few."

"Take a right at the first cross street heading north and follow the road to the end. Towering Trees Campground has showers. Some of the others don't. Enjoy your meal…er, what's your name, hon?"

"Jed. Thanks for the tip…and the mustard."

Claire's head snapped around. Jed. Memories swirled. A laughing boy with bright blue eyes sliding worms down her shirt, hollering over his shoulder at her to ride faster, licking a triple-decker chocolate ice cream cone—

"Careful of your drink."

She jerked her elbow back and slid the plastic glass away from the table's edge. "Thanks." Surely this man couldn't be—

"Are you just passing through?" He picked up his burger.

Collecting her scattered wits, she shook her head. "Actually, I have a reservation at the campground Augusta mentioned. Uh, you said your name's Jed?"

He nodded and popped an onion ring into his mouth. "Nice to meet you…"

"Claire."

His hand stilled over his plate. "Claire. Maybe we'll run into each other again while we're camping."

She worked her way through lettuce and an assortment of veggies while sneaking glances across the aisle. Jed wolfed down his burger then started on a chocolate shake topped with a cloud of whipped cream. The man might not have weight issues, but surely his cholesterol levels were as lofty as the dessert topping.

His gaze met hers again as he set down the glass. "I swear this isn't some kind of lame pick-up line, but you remind me of someone I used to know. I don't suppose you ever lived in Reno?"

She dropped her fork, eyes widening. "Oh, my God, it is you. Jed Lafferty. I can't believe it. You were skinny and obnoxious, and now you're…not."

His smile stopped her heart.

"Little Claire Templeton all grown up." His gaze swept downward. "Sort of. You're still pint-sized."

"I prefer vertically challenged."

His laugh turned the heads of the two old-timers at the counter who'd been eating blueberry pie and arguing about fishing. Augusta stepped through the kitchen doorway to glance in their direction with raised brows before retreating.

Claire pressed a hand to her chest. "I had the biggest crush on you despite all the nasty bugs and worms you tortured me with. I cried the whole way to Winnemucca when we moved."

"Your parents dragged you off to the middle of nowhere. I'd have cried, too."

"Good point. Not surprisingly, we didn't stay there long. After two more stops, I ended up here—" She spread her arms wide. "—for high school."

"No kidding?" He picked up his shake, crossed the aisle and slid onto the bench seat facing her. "How come you're camping if you're visiting your family?"

"I'm not. They left the area years ago. You remember my dad, always on the go, dragging my mom off to someplace new before she even had a chance to finish unpacking from the previous move. They're currently up in Oregon. How're your parents?"

His gaze dropped. "My mom died of breast cancer a few years ago. My dad's still in the same house, retired from the Reno police force. I see him on a regular basis."

She touched his arm. "I'm sorry. I loved your mom. She always had a smile and a cookie for the lonely, little girl from across the street. What about your brother?"

"Kane's married and has three stepdaughters. They live in the Napa Valley area."

His hand lay on the tabletop, ring finger conspicuously bare.

"You're not? Married, I mean."

He shook his head. "Not even close. What about you?"

"I've been within shouting distance a couple of times."

Leaning back in the booth, his gaze wandered over her face. The smile she remembered from the best time in her childhood grew.

"Those guys must have been crazy to let you get away."

"Augusta's right. You are a charmer." She wadded her napkin and dropped it next to her salad bowl. "How are you, Jed? Tell me all about your life for the last—what—twenty-five years?"

"Sounds about right. I was ten, and you were nine when you moved."

"Yet I still have vivid memories of following you around that summer. Apparently you leave a lasting impression on a girl."

He took a final swallow of his shake. "If you're finished with your rabbit food, let's go somewhere to catch up. The day's too beautiful to hang out in here. No fog or rain is a rare combination in the redwoods."

"It's not even very windy. We could drive through the woods to the beach." She dug her wallet out of her purse then glanced over to smile before dropping a few singles on the table. "I can't believe we met again, here of all places, after all these years."

"Must be fate or destiny or whatever."

Augusta lumbered out of the kitchen and headed toward the cash register. "If you're finished, I'll ring you up."

Jed tossed a five dollar tip next to his empty plate as he led the way through the diner. When her steps slowed, he turned. "What?"

She gripped her purse a little tighter. "You're not a serial killer on the run from the police or an escaped lunatic, are you? Going off alone into the forest with a relative stranger seems like something a dumb blonde in a horror flick would do. I may be blond, but I'm not stupid."

His smile flashed. "Want to call Kane? He's a small town sheriff. His endorsement should ease your mind."

She let out a breath then continued toward the register. "I'll take my chances and go with my gut. My gut tells me you're a good guy."

"That's because I am."

They paid for their meals, thanked the waitress then left the diner. Claire paused beside her compact motor home while he stopped next to an older SUV two spots over.

"Want to lead the way since you're familiar with the area?"

"Sure. There's a terrific beach not far from here. A twenty-minute drive at the most."

He nodded. "See you when we get there."

Claire backed out of the parking spot then turned onto the street. Heart thumping, she glanced in the rearview mirror. His SUV was right behind her. Pressing more firmly on the accelerator, she followed the highway through the tourist area of Shady Bend, past a gas station, a convenience store, several souvenir shops and a burl wood business into a thick grove of redwoods. Only a few rays of sunlight sifted through the trees, casting shadows across the narrow stretch of highway. She turned onto a rutted county road leading to the ocean.

Jed Lafferty—her first love. Not that he'd cared two shakes about the shy, scrawny girl next door. Although he might have felt sorry for her since he'd frequently let her tag along on his adventures. She'd peddled her heart out trying to keep up with him on his bike, endured skinned knees and elbows rollerblading down the steepest hill in their neighborhood and sprained her wrist bouncing off the trampoline in his backyard. Her family had moved to Reno late in the school year, and she'd never fit into any of the firmly established groups of girls in her class. Only when she was hanging out with Jed had she been happy.

A lot had changed in the last twenty-five years. She wasn't a sad preadolescent, and he wasn't an overactive little boy. Still, it would be interesting to see what he'd made of his life.

Turning into the sandy lot adjacent to the beach, Claire set the parking brake. When a thump sounded from the back of the motor home, she glanced over her shoulder and smiled.

"Did you have a nice nap...on my bed?"

Scoop yawned and shook then sauntered over to the door and plopped his butt on the mat in front of it. Leaning across him, Claire opened the door then waited for the dog to jump to the ground. She grabbed a windbreaker off the wall hook beside the table before following. Scoop walked over to a clump of waving sea grass and lifted his leg.

"Good God, what is that thing?" Jed stood next to his SUV, hands stuffed into the back pockets of his jeans, eyeing her dog like he might turn and charge.

"That *thing* is Scoop. Two years and one hundred pounds ago, he was a cute little rescue puppy. The shelter people weren't sure about his breed, some cross between a boxer, a Rottweiler and a hound."

"Interesting. Want to take a walk?"

"I'd love to. I'm stiff from driving all morning."

Slipping on her windbreaker to combat the light, autumn breeze, she strolled beside him down to the damp, packed sand. The tide was receding, leaving salt residue on the beach as the waves surged then retreated. High above in the endless stretch of blue, seagulls squawked and circled. Scoop ran ahead before pausing to sniff a pile of seaweed. Claire took a deep breath of tangy sea air then let it out slowly.

"Looks like we have the beach to ourselves."

She glanced his way. "I used to come here with friends for evening bonfires when I was in high school. The access road is crappy and unmarked, so not many tourists know about it."

Hands stuffed in his pockets, he squinted against the sun. "So, you're here to camp and visit your old stomping grounds?"

"Actually, I'm here for my job. I'm a nature photographer."

"Oh, yeah? Someone pays you to travel around to beautiful places and take pictures?"

She grinned. "Pretty much. I work for a magazine called *Rugged America.*"

"I want to be you when I grow up."

Her laugh set a flock of sandpipers running in all directions. "You look grown to me."

"Naw. I'm just a big kid. Up until a couple of weeks ago, I ran a wilderness camping retreat. Not the most adult job in the world."

"I'm not surprised in the least. The summer I lived across the street from you, you slept in a tent in your backyard most nights."

"Houses are overrated."

She smiled. "I don't know about that. You'll notice I have a motor home, not a tent. Where's this retreat?"

"It is—was up on Donner Summit in the middle of the Tahoe National Forest. Unfortunately, the government chose to revert the land to wilderness, so the camp's closed permanently and will soon be dismantled."

Stopping, she laid a hand on his arm. "I'm sorry."

"It was a good run, ten years, probably long past time for something new. In the winter, I work out of a ski rental shop offering backcountry skiing tours, so I have months before I need to worry about what to do next summer."

"This is your off season?"

He nodded. "I plan to spend the next few weeks hiking and camping along the coast."

"A busman's holiday."

"The best kind. Maybe we can hang out together while you're here photographing trees."

"Maybe."

They stepped across a shallow stream running through the sand then continued down the beach. Up ahead, Scoop wrestled with a giant chunk of driftwood before dropping it to trot back to her side. Claire reached down to rub his ears.

"I'll definitely be photographing trees, but that's not the focus of my story. I got a tip from an old friend who still lives in the area. A member of a research group camping in the woods swears he saw a Bigfoot."

Jed turned and stared. "You're writing a story about a bunch of crazies?"

She shrugged. "Could be. I intend to take a lot of cool pictures in addition to documenting the group's research. I'll let readers draw their own conclusions about whether or not Bigfoot is real or a hoax. To keep the magazine's core supporters happy, I'll mix in plenty of information on the area's flora and fauna along with spectacular photos. The Bigfoot angle is a twist to draw in a new group of readers. The marketing department is all over it."

He grinned. "Claire Templeton, does the heart of a rebel beat beneath that proper façade?"

She glanced down. "What's so proper about jeans and a T-shirt?"

"It's the *look but don't touch* aura you project."

"Hmm. Is that why your hands are jammed in your pockets?"

He nodded. "It helps me resist temptation and maintain my good guy persona. I wouldn't want you to think I grew up to be the sort of man who preys on lone, defenseless women."

"I'm not defenseless. I took classes. Besides, Scoop isn't just a pretty face. If you threatened me, he'd rip your arm off."

"Good to know. I'm in favor of keeping that mutt happy."

"You have something against dogs?"

"Only ones who look at me like I'm on the dinner menu."

Claire didn't blame Scoop one bit. The man was drool-worthy. She licked dry lips and turned when the beach ended at a rock cliff jutting into the water. They started back the way they'd come.

"Do you plan to camp with this research group?"

She glanced over. "Not right away, although I may spend the night out there at some point. I have an appointment with the director tomorrow, so I'll know more after that."

"I'd give my left—uh, arm to see a Bigfoot. Can I tag along?"

Pressing a hand to her mouth, she couldn't hold back a giggle. "You sound exactly like the ten-year-old boy I remember. I'll tell them I have an associate and ask permission for you to join me on any expeditions."

"Hot damn!"

The giggle erupted in a laugh. "You know it's all probably a big, fat farce, right?"

"Sure, but what if it isn't?"

"What if Santa Claus and the Easter Bunny and the Tooth Fairy are real?"

"If you're such a skeptic, why're you writing the story?"

"I'm writing about the process of hunting for a Bigfoot...and photographing a beautiful area of California. Anyway, I have an open mind." She swept a hand toward the forested hills rising away from the coast. "Who knows, any number of things could be hiding out there."

He reached over to snag her hand and squeeze. A tingle shot up her arm then fluttered around in her chest before moving on to heat her southern regions.

"This is great, Claire. Running into you just made my week." His grip tightened. "Unless you want me to take a hike, so to speak? If you'd prefer not to have company, I'll understand."

"I enjoy my dog, but having someone around who talks back is better." When he released her, she hesitated then stuffed her fist into the windbreaker pocket. "Okay, maybe not always better, but I'm looking forward to hanging out with you. Evening campfires should be a shared experience."

He stopped when they reached the trail to the parking area. "You're okay with continuing our get-reacquainted session at the campground? I don't want to be pushy or assume anything."

"You're not. We're both alone, so why not join forces?"

Brushing a strand of hair off her cheek, his finger moved in a soft caress. She held her breath until his hand fell away.

They turned together to walk side-by-side up the path from the beach, their arms touching.

"I like the sound of that. I'm pretty handy to have around camp. I promise you won't regret teaming up."

A hint of doubt crept to the surface. Once before, leaving Jed had broken her heart. She couldn't help wondering how the woman she'd become would fare when they parted ways this time. Looking into blue eyes full of light and laughter, she shrugged. It was a risk she was more than willing to take.

* * * *

At last!

He straightened in his seat and started the engine as a motor home rolled through town with Claire in the driver's seat and a big, brown mutt riding shotgun. With a smile stretching his lips, he pulled onto the street behind an older SUV.

She was finally here. As he'd hoped, the pull of a Bigfoot story was too strong for her to ignore. After waiting an eternity, they'd be together the way she'd promised all those years ago.

He was counting on her to keep her word.

Tapping his fingers on the steering wheel, he kept some distance between their vehicles then slowed when the RV pulled off the road into the lot of the supermarket on the far end of town. He edged up to the curb and parked. Turning in his seat, he held his breath as Claire stepped from the motor home and pushed the door shut behind her. Rays of late afternoon sun highlighted her beautiful blond hair.

The smile slipped from his face when she walked toward a man—one of those grunts who spent all his time in the gym from the looks of him—who slammed the door to the SUV that had been following her. *What the hell?* Claire wasn't dating anyone. He'd kept close tabs on her over the last few months as the big day drew closer, and he was one hundred percent positive there was no significant man in her life. Surely she hadn't picked up some guy on the drive to Shady Bend? One-night stands weren't her style.

His hands clenched around the wheel as the two strolled side-by-side into the store. Taking a deep breath, he let it out slowly, practicing the calming techniques his shrink had taught him. No point in panicking until he knew all the facts. No point in panicking, period. He'd simply adjust his plan to deal with any new circumstances.

Long minutes ticked by before Claire emerged carrying a bag of groceries. The stranger was still with her. He smacked his fist against the dashboard then closed his eyes and breathed deep. Opening them, he turned the key in the ignition and slouched lower in his seat when the woman he'd waited for—forever—drove past. Painful emotions churned in his gut as he flipped on his blinker to follow her through town. When she turned down the road leading to Towering Trees Campground, he continued past. Now was not the time to confront her. First, they'd get to know each other again. Maybe he'd leave a few more reminders of her promise.

Everything would have been perfect if the damned SUV hadn't turned toward the campground right behind her. No matter. No one, certainly not some fly-by-night boy toy, was going to stop him from getting what he wanted—the beautiful Claire. Not this time.

Meet the Author

Shady Grace makes Northern Ontario her home, where the bush is so thick you can't see two feet past the tree line. Perhaps the mystery of the woods was what initially sparked her need to write. She adores strong alpha males who fall for fiery, independent women, in settings with humorous dialogue and action-filled plots. Shady believes love and sex should be exciting and unforgettable. Being able to write about it is better than cheesecake.

Shady Grace is the new pen name of multi-published erotic author BL Bonita, who earned a starred review from Publishers Weekly for Dark Sun Rising. Visit her website at www.shadygrace.weebly.com, and find her on Facebook at www.facebook.com/shadygraceerotica.